Mrs Harris Goes to Paris
&
Mrs Harris Goes to New York

Paul Gallico

BLOOMSBURY PUBLISHING

NEW YORK • LONDON • OXFORD • NEW DELHI • SYDNEY

BLOOMSBURY PUBLISHING
Bloomsbury Publishing Inc.
1385 Broadway, New York, NY 10018, USA

BLOOMSBURY, BLOOMSBURY PUBLISHING, and the Diana logo
are trademarks of Bloomsbury Publishing Plc

Mrs Harris Goes to Paris first published as *Flowers for Mrs Harris* in
Great Britain by Michael Joseph 1958
Mrs Harris Goes to New York first published in Great Britain by Michael
Joseph 1960
This edition published 2022

Copyright © Paul Gallico, 1958, 1960
Cover artwork © 2022 Focus Features LLC

ISBN: PB: 978-1-63973-083-4

Library of Congress Cataloging-in-Publication Data is available.

2 4 6 8 10 9 7 5 3 1

Printed and bound in the U.S.A.

To find out more about our authors and books visit www.bloomsbury.com
and sign up for our newsletters.

Bloomsbury books may be purchased for business or promotional use. For
information on bulk purchases please contact Macmillan Corporate and
Premium Sales Department at specialmarkets@macmillan.com.

MRS HARRIS GOES TO PARIS

To the gallant and indispensable daily ladies who, year in, year out, tidy up the British Isles, this book is lovingly dedicated

The House of Dior is indubitably The House of Dior. But all the characters located on both sides of the Channel in this work of fiction are as indubitably fictitious and non-existent and resemble no living person or persons.

P.G.

THE small, slender woman with apple-red cheeks, greying hair, and shrewd, almost naughty little eyes sat with her face pressed against the cabin window of the BEA Viscount on the morning flight from London to Paris. As, with a rush and a roar, it lifted itself from the runway, her spirits soared aloft with it. She was nervous, but not at all frightened, for she was convinced that nothing could happen to her now. Hers was the bliss of one who knew that at last she was off upon the adventure at the end of which lay her heart's desire.

She was neatly dressed in a somewhat shabby brown twill coat and clean brown cotton gloves, and she carried a battered imitation leather brown handbag which she hugged close to her. And well she might, for it contained not only ten one-pound notes, the legal limit of currency that could be exported from the British Isles, and a return air ticket to Paris, but likewise the sum of fourteen hundred dollars in American currency, a thick roll of five, ten, and twenty dollar bills, held together by a rubber band. Only in the hat she wore did her ebullient nature manifest itself. It was of green straw and to the front of it was attached the flexible stem of a huge and preposterous rose which leaned this way and that, seemingly following the hand of the pilot upon the wheel as the plane banked and circled for altitude.

Any knowledgeable London housewife who had ever availed herself of the services of that unique breed of 'daily women', who come in to scrub and tidy up by the hour, or for that matter anyone English would have said: 'The woman under that hat could only be a London char,' and what is more, they would have been right.

On the Viscount's passenger list she appeared as Mrs Ada Harris, though she invariably pronounced it as 'Mrs 'Arris', Number 5 Willis Gardens, Battersea, London, SWII, and she was indeed a charwoman, a widow, who 'did' for a clientele living in and on the fringes of fashionable Eaton Square and Belgravia.

Up to that magic moment of finding herself hoisted off the face of the earth her life had been one of never-ending drudgery, relieved by nothing more than an occasional visit to the flicks, the pub on the corner, or an evening at the music hall.

The world in which Mrs Harris, now approaching the sixties, moved, was one of perpetual mess, slop, and untidiness. Not once, but half a dozen times a day she opened the doors of homes or flats with the keys entrusted to her, to face the litter of dirty dishes and greasy pans in the sink, acres of stale, rumpled, unmade beds, clothing scattered about, wet towels on the bathroom floor, water left in the tooth-glass, dirty laundry to be packed up and, of course, cigarette ends in the ashtrays, dust on tables and mirrors, and all the other litter that human pigs are capable of leaving behind them when they leave their homes in the morning.

Mrs Harris cleaned up these messes because it was her profession, a way of making a living and keeping body and soul together. And yet, with some chars there was more to it than just that, and particularly with Mrs Harris - a kind of perpetual house-proudness. And it was a creative effort as well, something in which a person might take pride and satisfaction. She came to these rooms to find them pigsties; she left them neat, clean, sparkling, and sweet-smelling. The fact that when she returned the next day they would be pigsties all over again, did not bother her. She was paid her three shillings an hour and she would again leave them immaculate. This was the life and professions of the little woman, one of thirty assorted passengers on the plane bound for Paris.

The green and brown checkered relief map of British soil slipped beneath the wings of the aircraft and gave way suddenly to the wind-ruffled blue of the English Channel. Where previously she had looked down with interest at the novelty of the tiny houses and farms below, these were now exchanged for the slender shapes of tankers and freighters ploughing the surface of the sea, and for the first time Mrs Harris realised that she was leaving England behind her and was about to enter a foreign country, to be amongst foreign people who spoke a foreign language and who, for all she had ever heard about them, were immoral, grasping, ate snails and frogs, and were particularly inclined to crimes of passion and dismembered bodies in trunks. She was still not afraid, for fear has no place in the vocabulary of the British char, but she was now all the more determined to be on her guard and not stand for any nonsense. It was a tremendous errand that was taking her to Paris, but she hoped in the accomplishing of it to have as little to do with the French people as possible.

A wholesome British steward served her a wholesome British breakfast and then would take no money for it saying that it came with the compliments of the airline, a little bit of all right.

Mrs Harris kept her face pressed to the window and her bag to her side. The steward came through saying: 'You will see the Eiffel Tower in the distance on your right.'

'Lumme,' said Mrs Harris to herself, when a moment later she discovered its pin point upthrust from what seemed to be an old patchwork quilt of grey roofs and chimney pots, with a single snake-like blue thread of a river running through it. 'It don't look as big as in the pictures.'

A minute or so later they landed without so much as a bump on die concrete of the French airport. Mrs Harris's spirits rose still further. None of her friend Mrs Butterfield's gloomy prognostications that the thing would either blow up in the sky or plunge with her to the bottom of the sea had been borne out. Paris perhaps might not prove so formidable after all. Nevertheless, from now on she was inclined to be suspicious and careful, a precaution not lessened by the long bus ride from Le Bourget through strange streets, lined with strange houses, and shops offering strange wares in a strange and unintelligible language.

The British European Airways man assigned to assist travellers confused by the hurly-burly of the Invalides Air Station in Paris took one look at the hat, the bag, the outsize shoes and, of course, the inimitable saucy little eyes, and recognised her immediately for what she was. 'Good Heavens,' he said to himself under his breath, 'a London char! What on earth is she doing here in Paris? The domestic help situation here can't be *that* bad.'

He noted her uncertainty, quickly consulted his list, and guessed right again. Moving smoothly to her side he touched his cap and asked: 'Can I help you in any way, Mrs Harris?'

The clever, roguish eyes inspected him carefully for any signs of moral depravity or foreign monkey business. Somewhat to her disappointment he seemed just like any Englishman. Since his approach was polite and harmless, she said cautiously: 'Ow, so they can speak the Queen's English over 'ere.'

The Airways man said: 'Well, ma'am, I ought to. I *am* British. But I think you will find most people over here speak a little English and you can get along. I see you are returning with us on the eleven o'clock plane this evening. Is there any particular place you wish to go now?'

Mrs Harris reflected upon just how much she was prepared to tell a stranger and then replied firmly: 'I'll just 'ave a taxi, if it's all the same to you. I've got me ten quid.'

'Ah, well then,' the Airways man continued, 'you'd better have some of it in French money. One pound comes to roughly a thousand francs.'

At the *bureau de change* a few of Mrs Harris's green pound notes were translated into flimsy, tattered, dirty blue paper with the figure 1000 on them and some greasy aluminium hundred-franc coins.

Mrs Harris was justly indignant. 'What's all this,' she demanded. 'Call this 'ere stuff money? Them coins feel like duds.'

The Airways man smiled. 'Well, in a sense they are, but only the Government's allowed to make them. The French just haven't caught up with the fact yet. They still pass, though.' He guided her through the crowd and up the ramp and placed her in a taxi. 'Where shall I tell him to take you?'

Mrs Harris sat up with her slender back, thin from hard work, ramrod straight, the pink rose pointing due north, her face as calm and composed as that of a duchess. Only the little eyes were dancing with excitement. 'Tell him to take me to the dress shop of Christian Dior,' she said.

The Airways man stared at her, refusing the evidence of his ears. 'I beg your pardon, ma'am?'

'The dress shop of Dior, you 'eard me!'

The Airways man had heard her all right, but his brain, used to dealing with all kind of emergencies and queer cases, could just not grasp the connexion between a London daily woman, one of that vast army that sallied forth every morning to scrub up the city's dirt in office and home, and the most exclusive fashion centre in the world, and he still hesitated.

'Come on then, get on with it,' commanded Mrs Harris sharply, 'what's so strange about a lydy going to buy 'erself a dress in Paris?'

Shaken to the marrow the Airways man spoke to the driver in French: 'Take madame to the House of Christian Dior in the Avenue Montaigne. If you try to do her out of so much as a sou, I'll take care you never get back on this rank again.'

As Mrs Harris was driven off he went back inside shaking his head. He felt he had seen everything now.

Riding along in the taxi, her heart pounding with excitement, Mrs Harris's thoughts went back to London and she hoped that Mrs Butterfield would be able to cope.

Mrs Harris's list of clients, whilst subject to change without notice - that is to say she might suddenly dismiss one of them, never they her - remained fairly static. There were some to whom she gave several hours every day and others who desired her services only three times a week. She worked ten hours a day, her labours beginning at eight in the morning and ending at six o'clock in the night with a half-day devoted to certain favoured customers on Saturdays. This schedule she maintained fifty-two weeks in the year. Since there were just so many hours in a day her patrons were limited to some six or eight and she herself restricted the area of her labours to the fashionable sector of Eaton and Belgrave Squares. For once she had arrived in that neighbourhood in the morning she was then able to walk quickly from house to flat to mews.

There was a Major Wallace, her bachelor, whom naturally she spoiled and in whose frequent and changing love affairs she took an avid interest.

She was fond of Mrs Schreiber, the somewhat muddled wife of a Hollywood film representative living in London, for her American warmth and generosity which displayed itself in many ways, but chiefly by her interest in and consideration for Mrs Harris.

She 'did' for fashionable Lady Dant, the wife of a wealthy industrial baron, who maintained a flat in London as well as a country manor - Lady Dant was always getting her picture in *The Queen* or *The Tatler* at hunt balls and charity affairs and this made Mrs Harris proud.

There were others, a White Russian Countess Wyszcinska, whom Mrs Harris liked because she was divinely mad, a young married couple, a second son, whose charming flat she loved because there were pretty things in it, Mrs Fford Foulks, a divorcée, who was a valuable mine of gossip as to what the idle rich were up to, and several others, including a little actress, Miss Pamela Penrose, who was struggling to gain recognition from her base in a two-room mews flat.

All of these establishments Mrs Harris looked after quite on her own. Yet in an emergency she could fall back on her friend and *alter ego* Mrs Violet Butterfield, like herself a widow and a char, and inclined to take the gloomy view of life and affairs wherever there was any choice.

Mrs Butterfield, who was as large and stout as Mrs Harris appeared to be thin and frail, naturally had her own set of clients, fortunately likewise in the same neighbourhood. But they helped one another out with a nice bit of teamwork whenever the necessity arose.

If either of them was ill or had pressing business elsewhere, the other would manage to pinch enough time from her clients to make the rounds of the other's customers sufficiently to keep them quiet and satisfied. Were Mrs Harris to be bedded with some malaise, as rarely happened, she would telephone her clients to advise them of this catastrophe and add: 'But don't you worry. Me friend, Mrs Butterfield, will look in on you and I'll be around again tomorrow,' and vice versa. Although they were different as night and day in character they were firm, loving, and loyal friends and considered covering one another a part of their duty in life. A friend was a friend and that was that. Mrs Harris's basement flat was at Number 5 Willis Gardens, Mrs Butterfield lived in Number 7 and rare was the day that they did not meet or visit one another to exchange news or confidences.

The taxi cab crossed a big river, the one Mrs Harris had seen from the air, now grey instead of blue. On the bridge the driver got himself into a violent altercation with another chauffeur. They shouted and screamed at one another. Mrs Harris did not understand the words but guessed at the language and the import and smiled happily to herself. This time her thoughts returned to Miss Pamela Penrose and the fuss she had kicked up when informed of Mrs Harris's intention to take a day off. Mrs Harris had made it a special point with Mrs Butterfield to see that the aspiring actress was not neglected.

Curiously, for all her shrewdness and judgement of character, Mrs Harris's favourite of all her clients was Miss Penrose.

The girl, whose real name, as Mrs Harris had gleaned from superficially inspecting letters that occasionally came so addressed, was Enid Suite, lived untidily in a mews flat.

She was a small, smooth blonde with a tight mouth and curiously static eyes that seemed fixed greedily upon but one thing - herself. She had an exquisite figure and clever tiny feet that had never tripped upon the corpses she had climbed over on her way up the ladder of success. There was nothing she would not do to further what she was pleased to call her career which up to that time had included a year or two in the chorus line, some bit parts in a few pictures, and several appearances on television. She was mean, hard, selfish, and ruthless, and her manners were abominable as well.

One would have thought that Mrs Harris would have penetrated the false front of this little beast and abandoned her, for it was so that when something about a client displeased Mrs Harris she simply dropped the key through the letter box and did not return. Like so many of her sisters who did not char for charring's sake alone, even though it was her living, she also brought a certain warmth to it. She had to like either the person or the person's home where she worked.

But it was just the fact that Mrs Harris had pierced the front of Miss Snite to a certain extent that made her stick to her, for she understood the fierce, wild, hungry craving of the girl to be something, to be somebody, to lift herself out of the rut of everyday struggle and acquire some of the good things of life for herself.

Before her own extraordinary craving which had brought her to Paris Mrs Harris had not experienced this in herself though she understood it very well. With her it had not been so much the endeavour to make something of herself as a battle to survive, and in that sense the two of them were not unalike. When Mrs Harris's husband had died some twenty years past and left her penniless she simply had to make a go of things, her widow's pension being insufficient.

And then too there was the glamour of the theatre which surrounded Miss Snite, or rather Penrose, as Mrs Harris chose to think of her, and this was irresistible.

Mrs Harris was not impressed by titles, wealth, position, or family, but she was susceptible to the enchantment that enveloped anything or anyone that had to do with the stage, the television, or the flicks.

She had no way of knowing how tenuous and sketchy was Miss Penrose's connexion with these, that she was not only a bad little girl but a mediocre actress. It was sufficient for Mrs Harris that from time to time her voice was heard on the wireless or she would pass across the television screen wearing an apron and carrying a tray. Mrs Harris respected the lone battle the girl was waging, humoured her, cosseted her, and took from her what she would not from anyone else.

The taxi cab entered a broad street, lined with beautiful buildings, but Mrs Harris had no eye or time for architecture.

''Ow far is it?' she shouted at the cab driver who replied, not slowing down one whit, by taking both hands off the steering wheel, waving his arms in the air, turning around and shouting back at her. Mrs Harris, of course, understood not a word, but his smile beneath a walrus moustache was engaging and friendly enough, and so she settled back to endure the ride until she should reach the so-long-coveted destination. She reflected upon the strange series of events that led to her being there.

IT had all begun that day several years back when during the course of her duties at Lady Dant's house, Mrs Harris had opened a wardrobe to tidy it and had come upon the two dresses hanging there. One was a bit of heaven in cream, ivory, lace, and chiffon, the other an explosion in crimson satin and taffeta, adorned with great red bows and a huge red flower. She stood there as though struck dumb, for never in all her life had she seen anything quite as thrilling and beautiful.

Drab and colourless as her existence would seem to have been, Mrs Harris had always felt a craving for beauty and colour which up to this moment had manifested itself in a love for flowers. She had the proverbial green fingers, coupled with no little skill, and plants flourished for her where they would not, quite possibly, for any other.

Outside the windows of her basement flat were two window boxes of geraniums, her favourite flower, and inside, wherever there was room, stood a little pot containing a geranium struggling desperately to conquer its environment, or a single hyacinth or tulip, bought from a barrow for a hard-earned shilling.

Then, too, the people for whom she worked would sometimes present her with the leavings of their cut flowers which in their wilted state she would take home and try to nurse back to health, and once in a while, particularly in the spring, she would buy herself a little box of pansies, primroses, or anemones. As long as she had flowers, Mrs Harris had no serious complaints concerning the life she led. They were her escape from the sombre stone desert in which she lived. These bright flashes of colour satisfied her. They were something to return to in the evening, something to wake up to in the morning.

But now as she stood before the stunning creations hanging in the wardrobe she found herself face to face with a new kind of beauty - an artificial one created by the hand of man the artist, but aimed directly and cunningly at the heart of woman. In that very instant she fell victim to the artist; at that very moment there was born within her the craving to possess such a garment.

There was no rhyme or reason for it, she would never wear such a creation, there was no place in her life for one. Her reaction was purely feminine. She saw it and she wanted it dreadfully. Something inside her yearned and reached for it as instinctively as an infant in the crib reaches at a bright object. How deeply this craving went, how powerful it was Mrs Harris herself did not even know at that moment. She could only stand there enthralled, rapt, and enchanted, gazing at the dresses, leaning upon her mop, in her music-hall shoes, soiled overall, and wispy hair down about her ears, the classic figure of the cleaning woman.

It was thus that Lady Dant found her when she happened to come in from her waiting room. 'Oh!' she exclaimed, 'my dresses!' And then noting Mrs Harris's attitude and the expression on her face said: 'Do you like them? I haven't made up my mind yet which one I am going to wear tonight.'

Mrs Harris was hardly conscious that Lady Dant was speaking, she was still engrossed in these living creations of silks and taffetas and chiffons in heart-lifting colours, daring cut, and stiff with cunning internal construction so that they appeared to stand almost by themselves like creatures with a life of their own. 'Coo,' she gasped finally, 'ain't they beauties. I'll bet they didn't 'arf cost a packet.'

Lady Dant had been unable to resist the temptation to impress Mrs Harris. London chars are not easily impressed, in fact they are the least impressionable people in the world. She had always been a little afraid of Mrs Harris and here was her chance to score. She laughed her brittle laugh and said: 'Well, yes, in a way. This one here - "*Ivoire*" - cost three hundred and fifty pounds and the big one, the red - it's called "Ravishing" - came to around four hundred and fifty. I always go to Dior, don't you think? Then, of course, you know you're right.'

'Four hundred and fifty quid,' echoed Mrs Harris, ''ow would anyone ever get that much money?' She was not unfamiliar with Paris styles, for she was an assiduous reader of old fashion magazines sometimes presented to her by clients, and she had heard of Fath, Chanel, and Balenciaga, Carpentier, Lanvin, and Dior, and the last named now rang a bell through her beauty-starved mind.

For it was one thing to encounter photographs of dresses, leafing through the slick pages of *Vogue* or *Elle* where, whether in colour or black and white, they were impersonal and as out of her world and her reach as the moon or the stars. It was quite another to come face to face with the real article to feast one's eyes upon its every clever stitch, to touch it, smell it, love it, and suddenly to become consumed with the fires of desire.

Mrs Harris was quite unaware that in her reply to Lady Dant she had already given voice to a determination to possess a dress such as this. She had not meant 'how would anyone find that much money?' but 'how would *I* find that much money?' There, of course, was no answer to this, or rather only one. One would have to win it. But the chances of this were likewise as remote as the planets.

Lady Dant was quite well pleased with the impression she seemed to have created and even took each one down and held it up to her so that Mrs Harris could get some idea of the effect. And since the char's hands were spotless from the soap and water in which they were immersed most of the time, she let her touch the materials which the little drudge did as though it were the Grail.

'Ain't it loverly,' she whispered again. Lady Dant did not know at that instant Mrs Harris had made up her mind that what she desired above all else on earth, and in Heaven thereafter, was to have a Dior dress of her own hanging in her cupboard.

Smiling slyly, pleased with herself, Lady Dant shut the wardrobe door, but she could not shut out from the mind of Mrs Harris what she had seen there: beauty, perfection, the ultimate in adornment that a woman could desire. Mrs Harris was no less a woman than Lady Dant, or any other. She wanted, she wanted, she wanted a dress from what must be surely the most expensive shop in the world, that of Mr Dior in Paris.

Mrs Harris was no fool. Not so much as a thought of ever wearing such a garment in public ever entered her head. If there was one thing Mrs Harris knew, it was her place. She kept to it herself, and woe to anyone who tried to encroach upon it. Her place was a world of unremitting toil, but it was illuminated by her independence. There was no room in it for extravagance and pretty clothes.

But it was possession she desired now, feminine physical possession; to have it hanging in her cupboard, to know that it was there when she was away, to open the door when she returned and find it waiting for her, exquisite to touch, to see, and to own. It was as though all she had missed in life through the poverty, the circumstances of her birth and class in life could be made up by becoming the holder of this one glorious bit of feminine finery. The same vast, unthinkable amount of money could be represented as well by a piece of jewellery, or a single diamond which would last for ever. Mrs Harris had no interest in diamonds. The very fact that one dress could represent such a huge sum increased its desirability and her yearning for it. She was well aware that her wanting it made no sense whatsoever, but that did not prevent her one whit from doing so.

All through the rest of that damp, miserable, and foggy day, she was warmed by the images of the creations she had seen, and the more she thought of them the more the craving grew upon her.

That evening as the rain dripped from the thick London fog, Mrs Harris sat in the cosy warmth of Mrs Butterfield's kitchen for the important ceremony of making out their coupons for the weekly football pool.

Ever since she could remember, it seemed that she and Mrs Butterfield had been contributing their threepence a week to this fascinating national lottery. It was cheap at the price, the hope and excitement and the suspense that could be bought for no more than three pennies each. For once the coupon was filled in and dropped into the pillar box it represented untold wealth until the arrival of the newspapers with the results and disillusionment, but never really disappointment since they actually did not expect to win. Once Mrs Harris had achieved a prize of thirty shillings and several times Mrs Butterfield had got her money back, or rather a free play for the following week, but, of course, that was all. The fantastic major prizes remained glamorous and ambition-inspiring fairy tales that occasionally found their way into the newspapers.

Since Mrs Harris was not sports-minded nor had the time to follow the fortunes of the football teams, and since as well the possible combinations and permutations ran into the millions, she was accustomed to making out her selections by guess and by God. The results of some thirty games, win, lose, or draw, had to be predicted, and Mrs Harris's method was to pause with her pencil poised over each line and to wait for some inner or outer message to arrive and tell her what to put down. Luck, she felt, was something tangible that floated around in the air and sometimes settled on people in large chunks. Luck was something that could be felt, grabbed at, bitten off; luck could be all around one at one moment and vanish in the next. And so, at the moment of wooing good fortune in the guise of the football pools, Mrs Harris tried to attune herself to the unknown. Usually, as she paused, if she experienced no violent hunches or felt nothing at all, she would mark it down as a draw.

On this particular evening as they sat in the pool of lamplight, their coupons and steaming cups of tea before them, Mrs Harris felt the presence of luck as thickly about her as the fog without. As her pencil hovered over the first line - 'Aston Villa v. Bolton Wanderers' - she looked up and said intensely to Mrs Butterfield: 'This is for me Dior dress.'

'Your what, dearie?' queried Mrs Butterfield who had but half heard what her friend said, for she herself was addicted to the trance method of filling out her list and was already entering into that state where something clicked in her head and she wrote her selections down one after the other without even stopping for a breath.

'Me Dior dress,' repeated Mrs Harris and then said fiercely as though by her very vehemence to force it to happen, 'I'm going to 'ave a Dior dress.'

'Are you now?' murmured Mrs Butterfield unwilling to emerge entirely from the state of catalepsy she had been about to enter, 'something new at Marks and Sparks?'

'Marks and Sparks me eye,' said Mrs Harris. ''Aven't you ever heard of Dior?'

'Can't say I 'ave, love,' Mrs Butterfield replied still half betwixt and between.

'It's the most expensive shop in the world. It's in Paris. The dresses cost four hundred and fifty quid.'

Mrs Butterfield came out of it with a bang. Her jaw dropped, her chins folded into one another like the sections of a collapsible drinking cup.

'Four hundred and fifty what?' she gasped, ''ave you gone barmy, dearie?'

For a moment even Mrs Harris was shocked by the figure, but then its very outrageousness, coupled with the force of the desire that had been born within her, restored her conviction. She said: 'Lady Dant 'as one of them in 'er cupboard. She brought it up for the charity ball tonight. I've never seen anything like it in me life before except perhaps in a dream or in a book.' Her voice lowered for a moment as she became reflective. 'Why, even the Queen ain't got a dress like that,' she said, and then, loudly and firmly, 'and I mean to 'ave one.'

The shock waves had now begun to subside in Mrs Butterfield and she returned to her practical pessimism. 'Where're you going to get the money, ducks?' she queried.

'Right 'ere,' replied Mrs Harris, tapping her coupon with her pencil so as to leave the fates in no doubt as to what was expected of them.

Mrs Butterfield accepted this since she herself had a long list of articles she expected to acquire immediately should her ticket come home. But she had another idea. 'Dresses like that ain't for the likes of us, dearie,' she gloomed.

Mrs Harris reacted passionately: 'What do I care what is or isn't for a likes of us; it's the most beautiful thing I've ever laid me eyes on and I mean to 'ave it.'

Mrs Butterfield persisted: 'What would you do with it when you got it?'

This brought Mrs Harris up short, for she had not even thought beyond the possession of such a wonderful creation. All she knew was that she craved it most fearfully and so to Mrs Butterfield's question she could not make other reply than: ''Ave it! Just 'ave it!'

Her pencil was resting on the first line of the pool coupon. She turned her attention to it and said: 'Now then, 'ere goes for it' And without another moment's hesitation, almost as though her fingers were working outside her own volition, she filled in line after line, win, lose, draw, win, win, draw, draw, draw, lose, and win, until the entire blank was completed. She had never done it like that before. 'There,' she said.

'Good luck to you, love,' said Mrs Butterfield. She was so fascinated by her friend's performance that she only paid perfunctory attention to her own and soon had it completed.

Still in the grip of something, Mrs Harris said hoarsely: 'Let's post them now, right now while me luck is running.'

They put on coats, wound scarves about their heads, and went off into the rain and the dripping fog to the red pillar box gleaming faintly on the corner beneath the street-lamp. Mrs Harris pressed the envelope to her lips for a moment, said ''Ere's for me Dior dress,' and slipped the letter through the slit, listening for its fall. Mrs Butterfield posted hers with less confidence. 'Don't expect nuffink and you won't get disappointed. That's me motto,' she said. They returned to their tea.

THE marvellous and universe-shattering discovery
was made that weekend not by Mrs Harris, but by
Mrs Butterfield who, flesh a-quivering, came storming
into the former's kitchen in such a state that she was
hardly able to speak and indeed seemed to be on the verge
of apoplexy.

'D-d-d-ducks– ,' she stammered - 'ducks, it's 'APPE-
NED!'

Mrs Harris who was engaged in ironing Major Wallace's
shirts after washing them - this was one of the ways in
which she spoiled him - said without looking up from the
nicety of turning the neckband: 'Take it easy, dear, or
you'll 'ave an attack. *Wot's* 'appened?'

Panting and snorting like a hippopotamus, Mrs Butterfield waved the newspaper - 'You've won!'

The full import of what her friend was saying did not
reach Mrs Harris at once, for having placed her ultimate
fate in the hands of the powerful feeling of luck, she had
then temporarily put the matter from her mind. But at last
the meaning of what Mrs Butterfield was shouting came to

her and she dropped her iron to the floor with a crash. 'Me Dior dress!' she cried, and the next moment she had seized her stout friend about the waist and the two of them were dancing like children about the kitchen.

Then, lest there be a mistake, they had to sit down, and minutely, score by score, figure by figure (for, of course, they kept duplicates of their selections), pore over the results of that Saturday's contests. It was true. But for two games, Mrs Harris had made a perfect score. There would be a prize, a rich one, certainly, perhaps even the jackpot, depending upon whether anyone else had surpassed or matched Mrs Harris's effort.

One thing seemed certain, however, the Dior dress, or at least the money for it, was assured, for neither could conceive that the prize for achieving twelve out of fourteen games could be less. But there was one great trial yet to be undergone by both. They would have to wait until Wednesday before being advised by telegram of the amount of Mrs Harris's swag.

'Whatever's over from what I need for me dress, I'll split with you,' the little charwoman told her stout friend in a moment of warm generosity and meant every word of it. In the first flush of excitement over the win Mrs Harris saw herself marching through this Dior's emporium, flanked by scraping and bowing sales staff. Her handbag would be crammed to bursting with the stuff. She would walk down aisle after aisle, past rack after rack of wondrous garments standing stiff with satin, lace, velvets, and brocades to make her choice finally and say - 'I'll 'ave *that* one.'

And yet - and yet - naturally gay optimist that she was, Mrs Harris could not help harbouring a suspicion gleaned from the precarious task of the living of daily life and making a go of things that it might not be all that easy.

To crave something exquisite but useless, a luxury wholly out of one's reach, to pin one's faith in getting it on a lottery, and to draw immediately the winning number, this was storybook stuff.

Still, it did seem to happen to people from time to time. One kept reading of such events in the newspapers every other day. Well, there was nothing to do but wait until Wednesday. But there was no gainsaying the facts and figures, or that she was a winner, for she had checked them over time and time again. The Dior dress would be hers, and perhaps much much more, even when she split with Mrs Butterfield. A top pool had been known to yield as much as a hundred and fifty thousand pounds.

Thus she dithered for three days until Wednesday morning when the fateful telegram from the pool head-quarters arrived. It was the measure of her affection for her friend that she did not tear it open at once to learn its contents, but held back until she was fully dressed and could run over to Mrs Butterfield, who braced herself in a chair for the big moment, fanning herself with her apron, crying: 'For the Lor's sake, love, open it or I'll die of excitement.'

At last, with trembling fingers, Mrs Harris opened the envelope and unfolded the message. It advised her briefly that her coupon had been a winning one and that her share would be one hundred and two pounds, seven shillings and ninepence halfpenny. It was well in a way that Mrs Harris had entertained the possibility of a let-down, for the sum was so much less than what she needed to become the possessor of a dress from Dior that the realisation of her dream was as far away and seemingly impossible as ever. Not even Mrs Butterfield's Job's comforting - 'Well, it's better than nothing; a lot of folks would be glad of the money' could help her to overcome her initial disappointment, even though she knew in her heart of hearts that that was what life was like.

What had happened? A list of winners sent to Mrs Harris a few days later made it plain enough. It had been a hard week in the football league with many upsets. While no one had picked all fourteen games correctly, or even thirteen, a considerable number had tied Mrs Harris's effort, shrinking the share for each one.

One hundred and two pounds, seven and ninepence halfpenny was a sum not to be sneezed at, and yet for several days it left Mrs Harris with rather a numb feeling about the heart and at night she would awaken with a feeling of sadness and unshed tears and then she would remember why.

Once the disappointment was over, Mrs Harris would have thought that the excitement of winning a hundred pounds in the football pool - a hundred pounds to be spent upon anything she liked - would have put an end to her desire for the Dior dress. Yet, the contrary proved to be the case. Her yearning was as strong as ever. She could not put it out of her mind. In the morning when she woke up, it was to a feeling of sadness and emptiness as though something unpleasant had happened to her, or something was missing which sleep had temporarily obliterated. Then she would realize that it was the Dior dress, or *a* Dior dress - just one, once in her lifetime that she was still craving and would never have.

And at night, when after her final cup of tea and chat with Mrs Butterfield she joined her old friends the hot-water bottles in her bed, and pulled the sheets up about her chin, there would begin a desperate struggle to think of something else - Major Wallace's new girl, introduced this time as his niece from South Africa (they were always either nieces, wards, secretaries, or friends of the family), or the latest oddity of the Countess Wyszcinska who had taken to smoking a pipe. She tried to concentrate upon her favourite flat, or upon the language Miss Pamela Penrose had used because she had broken an ashtray. She tried to invent and concentrate upon a flower garden. But it was no use. The more she tried to think of other things the more the Dior dress intruded into her consciousness, and she lay there in the darkness, shivering and craving for it.

Even with the light out and no more than the glimmer of the street-lamp filtering into the basement window, she could look right through the cupboard door and imagine it hanging there. The colour and the materials kept changing, sometimes she saw it in gold brocade, at other times in pink or crimson satin, or white with ivory laces. But always it was the most beautiful and expensive thing of its kind.

The originals that had started this strange desire had disappeared from the cupboard of Lady Dant and were no longer there to tantalise her. (Later there was a picture in the *Tatler* of Lady Dant wearing the one known as 'Ravishing'.) But Mrs Harris did not need to see them any longer. The desire to possess such a thing was indelibly embedded in her mind. Sometimes the longing was so strong that it would bring tears to her eyes before she fell asleep, and often it continued in some distorted dream.

But one night, a week or so later, Mrs Harris's thoughts took a new tack. She reflected upon the evening she had made out the football coupon with Mrs Butterfield and the curious sense of certainty she had experienced that this would win her the coveted dress. The results, it is true, had been in line with what she knew by experience. They were the disappointments of life, and yet, after all, were they?

She had won a hundred pounds, no, more, a hundred and two pounds, seven shillings and ninepence halfpenny.

Why then this curious sum, what was the message or the meaning it held for her? For Mrs Harris's world was filled with signals, signs, messages, and portents from On High. With the price of a Dior dress of four hundred and fifty pounds, three hundred and fifty pounds was still wholly out of her reach. But wait! A flash of insight and inspiration came to her and she snapped on the light and sat up in bed with the sheer excitement of it. It was not really three hundred and fifty pounds any longer. She had not only her hundred pounds in the bank, but a start of two pounds, seven shillings, and ninepence halfpenny on the second hundred, and once she had achieved that, the third hundred pounds would no longer be so difficult.

'That's it,' said Mrs Harris to herself aloud, 'I'll 'ave it if it's the last thing I do and it takes the rest of me life.' She got out of bed, secured pencil and paper and began to work it out.

Mrs Harris had never in her life paid more than five pounds for a dress, a sum she noted down on the paper opposite the utterly fantastic figure of four hundred and fifty pounds. Had Lady Dant named some such sum as fifty or sixty pounds as the price of the marvellous creations in her wardrobe it is quite possible that Mrs Harris would have put the entire matter out of her head immediately as not only a gap in price she was not prepared to consider, but also a matter of class upon which she preferred not to encroach.

But the very outrageousness of the sum put it all into a wholly different category. What is it that makes a woman yearn for chinchilla, or Russian sables, a Rolls-Royce, or jewels from Cartier, or Van Cleff and Arpels, or the most expensive perfume, restaurant, or neighbourhood to live in, etc.? It is this very pinnacle and preposterousness of price that is the guarantee of the value of her femininity and person. Mrs Harris simply felt that if one owned a dress so beautiful that it cost four hundred and fifty pounds, then there was nothing left upon earth to be desired. Her pencil began to move across the paper.

She earned three shillings an hour. She worked ten hours a day, six days a week, fifty-two weeks in the year. Mrs Harris screwed her tongue into her cheek and applied the multiplication table, reaching the figure of four hundred and sixty-eight pounds per annum, just the price of a Dior gala dress plus the amount of the fare to Paris and back.

Now, with equal determination and vigour Mrs Harris initiated a second column, rent, taxes, food, medicine, shoes, and all the little incidentals of living of which she could think. The task was a staggering one when she subtracted debits from credits. Years of saving lay ahead of her, two at the very least, if not three unless she had some other stroke of luck or a windfall of tips. But the figures shook neither her confidence nor her determination. On the contrary, they steeled them. 'I'll 'ave it,' she said once more and snapped out the light. She went to sleep immediately, peacefully as a child, and when she awoke the following morning she felt no longer sad but only eager and excited as one who is about to embark upon a great and unknown adventure.

The matter came out into the open next evening, their regular night to go to the cinema, when Mrs Butterfield appeared as usual shortly after eight, wrapped against the cold and was surprised to find Mrs Harris in her kitchen unprepared for any expedition, and examining some kind of prospectus entitled - EARN MONEY IN YOUR LEISURE TIME AT HOME.

'We'll be late, ducks,' admonished Mrs Butterfield.

Mrs Harris looked at her friend guiltily. 'I ain't going,' she said.

'Ain't going to the flicks?' echoed the astounded Mrs Butterfield. 'But it's Marilyn Monroe.'

'I can't 'elp it. I can't go. I'm syvin' me money.'

'Lor' bless us,' said Mrs Butterfield who occasionally, herself, submitted to a temporary economy wave. 'Whatever for?'

Mrs Harris gulped before she replied: 'Me Dior dress.'

'Lor' love you, ducks, you 'ave gone barmy. I thought you said the dress cost a ruddy four hundred and fifty quid.'

'I've already got a hundred and two poun', seven and ninepence halfpenny,' Mrs Harris said, 'I'm syvin' up for the rest.'

Mrs Butterfield's chins quivered as she shook her head in admiration. 'Character, that's what you've got,' she said. 'I could never do it meself. Tell you what, dear; you come along with me. I'll treat you.'

But Mrs Harris was adamant 'I can't,' she said, 'I wouldn't be able to treat you back.'

Mrs Butterfield sighed a heavy sigh and began to divest herself of her outer clothing. 'Oh, well,' she said, 'I guess Marilyn Monroe ain't everything. I'd just as soon 'ave a cup of tea and a quiet chat. 'Ave you seen Lord Klepper's been arrested again? Syme thing. It's 'is nephew I do for in Halker Street. As nice a lad as you could ever wish to know. Nothing wrong about 'im.'

Mrs Harris accepted the sacrifice her friend was making, but her glance travelled guiltily to the tea caddy. It was full enough now, but soon would be inhospitably empty. For this was one of the things on her list to cut down. She put the kettle on.

Thus began a long, hard period of scrimping, saving, and privation, none of which in the least interfered with Mrs Harris's good humour with the exception that she denied herself the occasional pot of flowers in season and more than ever watched over the health of her beloved geraniums lest she be unable to replace them.

She went without cigarettes - and a quiet smoke used to be a solace - and without gin. She walked instead of taking the bus or the underground and when holes appeared in her shoes she padded them with newsprint. She gave up her cherished evening papers and got her news and gossip a day late out of the waste-paper baskets of her clients. She scrimped on food and clothing. The former might have been injurious, except that Mrs Schreiber, the American woman, where she was usually working around lunch time was generous and always offered her an egg or something cold from the fridge.

This she now accepted.

But the cinema saw her no more, nor did The Crown, the pub on the corner; she went, herself, almost tea-less so that there might be some in the canister when it was Mrs Butterfield's turn to visit her. And she came near to ruining her eyes with some badly paid homework which she did at night, sewing zips on to the backs of cheap blouses. The only thing Mrs Harris did not give up was the threepence a week for the football pool, but, of course, lightning had no intention whatsoever of striking twice in this same place. Nevertheless she felt she could not afford not to continue playing it.

Through discarded six-months-old fashion magazines she kept up with the doings of Christian Dior, for all this took place before the sudden and lamented passing of the master, and always before her eyes, buoying her up and stiffening her backbone, was the knowledge that one of these days in the not too distant future, one of these unique creations would be hers.

And while Mrs Butterfield did not change her opinion that no good could come from wanting things above one's station and somewhere along the line Mrs Harris would encounter disaster, she nevertheless admired her friend's determination and courage, and stoutly supported her, helping her wherever she could, and, of course, keeping her secret, for Mrs Harris told no one else of her plans and ambitions.

MRS HARRIS jangled the bell of Mrs Butterfield's flat one mid-summer night during this period in a state of considerable excitement. Her apple cheeks were flushed and pinker than usual, and her little eyes were electric with excitement. She was in the grip of something bigger than herself, 'an 'unch', as she called it. The 'unch was guiding her to the Dog Track at White City, and she was calling upon Mrs Butterfield to accompany her.

'Going to take a plunge are you, dearie?' queried Mrs Butterfield. 'I don't mind a night out meself. 'Ow're you coming on with your savings?'

The excitement under which she was labouring made Mrs Harris's voice hoarse. 'I've got two hundred and fifty quid laid away. If I could double it, I'd have me dress next week.'

'Double it or lose it, dearie?' said Mrs Butterfield, the confirmed pessimist, who enjoyed looking upon the darker side of life.

'I've a 'unch,' whispered Mrs Harris. 'Come on then, the treat's on me.'

Indeed, to Mrs Harris it seemed almost more than a hunch - in fact, like a message from Above. She had awakened that morning with the feeling that the day was most propitious, and that her God was looking down upon her with a friendly and cooperative eye.

Mrs Harris's Deity had been acquired at Sunday school at an early age, and had never changed in her mind from a Being who combined the characteristics of a nannie, a policeman, a magistrate, and Santa Claus, an Omnipotence of many moods, who was at all times concerned with Mrs Harris's business. She could always tell which phase was uppermost in the Almighty by what was happening to her. She accepted her punishments from Above when she had been naughty without quibbling, as she would have accepted a verdict from the Bench. Likewise, when she was good, she expected rewards; when she was in distress she asked for assistance, and expected service; when things went well she was always prepared to share the credit with the Good Lord. Jehovah was a personal friend and protector, yet she was also a little wary of Him, as she might be of an elderly gentleman who occasionally went into fits of inexplicable tantrums.

That morning when she was awakened by the feeling that something wonderful was about to happen to her, she was convinced it could only have to do with her desire to own the dress, and that on this occasion she was to be brought nearer to the fulfilment of her wishes.

All that day at her work she had attuned herself to receive further communications as to what form the expected bounty would take. When she arrived at the flat of Miss Pamela Penrose to cope with the usual mess of untidiness left by the struggling actress, a copy of the *Evening Standard* was lying on the floor, and as she glanced at it she saw that the dogs were running at White City that evening. That was it! The message had been delivered and received. Thereafter there was nothing to do but to find the right dog, the right price, collect her winnings, and be off to Paris.

Neither Mrs Harris nor Mrs Butterfield was a stranger to the paradise that was White City, but that night the *mise en scène* that otherwise would have enthralled them - the oval track outlined in electric light, the rush and roar of the mechanical hare, the pulsating ribbon of the dogs streaming behind in its wake, the bustling crowds in the betting queues and the packed stands - was no more than the means to an end. Mrs Butterfield too, by this time, had caught the fever, and went waddling in Mrs Harris's wake from track to stands and back again without protest. They did not even pause for a cup of tea and a sausage at the refreshment room, so intent were they upon attuning themselves to the work in hand.

They searched the race cards for clues, they examined the long, thin, stringy animals, they kept their ears flapping for possible titbits of information, and it was this last precaution that eventually yielded results - results of such stunning portent that there could be no question of either authenticity or outcome.

Crushed in the crowd at the paddock where the entrants for the fourth race were being paraded, Mrs Harris listened to the conversation of two sporty-looking gentlemen standing just beside them.

The first gentleman was engaged in digging into his ear with his little finger and studying his card at the same time. 'Haute Couture, that's the one.'

The other gentleman, who was conducting similar operations on his nose, glanced sharply along the line of dogs and said: 'Number six. What the devil does "Haut Coutourie" mean?'

The first gentleman was knowledgeable. 'She's a French bitch,' he said, consulting his card again, 'owned by Marcel Duval. I dunno - ain't Haute Couture got something to do with dressmaking, or something like that?'

Mrs Harris and Mrs Butterfield felt cold chills run down their spines as they turned and looked at one another. There was no question, this was it. They stared at their cards, and sure enough there was the name of the dog, 'Haute Couture', and her French owner, and some of her record. A glance at the board showed them that her price was five to one.

'Come along,' cried Mrs Harris, making for the betting windows. She, like a tiny destroyer escorting the huge battleship of Mrs Butterfield, parted the crowds on either side of them, and arrived breathless at the queue.

'What will you put on her, dearie - five quid?' panted Mrs Butterfield.

'Five quid,' echoed Mrs Harris, 'after an 'unch like that? Fifty!'

At the mendon of this sum Mrs Butterfied looked as though she were going to faint. Pallor spread from chin to chin, until it covered all three. She quivered with emotion. 'Fifty quid,' she whispered, in case anyone should be listening to such folly. 'Fifty quid!'

'At five to one, that would be two hundred and fifty pounds,' asserted Mrs Harris calmly.

Mrs Butterfield's normal pessimism assailed her again. 'But what if she loses?'

'It can't,' said Mrs Harris imperturbably. ''Ow can it?'

By this time they were at the window. While Mrs Butterfield's eyes threatened to pop out of the folds of her face, Mrs Harris opened her battered brown handbag, extracted a sheaf of money, and said: 'Fifty quid on Howt Cowter, number six, to win.'

Mechanically the ticket-seller repeated: 'Haute Couture, number six, fifty pounds to win,' and then, startled by the amount, bent down to look through the wire screen at the heavy better. His eyes looked into the glowing blue beads of Mrs Harris, and the apparition of the little char startled him into an exclamation of 'Blimey', which he quickly corrected into 'Good luck, madam', and pushed the ticket to her. Mrs Harris's hand was not even trembling as she took it, but Mrs Butterfield stared at it as though it were a snake that might bite her. The two went off to the trackside to attend the fulfilment of the promised miracle.

The tragedy that they then witnessed was brief and conclusive. 'Haute Couture' led the first time around, running easily and smoothly, like the thoroughbred lady she was, but at the last turn she was assailed suddenly by an uncontrollable itch. She ran out into the middle of the track, sat down and scratched it to her relief and satisfaction. When she had finished, so was the race - and Mrs Harris.

It was not so much the loss of her hard-earned, hard-saved, so-valued fifty pounds that upset Mrs Harris and darkened her otherwise ebullient spirits in the following days, as the evidence that the policeman-magistrate God was uppermost, and that He was out of sorts with her. She had evidently misread his intentions, or perhaps it was only her own idea to take a plunge, and the Creator did not hold with this. He had sent swift and sure punishment in the form of a heavenly flea. Did it mean that He was not going to allow Mrs Harris to have her dress after all? Was she wishing for something so foolish and out of keeping with her position that He had chosen this method to indicate His disapproval?

She went about her work torn by this new problem, moody and preoccupied, and, of course, just because her Preceptor seemed to be against the idea, it made desire for the dress all the greater. She was of the breed who could defy even her Maker if it was necessary, though, of course, she had no notion that one could win out over Him. He was all-powerful, and His decisions final, but that did not say that Mrs Harris had to like them, or take them lying down.

The following week, when returning one evening from work, her eyes cast down due to the oppression that sat upon her, they were caught by a glitter in the gutter, as of a piece of glass reflecting in the lamplight overhead. But when she bent down, it was not a piece of glass at all, but a diamond clip, and one, as she saw at once, from the platinum frame and the size of the stones, of considerable value.

This time she had no truck either with hunches or communications. The thought that this piece of jewellery might be ten times the worth of the dress she longed for never entered her head. Because she was who she was and what she was, she responded almost automatically; she wended her way to the nearest police station and turned the article in, leaving her name and address, and a description of where she had found it. Within a week she was summoned back to the police station, where she received the sum of twenty-five pounds reward from the grateful owner of the lost clip.

And now all oppression was lifted from the soul of Mrs Harris, for the stern Magistrate Above had taken off His wig, reversed it and donned it as the beard of Santa Claus, and she was able to interpret both that which had happened to her, and the Divine Intention. He had returned half her money to show that He was no longer angry with her, and that if she were faithful and steadfast she might have her dress - but she was no longer to gamble; the missing twenty-five pounds said that. It was to be earned by work, sweat, and self-denial. Well, in the joy that filled her, she was prepared to give all that.

S OMEWHERE along the line without really trying - for Mrs Harris believed that by looking into things too energetically one could sometimes learn too much - the little charwoman had come across two pertinent bits of information. There were currency restrictions which forbade exporting more than ten pounds out of Great Britain and therefore no French shop would accept a large sum of money in pounds, but demanded another currency. So it would have done her no good to have smuggled out such a sum as four hundred and fifty pounds, nor would she have done so.

For Mrs Harris's code of ethics was both strict and practical. She would tell a fib but not a lie. She would not break the law, but she was not averse to bending it as far as it would go. She was scrupulously honest, but at the same time was not to be considered a mug.

Since pounds were forbidden as well as useless in quantities in Paris, she needed some other medium of exchange and hit upon dollars. And for dollars there was one person to whom she could turn, the friendly, kind, and not-too-bright American lady, Mrs Schreiber.

Mrs Harris conveniently invented a nephew in America who was apparently constitutionally impecunious, a kind of half-wit, unable to support himself and to whom, on a blood-is-thicker-than-water basis, she was compelled to send money. The name Mrs Harris cooked up for him was Albert, and he lived in Chattanooga, a place she bad picked out of the daily America column in the *Express*. She often held long conversations with Mrs Schreiber about this derelict relative. 'A good boy, my poor dead sister's son, but a bit weak in the 'ead, he was.'

Mrs Schreiber who was more than a bit muzzy herself with regard to British currency laws, saw no reason why she should not aid such a good-hearted person as Mrs Harris, and since she was wealthy and possessed an almost limitless supply of dollars, or could get fresh ones whenever she wanted them, Mrs Harris's slowly accumulating hoard of pounds got themselves translated into American currency. It became an accepted thing week by week, this exchange. Mrs Schreiber likewise paid her in dollars and tipped her in dollars and nobody was any the wiser.

Slowly but surely over a period of two years the wad of five-, ten-, and twenty-dollar bills grew in girth until one fresh morning, early in January, counting her hoard and thumbing her bank book, Mrs Harris knew that she was no longer too far away from the realisation of her dream.

She was well aware that anyone leaving the British Isles to travel abroad must hold a valid British passport, and she consulted Major Wallace as to what was necessary to obtain such a document, receiving explicit information as to where, how, and to whom she must apply in writing.

'Thinking of going abroad?' he asked with some amazement and no little alarm, since he considered Mrs Harris's ministrations indispensable to his comfort and well-being.

Mrs Harris tittered: "'Oo me? Where would I be going?' She hastily invented another relative. 'It's for me niece. She's going out to Germany to get married. Nice boy stationed in the Army there.'

And here you can see how Mrs Harris differentiated between a fib and a lie. A fib such as the above did nobody any harm, while a lie was deliberate, told to save yourself or to gain an unfair advantage.

Thus a never-to-be-forgotten moment of preparation was the day the instructions arrived from the Passport Office, a formidable blank to be filled in with '4 photographs of the applicant 2 inches by 2 inches in size, etc., etc.'

'Whatever do you think,' Mrs Harris confided to her friend Mrs Butterfield in a state of high excitement, 'I've got to 'ave me photograph tyken. They want it for me passport. You'd better come along and hold me 'and.'

The one and only time that Mrs Harris had ever faced the camera lens was upon the occasion of her wedding to Mr Harris and then she had the stout arm of that stout plumber to support her during the ordeal.

That picture in a flower-painted frame now adorned the table of her little flat. It showed Mrs Harris of thirty years ago, a tiny, thin-looking girl whose plain features were enhanced by the freshness of youth. Her hair was bobbed, the fashion of the day, and she wore a white muslin wedding dress tiered somewhat in the manner of a Chinese pagoda. In her posture there was already some hint of the courage and independence she was to display later when she became widowed. The expression on her face was one of pride in the man she had captured and who stood beside her, a nice-looking boy somewhat on the short side, wearing a dark suit, and with his hair carefully plastered down. As was becoming to his new status he looked terrified. And thereafter nobody had ever again troubled to reproduce Mrs Harris nor had she so much as thought about it.

'Won't it cost a packet?' was Mrs Butterfield's reaction to the dark side of things.

'Ten bob for 'arf a dozen,' Mrs Harris reported. 'I saw an ad in the paper. I'll give you one of the extra ones if you like.'

'That's good of you, dearie,' said Mrs Butterfield and meant it.

'Ow Lor'.' The exclamation was torn from Mrs Harris as she was suddenly riven by a new thought. 'Ow Lor',' she repeated, 'if I'm going to 'ave me photograph tyken, I'll 'ave to 'ave a new 'at.'

Two of Mrs Butterfield's chins quivered at the impact of this revelation. 'Of course you will, dearie, and that *will* cost a packet.'

Mrs Harris accepted the fact philosophically and even with some pleasure. It had been years since she had invested in a new hat. 'It can't be 'elped. Just as well I've got some of the stuff.'

The pair selected the following Saturday afternoon, invading the King's Road to accomplish both errands beginning, of course, with the choice of the hat. There was no doubt, but that Mrs Harris fell in love with it immediately she saw it in the window, but at first turned resolutely away for it was priced at a guinea, while all about it were others on sale, specials at ten and six, and even some at seven and six.

But Mrs Harris would not have been a true London char had she not favoured the one at one guinea, for it had been thought of, designed, and made for members of her profession. The hat was a kind of flat sailor affair of green straw, but what made it distinguished was the pink rose on a short but flexible stem that was affixed to the front. It was, of course, her fondness for flowers and the rose that got Mrs Harris. They went into the shop and Mrs Harris dutifully tried on shapes and materials considered to be within her price range, but her thoughts and her eyes kept roving to the window where the hat was displayed. Finally she could contain herself no longer and asked for it.

Mrs Butterfield examined the price tag with horror. 'Coo,' she said, 'a guinea! It is a waste of money, you that's been syving for so long.'

Mrs Harris set it upon her head and was lost. 'I don't care,' she said fiercely, 'I can go a week later.'

If a camera was to fix her features and person for all time, to be carried in her passport, to be shown to her friends, to be preserved in a little frame on Mrs Butterfield's dressing table, that was how she wanted it, with that hat and no other. 'I'll 'ave it,' she said to the sales girl and produced the twenty-one shillings. She left the shop wearing it contentedly. After all, what was one guinea to someone who was about to invest four hundred and fifty pounds in a dress.

The passport photographer was not busy when they arrived and soon had Mrs Harris posed before the cold eye of his camera while hump-backed he inspected her from beneath the concealment of his black cloth. He then turned on a hot battery of floodlights which illuminated Mrs Harris's every fold, line, and wrinkle etched into her shrewd and merry little face by the years of toil.

'And now, madam,' he said, 'if you would kindly remove that hat—'

'Not b—likely,' said Mrs Harris succinctly, 'what the 'ell do you think I've bought this 'at for if not to wear it in me photograph.'

The photographer said: 'Sorry, madam, against regulations. The Passport Office won't accept any photographs with hats on. I can make some specials at two guineas a dozen for you later, with the hat on, if you like.'

Mrs Harris told the photographer a naughty thing to do with his two-guinea specials, but Mrs Butterfield consoled her. 'Never mind, dearie,' she said, 'you'll have it to wear when you go to Paris. You'll be right in with the fashion.'

It was on a hazy May morning, four months later, or to be exact two years, seven months, three weeks, and one day following her resolve to own a Dior dress, that Mrs Harris, firm and fully equipped beneath the green hat with the pink rose, was seen off on the bus to the Air Station by a tremulous and nervous Mrs Butterfield. Besides the long and arduously hoarded fortune, the price of the dress, she was equipped with passport, return ticket to Paris, and sufficient funds to get there and back.

The intended schedule of her day included the selection and purchase of her dress, lunch in Paris, a bit of sightseeing, and return by the evening plane.

The clients had all been warned of the unusual event of Mrs Harris's taking a day off, with Mrs Butterfield substituting, and had reacted in accordance with their characters and natures. Major Wallace was, of course, dubious, since he could not so much as find a clean towel or a pair of socks without the assistance of Mrs Harris, but it was the actress, Miss Pamela Penrose, who kicked up the ugliest fuss, storming at the little char. 'But that's horrid of you. You can't. I won't hear of it. I pay you, don't I! I've a most important producer coming for drinks here tomorrow. You charwomen are all alike. Never think of anybody but yourselves. I do think, after all I've done for you, you might show me a little consideration.'

For a moment, in extenuation, Mrs Harris was tempted to reveal where she was off to and why - and resisted. The love affair between herself and the Dior dress was private. Instead she said soothingly: 'Now, now, ducks, no need for you to get shirty. Me friend, Mrs Butterfield, will look in on you on her way home tomorrow and give the place a good tidying up. Your producer friend won't know the difference. Well, dearie, 'ere's 'oping 'e gives you a good job,' she concluded cheerily and left Miss Penrose glowering and sulking.

ALL thoughts of the actress, and for that matter all of her meandering back into the past, were driven out of Mrs Harris's head when with a jerk and a squeal of brakes the cab came to a halt at what must be her destination.

The great grey building that is the House of Christian Dior occupies an entire corner of the spacious Avenue Montaigne leading off the Rond-Point of the Champs-Élysées. It has two entrances, one off the Avenue proper which leads through the Boutique where knick-knacks and accessories are sold at prices ranging from five to a hundred pounds, and another more demure and exclusive one.

The cab driver chose to deposit Mrs Harris at the latter, reserved for the genuinely rich clientele, figuring his passenger to be at the very least an English countess or milady. He charged her no more than the amount registered on the clock and forbore to tip himself more than fifty francs, mindful of the warning of the Airways man. Then crying to her gaily the only English he knew, which was - ''Ow do you do,' he drove off leaving her standing on the sidewalk before the place that had occupied her yearnings and dreams and ambitions for the past three years.

And a strange misgiving stirred in the thin breast beneath the brown twill coat. It was no store at all, like Selfridges in Oxford Street, or Marks and Spencer's where she did her shopping, not a proper store at all, with windows for display and wax figures with pearly smiles and pink cheeks, arms outstretched in elegant attitudes to show off the clothes that were for sale. There was nothing, nothing at all, but some windows shaded by ruffled grey curtains, and a door with an iron grille behind the glass. True, in the keystone above the arch of the entrance were chiselled the words CHRISTIAN DIOR, but no other identification.

When you have desired something as deeply as Mrs Harris had longed for her Paris dress, and for such a time, and when at last that deep-rooted feminine yearning is about to taste the sweetness of fulfilment, every moment attending its achievement becomes acute and indelibly memorable.

Standing alone now in a foreign city, assailed by the foreign roar of foreign traffic and the foreign bustle of foreign passers-by, outside the great, grey mansion that was like a private house and not a shop at all, Mrs Harris suddenly felt lonely, frightened, and forlorn, and in spite of the great roll of silver-green American dollars in her handbag she wished for a moment that she had not come, or that she had asked the young man from the Airlines to accompany her, or that the taxi driver had not driven away leaving her standing there.

And then, as luck would have it, a car from the British Embassy drove by and the sight of the tiny Union Jack fluttering from the mudguard stiffened her spine and brought determination to her mouth and eyes. She reminded herself who and what she was, drew in a deep breath of the balmy

Paris air laced with petrol fumes, and resolutely pushed open the door and entered.

She was almost driven back by the powerful smell of elegance that assailed her once she was inside. It was the same that she smelled when Lady Dant opened the doors to her wardrobe, the same that clung to the fur coat and clothes of the Countess Wyszcinska, for whom she cleaned from four to six in the afternoons, the one she sometimes sniffed in the streets when, as she passed, someone opened the door of a luxurious motor car. It was compounded of perfume and fur and satins, silks and leather, jewellery and face powder. It seemed to arise from the thick grey carpets and hangings, and fill the air of the grand staircase before her.

It was the odour of the rich, and it made her tremble once more and wonder what she, Ada 'Arris, was doing there instead of washing up the luncheon dishes for Mrs Fford Foulks at home, or furthering the career of a real theatrical star like Pamela Penrose by seeing that her flat was neat and tidy when her producer friends came to call.

She hesitated, her feet seemingly sinking into the pile of the carpet up to her ankles. Then her fingers crept into her handbag and tested the smooth feel of the roll of American bills. 'That's why you're 'ere, Ada 'Arris. That says you're ruddy well as rich as any of 'em. Get on with it then, my girl.'

She mounted the imposing and deserted staircase, it then being half-past eleven in the morning. On the first half-landing there was but a single silver slipper in a glass showcase let into the wall, on the second turn there was a similar showcase housing an outsize bottle of Dior perfume. But otherwise there were no goods of any kind on display, nor were there crowds of people rushing up and down the stairs as in Marks and Spencer's or Selfridges.

Nowhere was there any sign of anything that so much as resembled the shops to which she was accustomed.

On the contrary, the elegance and atmosphere of the deserted staircase gave her the feeling of a private house, and one on a most grand scale at that. Was she really in the right place? Her courage threatened to ooze again, but she told herself that sooner or later she must come upon some human being who would be able to direct her to the dresses, or at least put her right if she were in the wrong building. She pressed on and indeed on the first floor landing came upon a dark handsome woman in her early forties who was writing at a desk. She wore a simple black dress relieved by three rows of pearls at the neck, her coiffure was neat and glossy; her features were refined, her skin exquisite, but closer inspection would have revealed that she looked tired and care-worn and that there were dark hollows beneath her eyes.

Behind her, Mrs Harris noted a fair-sized room opening into a second one, grey-carpeted like the stairs, with fine silk hangings at the windows, and furnished only with several rows of grey and golden chairs around the perimeter. A few floor-to-ceiling pier mirrors completed the décor, but of anything to sell or even so much as to look at, there was not a sign.

Mme Colbert, the manageress, had had a bad morning. A usually kind and gracious lady, she had let herself quarrel with M. Fauvel, the young and handsome head of the accounts department, of whom otherwise she was rather fond, and had sent him upstairs again to his domain with his ears reddening.

It was merely a matter of his inquiring about a client whose bills seemed to run too long without payment. On any other day Mme Colbert might have favoured the accountant with a penetrating and not unhumorous summing-up of the client's characteristics, idiosyncrasies, and trustworthiness, since sooner or later they all bared themselves to her. Instead of which she railed angrily at him that it was her business to sell dresses and his to collect the money and she had not the time to inspect the bank accounts of clients. That was his affair.

Besides giving short answers all morning, she had ticked off several of the sales girls and even permitted herself to scold Natasha, the star model of the House, for being late for a fitting, when, as she knew well, the Métro and the buses were engaging in a go-slow strike. What made it worse was that the exquisite Natasha had responded to the sharp words in a most un-prima donna-like manner, she did not argue or snap back, only two large tears formed at her eyes and rolled down her cheeks.

And then besides, Mme Colbert was not at all sure that she had not muddled the invitations and seating for the afternoon's review of the collection. As head of the department she was an important and all-powerful person on the first floor. It was she who issued or denied invitations to see the collection, sorted out spies and curiosity seekers, and barred the undesirables. She was in charge of seating arrangements as complicated as those facing any head waiter of a fashionable restaurant, as clients must be placed according to importance, rank, title, and bankroll. She was the *directrice* of a fashion parade, having something to say as to the order in which the creations appeared, and likewise she was the commander-in-chief of a battalion of black-garbed sales women, deploying them on the staircase and taking great care to match them psychologically to their clients - a gay and gossipy sales girl for a gay and gossipy woman, a silent and respectful sales person for a mature and important customer, an English-speaking girl with a persuasive line for an American, a good bully with a commanding aspect for a German, etc.

When such a powerful person was out of sorts or ill-humoured, repercussions would ring far and wide. The crise which Mme Colbert was suffering had to do with her husband Jules, and the love, respect, and affection for him which had grown over the twenty years they had been together. Dear, good, decent, clever Jules, who had more knowledge in one fingertip than all the rest of them in the Foreign Office, with their rosettes and political connexions. But one thing Jules lacked, or rather two - he had not the ability to push himself and - he had no political friends or connexions.

Beginning as a poor boy, he had achieved his position by brilliance and application. Yet, whenever there was a better or higher position opening he was rejected in favour of someone of lesser intellect but greater connexions who then from his new position of eminence used Jules's experience to handle his job. As his wife, and an intelligent woman *au courant* with affairs in France, Mme Colbert knew that many a difficult problem had been solved by her husband's brains and intuition. Yet, time and time again he had been passed over for promotion, time and time again his eager optimism and enthusiasm had been shattered. In the past year for the first time Mme Colbert had become aware of a growing hopelessness and misanthropy in her husband. Now a man of fifty, he felt he could look forward to nothing but the existence of a Foreign Office hack. He had all but given up, and it broke her heart to see the changes in the man to whom she had given her devotion.

Recently, there had been a sudden death at the Quai d' Orsay; the chief of an important department had succumbed to heart failure. Speculation was rife as to who would replace him. Jules Colbert was one of those in line for the job and yet—

It saddened Mme Colbert almost to the point of desperation to see how her husband's buoyancy from his younger days struggled to break through the weight of pessimism that experience had laid upon his shoulders. He dared to hope again, even against all of the political corruption which would shatter his hopes and this time leave him an old and broken man.

This then was the burden that Mme Colbert carried about with her. She had helped her husband by working and taking financial strain off him and so had built herself into her position in the great dressmaking house. But she realised now that this was not enough and that in another way she had failed. The wife of a diplomat or a politician must herself be a diplomat or politician, conduct a *salon* to which the great and the might-be great would be invited; she would wheedle, flatter, intrigue, even if need be, give herself to advance her husband's interests. Here was the ideal situation for such assistance; a plum was ready to fall to the right man and there was no way she could influence it into the lap of Jules. There was no one in those circles who cared a fig for her or her husband.

This knowledge drove Mme Colbert almost frantic with unhappiness, for she loved her husband and could not bear to see him destroyed, but neither could she do anything to prevent it and break the ugly pattern of his being shunted aside in favour of someone who had the right connexions of money, family, or political power. She lay awake at nights racking her brains for some means to help him. By day she could only become more and more convinced of the futility of her efforts, and thus her bitterness was carried on into the life of her daily work and began to affect those about her. She was not unaware of the change in herself; she seemed to be going about in some kind of nightmare from which she could not awake.

Seated now at her desk on the first floor landing and trying to concentrate on the placing of the guests for the afternoon show, Mme Colbert looked up to see an apparition ascending the stairs which caused a shudder to pass through her frame and led her to brush her hand across her brow and eyes as though to clear away an hallucination, if it was one. But it was not. She was real enough.

One of Mme Colbert's assets was her unvarying judgement in estimating the quality of would-be customers or clients, divining the genuine article from the time-wasters, penetrating the exterior of eccentrics to the bankrolls within. But this woman ascending the stairs in the worn, shabby coat, gloves of the wrong colour, shoes that advertised only too plainly her origin, the dreadful glazed imitation leather handbag, and the wholly preposterous hat with its jiggling rose, defied her.

Swiftly Mme Colbert's mind raced through all the categories of clients she had ever seen and known. If the creature had been what she looked like, a cleaning woman (and here you see how marvellous Mme Colbert's instincts were), she would have been entering by the back way. But, of course, this was absurd since all of the cleaning was done there at night, after hours. It was impossible that this could be a client of or for the House of Dior.

And yet she waited for the woman to speak, for she realised that she was so upset by her own personal problems that her judgement might be warped. She had not long to wait.

'Ah, there you are, dearie,' the woman said, 'could you tell me which way to the dresses?'

Madame Colbert no longer had any doubts as to her judgement. Such a voice and such an accent had not been heard inside the walls of the House of Dior since its inception.

'The dresses?' inquired Mme Colbert in chilled and flawless English, 'what dresses?'

'Oh come now, duckie,' admonished Mrs Harris, 'aren't you a bit on the slow side this morning? Where is it they 'angs up the dresses for sale?'

For one moment Mme Colbert thought that this weird person might have strayed from looking for the little shop below. 'If you mean the Boutique—'

Mrs Harris cocked an ear. 'Bou - what? I didn't ask for any booties. It's them dresses I want, the expensive ones. Pull yourself together, dearie, I've come all the way from London to buy meself one of your dresses and I 'aven't any time to waste.'

All was as clear as day to Mme Colbert now. Every so often, an error came marching up the grand staircase, though never before one quite so obviously and ghastly as this one, and had to be dealt with firmly. Her own troubles and frustrations rendered the manageress colder and more unsympathetic than usual in such circumstances. 'I am afraid you have come to the wrong place. We do not display dresses here. The collection is only shown privately in the afternoons. Perhaps if you go to the Galeries Lafayette—'

Mrs Harris was completely bewildered. 'Wot Galleries,' she asked, 'I don't want no galleries. Is this Dior or ain't it?' Then, before the woman could reply she remembered something. She used to encounter the word 'collections' in the fashion magazines, but thought they had something to do with charity, such as the collection in the church on Sunday. Now her native shrewdness cut through the mystery. 'Look 'ere,' she said, 'maybe it's this 'ere collection I want to see, what about it?'

Impatience seized Mme Colbert who was anxious to return to the miseries of her own thoughts. 'I am sorry,' she said coldly, 'the salon is filled for this afternoon and the rest of the week.' To get rid of her finally she repeated the usual formula: 'If you will leave the name of your hotel, perhaps next week some time we can send you an invitation.'

Righteous anger inflamed the bosom of Mrs Harris. She moved a step nearer to Mme Colbert and the pink rose attached to the front of the hat bobbed vigorously as she cried: 'Coo, that's a good one. You'll send me a invitytion to spend me money hard-earned dusting and mopping and ruinin' me 'ands in dirty dish water, next week, perhaps - me that's got to be back in London tonight. 'Ow do you like that?'

The rose bobbed menacingly a foot from Mme Colbert's face. 'See 'ere, Miss Snooty-at-the-Desk, if yer don't think I've got the money to pay for what I want - 'ERE!' And with this Mrs Harris opened the imitation leather bag and up-ended it The rubber band about her roll chose that moment to burst, dramatically showering a green cascade of American five-, ten-, and twenty-dollar notes. 'There!' at which point Mrs Harris raised her indignant voice to roof level, 'what's the matter with that? Ain't my money as good as anybody else's?'

Caught by surprise Mme Colbert stared at the astonishing and, truth to tell, beautiful sight, murmuring to herself '*Mon dieu*! Better than most people's.' Her mind had turned suddenly to her recent quarrel with young André Fauvel who had complained about the fall of the French franc and clients not paying their bills, and she thought ironically that here was a genuine cash customer and how would he like that. There was no gainsaying that the mound of dollars on the desk was real money.

But Mme Colbert was now confused as well as taken aback by the appearance and manner of this weird customer. How had she, who professed to scrub floors and wash dishes for her living, come by so much money and in dollars at that? And what on earth did she want with a Dior dress? The whole business smacked of irregularity leading to trouble. Nowhere did it add up or make sense, and Mme Colbert felt she had enough trouble as it was without becoming involved with this impossible British visitor who had more money on her person than she ought.

Adamantly, in spite of the sea of green dollars covering her desk, Mme Colbert repeated: 'I am sorry, the salon is full this afternoon.'

Mrs Harris's lip began to tremble and her little eyes screwed up as the implications of the disaster became clear. Here, in this apparently empty, hostile building, before cold hostile eyes, the unimaginable seemed about to happen. They didn't seem to want her, they didn't even appear to want her money. They were going to send her away and back to London without her Dior dress.

'Lumme!' she cried, 'ain't you Frenchies got any 'eart? You there, so smooth and cool! Didn't you ever want anything so bad you could cry every time you thought about it? Ain't you never stayed awake at nights wanting somefink and shivering, because maybe you couldn't never 'ave it?'

Her words struck like a knife to the heart of Mme Colbert who night after night had been doing just that, lying awake and shivering from the ache to be able to do something for her man. And the pain of the thrust forced a little cry from the manageress. 'How did you know? How ever could you guess?'

Her own dark unhappy eyes suddenly became caught up in the small vivid blue ones of Mrs Harris which were revealing the first glint of tears. Woman looked into woman, and what Mme Colbert saw filled her first with horror and then a sudden rush of compassion and understanding.

The horror was directed at herself, at her own coldness and lack of sympathy. In one moment it seemed this odd little woman facing her had held a mirror up and let her see herself as she had become through self-indulgence and yielding to her personal difficulties. She thought with shame how she had behaved towards M. Fauvel, and with even more contrition her feckless scolding of the sales girls and even Natasha, the model, who was one of her pets.

But above all she was appalled at the realisation that she had let herself be so encrusted, so hardened by the thoughts with which she lived daily that she had become both blind and deaf to human needs and cries emanating from the human heart. Wherever she came from, whatever her walk in life, the person opposite her was a woman, with all of a woman's desires, and as the scales fell thus from her own eyes, she whispered: 'My dear, you've set your heart on a Dior dress.'

Mrs Harris would not have been a veteran member in good-standing of her profession had she forborne to reply: 'Well, now, 'ow did you know?'

Mme Colbert ignored the sarcasm. She was looking now at the pile of money and shaking her head in amazement. 'But however did you— ?'

'Scrimped and syved,' said Mrs Harris. 'It's took me three years. But if you wants somefink bad enough, there's always ways. Mind you, you've got to 'ave a bit o' luck as well. Now tyke me, after I won a hundred pounds on a football pool

I said to meself, "That's a sign, Ada 'Arris," so I started syving and 'ere I am.'

Mme Colbert had a flash of intuition as to what 'Syving' meant to such a person and a wave of admiration for the courage and gallantry of the woman passed through her. Perhaps if she herself had shown more of this kind of courage and tenacity, instead of taking out her frustration on innocent and helpless sales girls, she might have been able to accomplish something for her husband. She passed her hand over her brow again and came to a quick decision. 'What is your name, my dear?' When Mrs Harris told her she filled it in quickly on an engraved card that said that Monsieur Christian Dior, no less, would be honoured by her presence at the showing of his collection that afternoon. 'Come back at three,' she said and handed it to Mrs Harris. 'There really is no room, but I will make a place for you on the stairs from where you will be able to see the collection.'

All rancour and sarcasm vanished from the voice of Mrs Harris as she gazed in ecstasy at her admission to Paradise. 'Now, that's kind of you, love,' she said. 'It looks like me luck is 'olding out.'

A curious feeling of peace pervaded Mme Colbert and a strange smile illuminated her countenance as she said: 'Who can say, perhaps you will be lucky for me too.'

A T five minutes to three that afternoon three people
whose lives were to become strangely entangled, found
themselves within a whisper of one another by the grand staircase in the House of Dior, now crowded with visitors, clients,
sales girls, staff, and members of the press, all milling about.

The first of these was M. André Fauvel, the young chief
accountant. He was well set up and handsome in a blond
way, in spite of a scar upon his cheek honourably acquired,
and the source of a military medal won during his army
service in Algeria.

It was sometimes necessary for him to descend from the
chilling regions of his account books on the fourth floor
to the warmth of the atmosphere of perfumes, silks, and
satins, and the females they encased, on the first floor. He
welcomed these occasions and even sought excuses for them
in the expedition of catching a glimpse of his goddess, the
star model, with whom he was desperately and, of course,
quite hopelessly in love.

For Mlle Natasha, as she was known to press and public
in the fashion world, was the toast of Paris, a dark-haired,

dark-eyed beauty of extraordinary attraction and one who surely had a brilliant career before her either in films or a rich and titled marriage. Every important bachelor in Paris, not to mention a considerable quota of married men, were paying her court.

M. Fauvel came from a good middle class family; his was a good position with a good wage, and he had a little money besides, but his world was as far removed from the brilliant star of Natasha as was the planet earth from the great Sirius.

He was fortunate, for that moment he did catch a sight of her in the doorway of the dressing room, already encased in the first number she was to model, a frock of flame-coloured wool, and on her glossy head perched a flame-coloured hat. A diamond snowflake sparkled at her throat, and a sable stole was draped carelessly over one arm. M. Fauvel thought that his heart would stop and never beat again, so beautiful was she and so unattainable.

Glancing out of her sweet, grave eyes set wide apart in narrowing lids, Mlle Natasha saw M. Fauvel and yet saw him not, as, showing a sliver of pink tongue, she stifled a yawn. For truth to tell, she was prodigiously bored. None but a few at Dior's knew the real identity much less the real personality of the long-limbed, high-waisted, raven-haired Niobe who attracted the rich and famous to her side like flies.

Her real name then was Suzanne Petitpierre. Her origin was a simple bourgeois family in Lyons and she was desperately weary of the life her profession forced her to lead, the endless rounds of cocktail parties, dinners, theatres, and cabarets, as companion to film men, motor manufacturers, steel men, titled men, all of whom wished to be seen with the most glamorous and photographed model in the city. Mlle Petitpierre wanted nothing of any of them. She had no ambition for a career in films, or on the stage, or to take her place as the châtelaine of some noble château. What she desired more than anything else was somehow to be able to rejoin that middle class from which she had temporarily escaped, marry someone for love, some good, simple man, who was not too handsome or clever, settle down in a comfortable bourgeois home, and produce a great many little bourgeois offspring. Such men existed, she knew, men who were not consistently vain, boastful, or super-intellectual to the point where she could not keep up with them. But they were somehow now all outside of her orbit. Even at that very moment when she was beneath the gaze of many admiring eyes she felt lost and unhappy. She remembered vaguely having seen the young man who was regarding her so intently, somewhere before, but could not place him.

Finally, Mrs Harris, of Number 5 Willis Gardens, Battersea, London, came bustling up the staircase already crowded with recumbent figures, to be received by Mme Colbert. And then and there an astonishing thing took place.

For to the regulars and *cognoscenti* the staircase at Christian Dior's is Siberia, as humiliating a spot as when the head waiter of a fashionable restaurant seats you among the yahoos by the swinging doors leading to the kitchen. It was reserved strictly for boobs, nosies, unimportant people, and the minor press.

Mme Colbert regarded Mrs Harris standing there in all her cheap clothing, and she looked right through them and saw only the gallant woman and sister beneath. She reflected upon the simplicity and the courage that had led her thither in pursuit of a dream, the wholly feminine yearning for an out-of-reach bit of finery, the touching desire, once in her drab cheerless life, to possess the ultimate in a creation. And she felt that somehow Mrs Harris was quite the most important and worthwhile person in the gathering there of chattering females waiting to view the collection that day.

'No,' she said to Mrs Harris. 'Not on the staircase. I will not have it. Come. I have a seat for you inside.'

She threaded Mrs Harris through the throng, holding her by the hand, and took her into the main salon where all but two of the gold chairs in the double rows were occupied. Mme Colbert always kept one or two seats in reserve for the possible unexpected arrival of some V.I.P., or a favoured customer bringing a friend.

She towed Mrs Harris across the floor and seated her on a vacant chair in the front row. 'There,' said Mme Colbert 'You will be able to see everything from here. Have you your invitation? Here is a little pencil. When the models enter, the girl at the door will call out the name and number of the dress - in English. Write down the numbers of the ones you like best, and I will see you afterwards.'

Mrs Harris settled herself noisily and comfortably on the grey and gold chair. Her handbag she parked on the vacant seat at her left, the card and pencil she prepared for action. Then with a pleased and happy smile she began taking stock of her neighbours.

Although she had no means of identifying them, the main salon contained a cross-section of the *haut monde* of the world, including a scattering of the nobility, ladies and honorables from England, marquises and countesses from France, baronesses from Germany, principessas from Italy, new-rich wives of French industrialists, veteran-rich wives of South American millionaires, buyers from New York, Los Angeles, and Dallas, stage actresses, film stars, playwrights, playboys, diplomats, etc.

The seat to Mrs Harris's right was occupied by a fierce-looking old gentleman with snow-white hair and moustaches, tufted eyebrows that stood out like feathers from his face, and dark pouches under his eyes which were, however, of a penetrating blue and astonishingly alert and young looking. His hair was combed down over his brow in a sort of fringe; his boots were magnificently polished; his waistcoat was edged with white, and in the lapel of his dark jacket was fastened what seemed to Mrs Harris to be a small rosebud which both fascinated and startled her, since she had never seen a gentleman wearing any such thing before and so she was caught by him staring at it.

The thin, beak nose aimed itself at her; the keen blue eyes scrutinised her, but the voice that addressed her in perfect English was sere and tired. 'Is there something wrong, madam?'

It was not in the nature of Mrs Harris to be abashed or put out of countenance by anyone, but the thought that she might have been rude stirred her to contrition and she favoured the old gentleman with a self-deprecating smile.

'Fancy me gawking at you like you was a waxworks,' she apologised, 'where's me manners? I thought that was a rose in yer buttonhole. Jolly good idea too.' Then in explanation she added - 'I'm very fond of flowers.'

'Are you,' said the gentleman. 'That is good.' Whatever hostility had been engendered by her stare was dispelled by the engaging innocence of her reply. He looked upon his neighbour with a new interest and saw now that she was a most extraordinary creature and one he could not immediately place. 'Perhaps,' he added, 'it would be better if this were indeed a rose instead of a - rosette.'

Mrs Harris did not understand this remark at all, but the pleasant manner in which it had been delivered showed her that she had been forgiven for her rudeness and the tiny shadow that had fallen across her mood was dispelled. 'Ain't it loverly 'ere?' she said by way of keeping the conversation going.

'Ah, you feel the atmosphere too.' Puzzled, the old gentleman was racking his brain, trying to catch or connect with something that was stirring there, something that seemed to be connected vaguely with his youth and his education which had been rounded out by two years at an English University. He was remembering a dark and dingy closet, dark-panelled, that had been his bedroom and study, cold and austere, opening off a dark hallway, and incongruously, as the picture formed in his mind, there was a pail standing in the hall at the head of the stairs.

Mrs Harris's alert little eyes now dared to engage those of the old gentleman. They penetrated the fierceness of his exterior, peering through the fringe of white hair and menacing eyebrows and the immaculate front of his clothing to a warmth that she felt within. She wondered what he was doing there, for his attitude of hands folded over a gold-headed cane was of one who was unaccompanied. Probably looking for a dress for his granddaughter, she thought and, as always, with her kind, resorted to the direct question to satisfy her curiosity. She did, however, as a gesture of benevolence advance the prospective recipient a generation.

'Are you looking for a dress for your daughter?' Mrs Harris inquired.

The old man shook his head, for his children were scattered and far removed. 'No,' he replied, 'I come here from time to time because I like to see beautiful clothes and beautiful women. It refreshes me and makes me feel young again.'

Mrs Harris nodded assent. 'No doubt abaht that!' she agreed. Then with the pleasant feeling that she had found someone else in whom she might confide she leaned towards him and whispered: 'I've come all the way from London to buy meself a Dior dress.'

A flash of insight, half a Frenchman's marvellous perspicacity, half the completion of the memory he had been trying to dredge up, illuminated the old gentleman, and he knew now who and what she was. The old picture of the dark-stained hallway and creaking stairs with the pail at the top, returned, but now a figure stood beside the bucket, a large slatternly woman in a bedraggled overall, outsize shoes, reddish-grey hair, and freckled skin, sole commander of battery of brooms, mops, dusters, and brushes. She had been for him the only cheerful note throughout the gloomy precincts of the college rooms.

A slattern whose husband had deserted her, the sole support of five children, she exuded unfailing good humour and a kind of waspish but authentic and matter-of-fact philosophy sandwiched in between comments upon the weather, the government, the cost of living, and the vicissitudes of life 'Tyke what you can get and don't look no gift 'orse in the eye,' was one of her sayings. He remembered that her name had been Mrs Maddox, but to him and another French boy in the college she had always been Madame Mops, and as such had been their friend, counsellor, bearer of tidings, source of gossip and intramural news.

He remembered too that beneath the brash and comic exterior he had recognised the intrepid bravery of women who lived out lives of hardship and ceaseless toil to render their simple duties to their own, leavened with no more than the sprinkling of the salt of minor grumbling, and acid commentary upon the scoundrels and scallywags who ran things. He could see her again now, the reddish-grey hair hanging down about her eyes, a cigarette tucked behind one ear, her head bobbing with concentrated energy as she charred the premises. He could almost hear her speak again. And then realised that he *had.*

For seated next to him in the most exclusive and sophisticated dress salon in Paris, was the reincarnation of his Madame Mops of half a century ago.

True there was no physical resemblance, for his neighbour was slight and worn thin by work - the old gentleman's eyes dropping to her hands confirmed the guess - but that was not how he recognised her; it was by the bearing, the speech, of course, and the naughty little eyes, but above all by the aura of indomitable courage and independence and impudence that surrounded her.

'A Dior dress,' he echoed her - 'a splendid idea. Let us hope that you will find here this afternoon what you desire.'

There was no need in him to question her as to *how* it was possible for her to fulfil such a wish. He knew from his own experience something of the nature of these special Englishwomen and simply assumed that she had been left a legacy, or had suddenly acquired a large sum of money through one of those massive and extraordinary football lotteries he was always reading about in the papers as conferring untold wealth upon British railroad porters, coal miners, or grocery assistants. But had he known just how Mrs Harris had come by the entire sum needed to satisfy her ambition he would not have been surprised either.

They now understood one another as did old friends who had much in life behind them.

'I wouldn't let on to anyone else,' Mrs Harris confessed from the comfort of her new-found friendship, 'but I was frightened to death to come 'ere.'

The old man looked at her in astonishment - 'You? Frightened?'

'Well,' Mrs Harris confided, 'you know the French . . .'

The gentleman emitted a sigh. 'Ah yes. I know them very well. Still there is nothing now but for you to choose the gown that you like the best. It is said the collection this spring is superb.'

There was a stir and a rustle. A chic, expensively-dressed woman came in acolyted by two sales ladies and made for the seat beside Mrs Harris where the brown rexine handbag containing the latter's fortune reposed momentarily.

Mrs Harris snatched it away with an 'Oops, dearie, sorry!' then brushed the seat of the chair with her hand, and smiling cheerily said: 'There you are now. All ready for you.'

The woman who had close-set eyes and a too small mouth sat down with a jangle of gold bracelets, and immediately Mrs Harris felt herself enveloped in a cloud of the most delectable and intoxicating perfume. She leaned closer to the woman for a better sniff and said with sincere admiration: 'My, you do smell good.'

The newcomer made a testy motion of withdrawal and a line appeared between the narrow eyes. She was looking towards the door as though searching for someone.

It would be time to begin soon. Mrs Harris felt as eager and excited as a child and mentally apostrophized herself: 'Look at you, Ada 'Arris! Whoever would have thought you'd be sitting in the parlour at Dior's in Paris one day, buying a dress with all the toffs? And yet 'ere you are, and noffink can stop you now—'

But the woman next to her, the wife of a speculator, had found whom she sought - Madame Colbert, who had just emerged from the dressing rooms leading off from the stairs, and she beckoned her over, speaking sharply and loudly to her in French as she neared: 'What do you mean by seating a vulgar creature like this next to me? I wish her removed at once. I have a friend coming later who will occupy her chair.'

Mme Colbert's heart sank. She knew the woman and the breed. She bought not for love of clothes, but for the ostentation of it. Nevertheless she spent money. To temporize, Mme Colbert said: 'I am sorry, madame, but I have no recollection of reserving this seat for a friend of yours, but I will look.'

'It is not necessary to look. I told you I wished this seat for a friend. Do as I say at once. You must be out of your mind to place such a person next to me.'

The old gentleman next to Mrs Harris was beginning to colour, the crimson rising from the neckline of his collar and spreading to his ears. His blue eyes were turning as frosty as his white fringe.

For a moment Mme Colbert was tempted. Surely the little cleaning woman from London would understand if she explained to her that there had been an error in the reservations and the seat was taken. She would be able to see just as much from the head of the stairs. Her glance travelled to Mrs Harris sitting there in her shabby coat and preposterous hat. And the object of this contretemps, not understanding a word of the conversation, looked up at her with her sunniest and most trusting apple-cheeked smile. 'Ain't you a dear to put me 'ere with all these nice people,' she said, 'I couldn't be 'appier if I was a millionaire.'

A worried-looking man in striped trousers and frock coat appeared at the head of the salon. The angry woman called to him: 'Monsieur Armand; come here at once, I wish to speak to you. Mme Colbert has had the impertinence to seat me next to this dreadful woman. Am I forced to put up with this?'

Flustered by the vehemence of the attack, M. Armand took one look at Mrs Harris and then to Mme Colbert he made secret ousting movements with his hands and said: 'Well, well. You heard. Get rid of her at once.'

The angry red in the face of the fierce old gentleman turned to purple, he half arose from his chair, his mouth opening to speak when Mme Colbert preceded him.

Many thoughts and fears had raced through the French-woman's mind, her job, prestige of the firm, possible loss of a wealthy client, consequences of defiance of authority. Yet she also knew that though M. Armand was her superior, on this floor she was in supreme command. And now that the unwitting Mrs Harris was the subject of a cruel attack the manageress experienced more than ever the feeling of kinship and sisterhood with this strange visitor from across the Channel returning overpoweringly. Whatever happened, oust her she could not and would not. It would be like beating an innocent child. She thrust out her firm round chin at M. Armand and declared: 'Madame has every right to be seated there. She has journeyed here from London especially to buy a dress. If you wish her removed, do it yourself, for I will not.'

Mrs Harris guessed she was being discussed and identified too the city of her birth, but took no hint as to the import of the discussion. She gathered that Mme Colbert had acquainted the gentleman in the frock coat with the story of her ambitions. She therefore favoured him with her most engaging smile and, in addition, tipped him a large and knowing wink.

The old gentleman had in the meantime resumed both his seat and his normal colour, but he was staring at Mme Colbert, his face lit up with a kind of fierce and angry joy. He had momentarily forgotten Mrs Harris in his discovery of something new, or rather on the contrary, something very old and almost forgotten - a Frenchwoman of selfless courage, honour, and integrity.

As for M. Armand, he hesitated - and was lost. Mme Colbert's firm stand as well as Mrs Harris's wink had unnerved him. Some of Dior's best clients, he was aware, were frequently most odd-appearing and eccentric women. Mme Colbert was supposed to know what she was doing. Throwing up his hands in a gesture of surrender, he fled the battlefield.

The wife of the speculator snapped: 'You will hear further about this. I think, Mme Colbert, this will cost you your position,' got up, and stalked from the room.

'Ah, but I think it will not!' The speaker was now the old gentleman with the tufted eyebrows, fiercely prominent nose, and the rosette of the Légion d'Honneur in his buttonhole. He arose and declaimed somewhat dramatically: 'I am proud to have been a witness that the spirit of true democracy is not entirely extinguished in France and that decency and honour still have some adherents. If there are any difficulties over this I will speak to the patron myself.'

Mme Colbert glanced at him and murmured: 'Monsieur is very kind.' She was bewildered, sick at heart, and not a little frightened, as she peered momentarily into the dark abyss of the future - Jules passed over again, a broken man, she dismissed from her job and no doubt blacklisted by a malicious woman.

A girl stationed at the door called out: 'Number wan, "Nocturne",' as a model in a beige suit with wide lapels and flaring skirt minced into the room.

A little shriek of excitement was torn from Mrs Harris. 'Lumme. It's begun!'

In spite of her state of mind Mme Colbert felt suddenly an inexplicable welling up in her of love for the charwoman and bending over her she gave her a little squeeze. 'Look well now,' she said, 'so that you may recognise your heart's desire.'

THEREAFTER, for the next hour and a half, before the enthralled eyes of Mrs Harris, some ten models paraded one hundred and twenty specimens of the highest dressmaker's art to be found in the most degenerately civilised city in the world.

They came in satins, silks, laces, wools, jerseys, cottons, brocades, velvets, twills, broadclothes, tweeds, nets, organzas, and muslins—

They showed frocks, suits, coats, capes, gowns, clothes for cocktails, for the morning, the afternoon, for dinner parties, and formal and stately balls and receptions.

They entered trimmed with fur, bugle beads, sequins, embroidery with gold and silver thread, or stiff with brocades, the colours were wonderfully gay and clashed in daring combinations; the sleeves were long, short, medium, or missing altogether. Necklines ranged from choke to plunge, hemlines wandered at the whim of the designer. Some hips were high, others low, sometimes the breasts were emphasized, sometimes neglected or wholly concealed. The theme of the show was the high waist and hidden hips.

There were hints and forecasts of the sack and trapeze to come. Every known fur from Persian lamb, mink, and nutria to Russian baumarten and sable were used in trimming or in the shape of stoles or jackets.

It was not long before Mrs Harris began to become accustomed to this bewildering array of richness and finery and soon came to recognise the various models upon their appearance in rotation.

There was the girl who walked slinky-sly with her stomach protruding a good six inches before her, and the petite one with the come-hither eyes and provocative mouth. There was the model who seemed to be plain until Mrs Harris noted her carriage and quiet air of elegance, and another who was just sufficiently on the plump side to convey the idea to a stout customer. There was the girl with her nose in the air and disdain at her lips, and an opposite type, a red-haired minx who wooed the whole salon as she made her rounds.

And then, of course, there was the one and only Natasha, the star. It was the custom in the salon to applaud when a creation made a particular hit, and Mrs Harris's palms, horny from application to scrubbing brush and mop, led the appreciation each time Natasha appeared looking lovelier than the last. Once, during one of her appearances, the charwoman noticed a tall, blond, pale young man with an odd scar on his face standing outside, staring hungrily as Natasha made an entrance and said to herself: 'Coo, he ain't arf in love with her, he ain't . . .'

She was in love herself, was Mrs Harris, with Natasha, with Mme Colbert, but above all with life and the wonderful thing it had become. The back of her card was already covered with pencilled numbers of frocks and dresses and frantic notes, messages and reminders to herself that she would never be able to decipher. How could one choose between them all?

And then Natasha glided into the salon wearing an evening gown, Number 89, called 'Temptation'. Mrs Harris had just a fleeting instant in which to note the enraptured expression on the face of the young man by the door before he turned away quickly as though that was what he had come for, and then it was all up with her. She was lost, dazzled, blinded, overwhelmed by the beauty of the creation. This was IT!!! Thereafter there were yet to come further stunning examples of evening gowns until the traditional appearance of the bridal costume brought the show to a close, but the char saw none of them. Her choice was made. Feverish excitement accelerated her heartbeat. Desire coursed like fire in her veins.

'Temptation' was a black velvet gown, floor length, encrusted half-way from the bottom up with a unique design picked out in beads of jet that gave to the skirt weight and movement. The top was a froth of cream, delicate pink, and white chiffon, tulle and lace from which arose the ivory shoulders and neck and dreamy-eyed dark head of Natasha.

Rarely had a creation been better named. The wearer appeared like Venus arising from the pearly sea, and likewise she presented the seductive figure of a woman emerging from tousled bedclothes. Never had the upper portion of the female form been more alluringly framed.

The salon burst into spontaneous applause at Natasha's appearance and the clacking of Mrs Harris's palms rounded like the beating upon boards with a broomstick.

Cries and murmurs of 'La, la!' and 'Voyez, c'est formidable!' arose on all sides from the males present while the fierce old gentleman thumped his cane upon the floor and beamed with ineffable pleasure. The garment covered Natasha most decently and morally and yet was wholly indecent and overwhelmingly alluring.

Mrs Harris was not aware that there was anything extra-ordinary as to the choice she had made. For she was and eternally would be a woman. She had been young once and in love. She had had a husband to whom her young heart had gone out and to whom she had wished to give and be everything. Life in that sense had not passed her by. He had been shy, embarrassed, tongue-tied, yet she had heard the love words forced haltingly from his lips whispered into her ear. Incongruously, at that moment she thought of the photograph upon her dressing table with herself in the tiered muslin dress that had seemed so grand then, only now she saw herself clad in 'Temptation' in the picture instead.

The bridal model showed herself perfunctorily; the gath-ering, buzzing as it emerged from the two salons were sucked towards the exit leading to the grand staircase where, lined up like ravens, the *vendeuses,* the black-clad sales women with their little sales books under their arms waited to pounce upon their customers.

Mrs Harris, her small blue eyes glittering like aquamar-ines, found Mme Colbert. 'Number eighty-nine, Tempty-tion,' she cried, and then added, 'oh Lor', I 'ope it don't cost more'n what I've got.'

Mme Colbert smiled a thin, sad smile. She might almost have guessed it. 'Temptation' was a poem created in materials by a poet of women, for a young girl in celebration of her freshness and beauty and awakening to the mysterious power of her sex. It was invariably demanded by the faded, the middle-aged, the verging-on-passé women. 'Come,' she said, 'we will go to the back and I will have it brought to you.'

She led her through grey doors into another part of the building, through endless meadows of the soft grey carpeting until at last Mrs Harris came into yet another world that was almost stifling with excitement.

She found herself in a curtained-off cubicle on a corridor that seemed to be a part of an endless maze of similar corridors and cubicles. Each cubicle held a woman like a queen bee in a cell, and through the corridors rushed the worker bees with the honey - armfuls of frilly, frothy garments in colours of plum, raspberry, tamarind, and peach, gentian-flower, cowslip, damask rose, and orchid, to present them where they had been ordered for trial and further inspection.

Here was indeed woman's secret world, where gossip and the latest scandal was exchanged, the battlefield where the struggle against the ravages of age was carried on with the weapons of the dressmaker's art and where fortunes were spent in a single afternoon.

Here, attended by sales women, seamstresses, cutters, fitters, and designers, who hovered about them with tape, scissors, basting needle and thread, and mouths full of pins, rich French women, rich American women, rich German women, super-rich South American women, titled women from England, maharanees from India, and even, it was rumoured, the wife or two of an ambassador or commissar from Russia, spent their afternoons - and their husband's money.

And here too, in the midst of this thrilling and entrancing hive, surrounded by her own entourage, stood the London charwoman, encased in 'Temptation' - whom it fitted astonishingly, yet logically, since she too was slender, thinned by occupational exercise and too little food.

She issued from the wondrous, frothy foam of seashell pink, sea-cream and pearl white like - Ada 'Arris from Battersea. The creation worked no miracles except in her soul. The scrawny neck and greying head that emerged from the shoulder *décolleté* of the gown, the weathered skin, small button-bright blue eyes, and apple cheeks contrasted with the classic fall of jet-encrusted black velvet panels were grotesque - but still, not wholly so, for the beautiful gown as well as the radiance of the person in it yet managed to lend an odd kind of dignity to this extraordinary figure.

For Mrs Harris had attained her Paradise. She was in a state of dreamed-of and longed-for bliss. All of the hardships, the sacrifices, the economies, and hungers and doings-without she had undergone faded into insignificance. Buying a Paris dress was surely the most wonderful thing that could happen to a woman.

Mme Colbert was consulting a list 'Ah, *oui*,' she murmured, 'the price is five hundred thousand francs.' The apple cheeks of Mrs Harris paled at this announcement. There was not that much money in the whole world. 'That is five hundred English pounds,' Mme Colbert continued, which is one thousand four hundred American dollars, and with our little discount for cash—'

Mrs Harris's yell of triumph interrupted her. 'Blimey! That's exactly what I've got. I'll 'ave it! Can I pye for it now?' and moving stiffly beneath the crinolines, jet, and interior reinforcements of the dress, she reached for her purse.

'Of course - if you wish. But I do not like to handle such an amount of cash. I will ask M. Fauvel to descend,' Mme Colbert replied and reached for a telephone.

A few minutes later, the young, blond, M. André Fauvel appeared in the cubicle, where the shrewd appraising eyes recognised him at once as the man who had gazed with such a hopelessly lovelorn expression upon Natasha.

As for M. Fauvel, he looked upon Mrs Harris rising out of 'Temptation', registering sheer and almost unconcealed horror at the picture of this earthy person desecrating the gown modelled in the collection by his goddess. To the inflamed mind of young Fauvel it was as though one of the girls from the Rue Blanche or the Place Pigalle had wrapped herself in the flag of France.

The creature smiled at him, revealing missing and imperfect teeth and wrinkling the cheeks so that they looked like fruit shrunken by frost, as she said: 'It's all 'ere ducks. Fourteen hundred dollars, and that's me last penny. Strewth!' And she handed him the sheaf of dollars.

Mme Colbert caught the look upon the face of the young accountant She could have told him this was something they went through a hundred times each week, watching exquisite creations meant for beautiful women carried off by raddled old frumps. She touched his arm gently, distracting him, and explained in a few swift sentences in French. It failed to abate his anger at seeing the outer shell of his beloved so mocked and burlesqued.

'It don't need no altering,' Mrs Harris was saying. 'I'll take it just as it is. 'Ave it wrapped for me.'

Mme Colbert smiled. 'But, my dear, surely you must know we cannot let you have *this* dress. This is the model and there is yet another month of summer showings. We will make you one, of course, exactly like—'

Alarm squeezed the heart of Mrs Harris as the import of what Mme Colbert was saying struck home. 'Lumme! Myke me one—' she repeated, and suddenly looking like an older travesty of herself, asked, ''ow long does it take?'

Mme Colbert felt alarm now too: 'Ten days to two weeks ordinarily - but for you we would make an exception and rush it through in a week—'

The awful silence following upon this revelation was broken by the cry torn from the depth of Mrs Harris - 'But don't you understand? I can't stay in Paris. I've just enough money to get me 'ome! It means I can't 'ave it!' She saw herself back in the gloomy Battersea flat, empty-handed, possessed only of her useless money. What did she want with all that money? It was ownership of 'Temptation' for which she craved, body and soul, even though she never again put it on her back.

Horrible, dreadful, common woman, thought M. André. *Serves you right, and I shall enjoy handing your vulgar money back to you.*

Thereupon, to the horror of all, they saw two tears form at the corners of her eyes, followed by others that coursed down the red-veined cheeks as Mrs Harris stood there in the midst of them, in the exquisite ball gown, miserable, abandoned, desperately unhappy.

And M. André Fauvel, accountant and money-man, supposedly with heart of stone, suddenly felt himself moved as he had never thought possible, deeply and unbearably touched and, with one of those flashes of insight of which the French are so capable, knew that it was the hopeless love he felt for the girl Natasha whose sweet and dear body had inhabited this garment that had brought him so suddenly to an understanding of the tragedy of this stranger who, on the brink of realising her greatest desire, was to suffer frustration.

Thereupon he dedicated his next remark to that girl who would never know how much or greatly he had loved her, or that he had loved her at all, for that matter. He presented himself to Mrs Harris with a formal little bow: 'If madame would care, I invite her to come to my home and remain with me during this period as my guest. It is not much - only a small house, but my sister has had to go to Lille and there would be room—'

His reward was almost immediate in the expression that came over the little woman's face and her cry of 'Oh Lor' love yer! Do yer really mean it?' and the odd gesture of Mme Colbert which might have been the brushing away of something from the corner of her eyes as she said - 'Oh *André, vous êtes un ange!*'

But then Mrs Harris gave a little shriek. 'Oh lumme - my jobs . . .'

'Haven't you a friend,' suggested Mme Colbert helpfully, 'someone who would help you out while you were away?'

'Mrs Butterfield,' Mrs Harris replied immediately - 'but a whole week—'

'If she is a real friend she will not mind,' Mme Colbert counselled. 'We could send her a telegram from you.'

Mrs Butterfield would not mind, particularly when she heard all about it, Mrs Harris felt certain. Her conscience smote her when she thought of Pamela Penrose and her important producer friends and her career. Yet there was 'Temptation'. 'I'll do it,' she cried. 'I've got to 'ave it.'

Thereupon to her excitement and delight, *her* horde of fitters, cutters, dressmakers, and seamstresses descended upon her with tape, pattern muslin, pins, basting thread, scissors, and all the wondrous exciting paraphernalia that was connected with making up the most expensive dress in the world.

By late afternoon, when at last Mrs Harris was done with measuring and fitting, the most remote corner of the establishment had heard the tale of the London charwoman who had saved her wages and journeyed to Paris to buy herself a Dior dress and she was in the way of becoming something of a celebrity. Members of the staff from the lowest to the highest, including the Patron himself, had managed an excuse to pass by the cubicle to catch a glimpse of this remarkable Englishwoman.

And later, while for the last time Mrs Harris was encased in the model, Natasha herself, clad in a neat cocktail frock, for she was about to start out on a round of evening's eng-agements, came and saw nothing unusual or grotesque in the figure of the charwoman in the beautiful creation, for she had heard the story and felt herself touched by it. She understood Mrs Harris. 'I am so glad you have chosen that one,' she said simply.

When the latter suddenly said - 'Coo, 'owever am I going to get to this Mr Fauvel. He gave me 'is address, but I wouldn't know where it was—' Natasha was the first to offer to take her thither.

'I have a leetle car; I will drive you there myself. Let me see where it is.'

Mrs Harris handed her the card M. Fauvel had given her with the address, 'Number 18, Rue Dennequin.' Natasha wrinkled her pretty forehead over the name. 'Monsieur André Fauvel,' she repeated. 'Now where have I seen that name before?'

Madame Colbert smiled indulgently - 'It is only the accountant of our company, *chérie*,' she said, 'he is the one who pays out your salary.'

'*Tiens!*' laughed Natasha - 'One might love such a one. Very well, Madame Harris, when you are ready I will take you to heem.'

THUS it was that, shortly after six, Mrs Harris found herself in Natasha's sporty little Simca, negotiating the traffic rapids of the Étoile and then sailing down the broad stream of the Avenue de Wagram, bound for the home of M. Fauvel. A telegram had already been dispatched to London, asking her friend to cope with her clients as best she could until her return; a telegram calculated to shake Mrs Butterfield to her very marrow, emanating from Paris as it did. But Mrs Harris cared not. She was still exploring Paradise.

Number 18 rue Dennequin was a small, two-storey grey house with mansard roof, built in the nineteenth century. When they rang the doorbell, M. Fauvel cried: '*Entrez, entrez* - come in,' from within, believing it to be Mrs Harris by herself. They pushed through the door that was ajar and found themselves in a home in exactly that state of chaos to be expected when a bachelor's sister has gone away leaving explicit instructions with the daily cleaning woman, who would naturally choose that moment to become ill.

Dust lay thick; nothing had been touched for a week; books and clothes were scattered about. It took no trick of the imagination to estimate the piled-up dishes in the kitchen sink, the greasy pans on the stove, as well as the condition of the bathroom and the unmade beds above.

Never was a man in such confusion. His honourable scar gleaming white in a face crimson with shame - the cicatrice rather made him attractive looking - M. Fauvel appeared before them stammering: 'Oh, no - no - Mademoiselle Natasha - you of all people - I cannot permit you to enter - I, who would have given anything to have welcomed - I mean, I have been living alone here for a week - I am disgraced—'

Mrs Harris saw nothing unusual in the condition of the place. If anything, it was comfortably like old times, for it was exactly the same as greeted her in every house, flat, or room when she came to work daily in London.

''Ere, 'ere, duckie,' she called out genially. 'What's all the fuss about? I'll 'ave all this put right in a jiffy. Just you show me where the mop cupboard is, and get me a bucket and a brush—'

As for Natasha - she was looking right through and past the dirt and disorder to the solid, bourgeois furniture she saw beneath it, the plush sofa, the what-not cabinet, the huge portrait-size framed photographs of M. Fauvel's grandfather and mother in stiff, beginning-of-the-century clothes, the harpsichord in one corner, the great tub with the plant in another, the lace on the sofa pillows, the chenille curtains, and the overstuffed chairs - comfort without elegance - and her heart yearned towards it. This was a home, and she had not been in one like it since she had left her own in Lyons.

'Oh, please,' she cried, 'may I remain and help? Would you permit it, monsieur?'

M. Fauvel went into a perfect hysteria of abject apologies - 'But mademoiselle - you of all people - in this pigsty, for which I could die of shame - to spoil those little hands - never in a thousand years could I permit—'

'Ow - come off it, dearie,' ordered Mrs Harris succinctly. 'Blimey, but all the thick 'eads ain't on our side of the Channel. Can't you see the girl WANTS to? Run along now and keep out of the way and let us get at it.'

Dear me, Mrs Harris thought to herself as she and Natasha donned headcloths and aprons and seized upon brooms and dustcloths, *French people are just like anyone else, plain and kind, only maybe a little dirtier. Now 'oo would have thought it after all one 'ears?*

That particular evening, Natasha had a rendezvous for drinks with a count, an appointment for dinner with a duke, and a late evening date with an important politico. It gave her the most intense pleasure she had known since she came to Paris to leave the count standing and, with the professional and efficient Mrs Harris, make the dirt fly at number 18 Rue Dennequin, as it had never flown before.

It seemed no time at all before everything was in order again. The mantelpieces and furniture gleamed, the plant was watered, the beds stiff with clean sheets and pillowcases, the ring around the bath tub banished, pots, pans, dishes, glasses, and knives and forks washed-up.

'*Oh, it is good to be inside a home again, where one can be a woman and not just a silly little doll,*' Natasha said to herself as she attacked the dust and cobweb salients in the corners and contemplated the horrors that M. Fauvel, manlike, had brushed under the carpet.

And as she stood there for a moment, reflecting upon the general hopelessness of the male species, she found herself suddenly touched by the plight of M. Fauvel and thought, *That must be a fine sister he has, poor boy, and he is so ashamed* - and suddenly in her mind's eye she saw herself holding this blond head with the blushing face and the white scar - surely acquired in some noble manner - to her breast while she murmured, 'Now, now, my little one, do not take on so. Now that I am here everything will be all right again.' And this to a perfect stranger she had seen only vaguely before as he appeared occasionally in the background of the establishment for which she worked. She stood stock-still for a moment with astonishment at herself, leaning upon her broom, the very picture of housewifely grace, to be discovered so by the sudden return of the enchanted M. Fauvel himself.

So busy had been the two women that neither had noticed the absence of the accountant until he suddenly re-appeared but half-visible behind the mountain of parcels with which he was laden.

'I thought that after such exhausting labours you might be hungry—' he explained. Then, regarding a dishevelled, smudged, but thoroughly contented Natasha, he stammered: 'Would you - could you - dare I hope that you might remain?'

The count and his date were already dead pigeons. Bang, bang, went both barrels and the duke and the politico joined him. With the utmost simplicity and naturalness, and quite forgetting herself, Natasha, or rather Mme Petitpierre of Lyons, threw her arms about M. Fauvel's neck and kissed him. 'But you are an angel to have thought of this, André I am ravenous. First I will allow myself a bath in that wonderful deep old tub upstairs and then we will eat and eat and eat.'

M. Fauvel thought too that he had never been so happy in his life. What an astonishing turn things had taken ever since - why, ever since that wonderful little Englishwoman had come to Dior's to buy herself a dress.

Mrs Harris had never tasted caviar before, a *pâté de foie gras* fresh from Strasbourg, but she very quickly got used to them both, as well as the lobster from the Pas-de-Calais and the eels from Lorraine in jelly. There was *charcuterie* from Normandy, a whole cold roast *poulet de Bresse* along with a crispy skinned duck from Nantes. There was a Chassagne Montrachet with the lobster and *hors d'œuvre*, champagne with the caviar, and Vosne Romanée with the fowl, while an Yquem decorated the chocolate cake.

Mrs Harris ate for the week before, for this, and the next as well. There had never been a meal like it before and probably never would again. Her eyes gleamed with delight as she crowed: 'Lumme, if there's anything I like it's a good tuck in.'

'The night without is heavenly,' said M. Fauvel, his eyes meltingly upon the sweet, well-fed-pussy-cat face of Natasha, 'perhaps afterwards we will let Paris show herself to us—'

'Ooof!' grunted Mrs Harris, stuffed to her wispy eyebrows. 'You two go. I've 'ad a day to end all days. I'll just stay 'ome 'ere and do the dishes and then get into me bed and try not to wake up back in Battersea.'

But now, a feeling of restraint and embarrassment seemed suddenly to descend upon the two young people and which Mrs Harris in her state of repletion failed to notice. Had his guest consented to go, M. Fauvel was thinking, all would have been different, and the exuberance of the party plus the glorious presence of Natasha might have been maintained. But, of course, without this extraordinary person the thought of his showing Dior's star model the sights of Paris suddenly seemed utterly ridiculous.

To Natasha, Paris at night was the interior of a series of smoky *boîtes*, or expensive nightclubs, such as Dinazard, or Shéhérazade, and of which she was heartily sick. She would have given much to have been enabled to stand on the Grand Terrasse of Le Sacré-Cœur, under the starry night, and look out over these stars reflected in the sea of the light of Paris - and in particular with M. Fauvel at her side.

But with Mrs Harris's plumping for bed there seemed no further excuse for her presence. She had already intruded too much into his privacy. She had shamelessly pried into his quarters with broom and duster, seen the squalor in his sink, permitted herself the almost unthinkable intimacy of washing out his bath tub, and, in her exuberance, the even more unpardonable one of bathing in it herself.

She became suddenly overcome with confusion, and blushing murmured: 'Oh, no, no, no. I cannot, it is impossible. I am afraid I have an appointment. I must be going.'

M. Fauvel accepted the blow which was expected. *'Ah, yes'* he thought, *'you must return, little butterfly, to the life you love best. Some count, marquis, duke, or even prince will be waiting for you. But at least I have had this one night of bliss and I should be content.'* Aloud he murmurmured 'Yes, yes, of course, Mademoiselle has been too kind.'

He bowed, they touched hands lightly and their glances met and for a moment lingered. And this time the sharp knowing eyes of Mrs Harris twigged: 'Oho,' she said to herself, *'so that's 'ow it is. I should have went with them.'*

But it was too late to do anything about it now and the fact was that she really was too stuffed to move. 'Well, good night, dears,' she said loudly and pointedly, and tramped up the stairs, hoping that with her presence removed they might still get together on an evening out. But a moment later she heard the front door opened and shut and then the clatter as the motor of Natasha's Simca came to life. Thus ended Mrs Ada 'Arris's first day in a foreign land and amidst a foreign people.

The following morning, however, when M. Fauvel proposed that in the evening he show her something of Paris, Mrs Harris lost no time in suggesting that Natasha be included in the party. Flustered, M. Fauvel protested that sightseeing was not for such exalted creatures as Mlle Natasha.

'Garn,' scoffed Mrs Harris. 'What makes you think she's different from any other young girl when there is an 'andsome man about? She'd 'ave gone with you last night if you 'ad 'ad the brains to ask 'er. You just tel 'er I said she was to come.'

That morning the two of them encountered briefly upon the grey carpeted stairs at Dior. They paused for an instant uncomfortably. M. Fauvel managed to stammer: 'Tonight I shall be showing Mrs Harris something of Paris. She has begged that you would accompany us.'

'Oh,' murmured Natasha, 'Madame Harris has asked? She wishes it? Only she?'

M. Fauvel could only nod dumbly. How could he in the chill austerity of the grand staircase of the House of Christian Dior cry out 'Ah, no, it is I who wish it, crave it, desire it, with all my being. It is I who worship the very nap of the carpet on which you stand.'

Natasha finally said: 'If she desires it then, I will come. She is adorable, that little woman.'

'At eight then.'

'I will be there.'

They continued on their routes, he up, she down.

The enchanted night duly took place. It began for the three of them with a ride up the Seine on a *bateau-mouche* to a riverside restaurant in a tiny suburb. With a wonderful sense of tact and feeling M. Fauvel avoided those places where Mrs Harris might have felt uncomfortable, the expensive luxury and glitter spots, and never knew how happy Natasha herself felt in this more modest environment.

This was a little family restaurant. The tables were of iron, the tablecloths checkered, and the bread wonderfully crisp and fresh. Mrs Harris took it all in, the simple people at neighbouring tables, the glassy, shimmering surface of the river with boating parties gliding about and the strains of accordion music drifting over from the water, with a deep sigh of satisfaction. She said: 'Lumme, if it ain't just like 'ome. Sometimes, on a hot night, me friend Mrs Butterfield and I go for a ride up the river and drop in for a pint at a little plyce near the brewery.'

But at the eating of a snail she firmly baulked. She examined them with interest in their steaming fragrant shells. The spirit was willing but her stomach said no.

'I can't,' she finally confessed, 'not arter seeing them walkin' about.'

From that time on, unspoken, the nightly gathering of the three for roamings about Paris became taken for granted. In the daytime, while they worked, except for her fittings which took place at eleven-thirty in the mornings, and her tidying of Fauvel's premises, Mrs Harris was free to explore the city on her own, but the evenings were heralded by the arrival of Natasha in her Simca, and they would be off.

Thus Mrs Harris saw Paris by twilight from the second landing of the Tour Eiffel, by milky moonlight from Le

Sacré-Cœur, and waking up in the morning at dawn when the market bustle at Les Halles began, and after a night of visiting this or that part of the city of never-ending wonder, they breakfasted there on eggs and garlic sausages surrounded by workmen, market porters, and lorry drivers.

Once, instigated somewhat in a spirit of mischief by Natasha, they took Mrs Harris to the *Revue des Nudes*, a cabaret in the Rue Blanche, but she was neither shocked nor impressed. There is a curiously cosy kind of family atmosphere at some of these displays; whole groups, including grandmothers, fathers, mothers, and the young come up from the country for a celebration or anniversary of some kind, bringing along a picnic hamper; they order wine and settle down to enjoy the fun.

Mrs Harris felt right at home in this milieu. She did not consider the parade of stitchless young ladies immoral. Immoral in her code was doing someone the dirty. She peered interestedly at the somewhat beefy naiads and remarked: 'Coo - some of them don't arf want a bit o' slimming, what?' Later when an artiste adorned with no more than a *cache sexe* consisting of a silver fig leaf performed rather a strenuous dance, Mrs Harris murmured: 'Lumme, I don't see 'ow she does it.'

'Does which?' queried M. Fauvel absent-mindedly, for his attention was riveted upon Natasha.

'Keeps that thing on 'oppin about like that.'

M. Fauvel blushed crimson and Natasha shouted with laughter, but forbore to explain.

And in this manner, Mrs Harris lost all fear of the great foreign capital, for they showed her a life and a city teeming with her own kind of people - simple, rough, realistic, and hard-working, and engaged all of them in the same kind of struggle to get along as she herself back home.

FREE to wander where she would during the day in Paris
except for her fittings, Mrs Harris never quite knew
where her footsteps would lead her. It was not the glittering
shopping sections of the Champs Élysées, the Faubourg
St Honoré, and the Place Vendôme that interested her, for
there were equally shimmering and expensive shopping
sections in London which she never visited. But she loved
people and odd *quartiers*, the beautiful parks, the river, and
the manner in which life was lived in the poorer section by
the inhabitants of the city.

She explored thus the Left Bank and the Right and eventually through accident stumbled upon a certain paradise in
the Middle, the Flower Market located by the Quai de la
Corse on the Île de la Cité.

Often back home Mrs Harris had peered longingly into
the windows of flower shops, at the display of hot-house
blooms, orchids, roses, gardenias, etc., on her way to and
from her labours, but never in her life had she found herself
in the midst of such an intoxicating profusion of blossoms

of every kind, colour, and shape, ranged upon the footpaths and filling stalls and stands of the Flower Market within sight of the twin towers of Notre-Dame.

Here were streets that were nothing but a mass of azaleas in pots, plants in pink, white, red, purple, mingling with huge bunches of cream, crimson, and yellow carnations. There seemed to be acres of boxes of pansies smiling up into the sun, blue irises, red roses, and huge fronds of gladioli forced into early bud in hot-houses.

There were many plants and flowers Mrs Harris did not even know the name of, small rubbery-looking pink blooms, or flowers with yellow centres and deep blue petals, every conceivable kind of daisy and marguerite, bushy-headed peonies and, of course, row upon row of Mrs Harris's own very dearest potted geraniums.

But not only were her visual senses enthralled and over-whelmed by the masses of shapes and colours, but on the soft breeze that blew from the Seine came as well the intoxication of scent to transport the true lover of flowers into his or her particular heaven, and such a one was Mrs Harris. All the beauty that she had ever really known in her life until she saw the Dior dress had been flowers. Now, her nostrils were filled with the scent of lilies and tuberoses. From every quarter came beautiful scents, and through this profusion of colour and scent Mrs Harris wandered as if in a dream.

Yet another familiar figure was promenading in that same dream, none other than the fierce old gentleman who had been Mrs Harris's neighbour at the Dior show and whose name was the Marquis de Chassagne, of an ancient family. He was wearing a light brown spring coat, a brown homburg, and fawn-coloured gloves. There was no fierceness in his face now and even his tufted wild-flung eyebrows seemed at peace as he strolled through the lanes of fresh, dewy blossoms and breathed deeply and with satisfaction of the perfumes that mounted from them.

His path crossed that of the charwoman, a smile broke out over his countenance, and he raised his homburg with the same gesture he would have employed doffing it to a queen. 'Ah,' he said, 'our neighbour from London who likes flowers. So you have found your way here.'

Mrs Harris said: 'It's like a bit of 'eaven, ain't it? I wouldn't have believed it if I 'adn't seen it with me own eyes.' She looked down at a huge jar bulging with crisp white lilies and another with firm, smooth, yet unopened gladioli with but a gleam of mauve, crimson, lemon, or pink showing at the stalks to indicate what colours they would be. Drops of fresh water glistened on them. 'Oh, Lor'!' murmured Mrs Harris, 'I do 'ope Mrs Butterfield won't forget to water me geraniums.'

'Ah, madame, you cultivate geraniums?' the marquis inquired politely.

'Two window boxes full and a dozen or so pots wherever I can find a place to put one. You might say as it was me 'obby.'

'*Épatant!*' the marquis murmured to himself and then inquired: 'And the dress you came here to seek. Did you find it?'

Mrs Harris grinned like a little imp. 'Didn't I just! It's the one called "Temptytion", remember? It's black velvet trimmed wiv black bugle beads and the top is some sort of pink soft stuff.'

The marquis reflected for a moment and then nodded: 'Ah, yes, I do remember. It was worn by that exquisite young creature— '

'Natasha,' Mrs Harris concluded for him. 'She's me friend. It's being myde for me, I've got three more days to wait.'

'And so, with infinite good sense, you acquaint yourself with the genuine attractions of our city.'

'And you—' Mrs Harris began and broke off in the middle of her sentence, for intuitively she knew the answer to the question she had been about to ask.

But the Marquis de Chassagne was not at all put out, and only remarked gravely: 'You have guessed it. There is so little time left for me to enjoy the beauties of the earth. Come, let us sit on this seat in the sun, a little, you and I, and talk.'

They sat then, side by side on the green wooden bench, in the midst of the sensuous colours and ravishing perfumes, the aristocrat and the charwoman, and conversed. They were worlds apart in everything but the simplicity of their humanity, and so they were really not apart at all. For all his title and eminent position, the marquis was a lonely widower, his children married and scattered. And what was Mrs Harris but an equally lonely widow, but with the courage to embark upon one great adventure to satisfy her own craving for beauty and elegance. They had much in common these two.

Besides her geraniums, Mrs Harris remarked, she also received cut flowers from time to time with which to brighten her little basement flat, from clients about to leave for a weekend in the country, or who received presents of fresh flowers and would make it a point to present Mrs Harris with their old and half-wilted blooms. 'I get them 'ome as fast as ever I can,' she explained, 'cut off their stems and put them in a fresh jug of water with a penny at the bottom.'

The marquis looked astounded at this piece of intelligence.

''Ow, didn't you know?' Mrs Harris said. 'If you put a copper in the water with wilted flowers it brings them right back.'

The marquis, full of interest, said: 'Well now, it is indeed true that one is never too old to learn.' He went on to another subject that had interested him. 'And you say that Mademoiselle Natasha has become your friend?'

'She's a dear,' said Mrs Harris, 'not at all like you might expect, high and mighty with all the fuss that's made over her. She's as unspoiled as your own daughter would be. They're all me friends, I do believe - that nice young Monsieur Fauvel, the cashier - it's his 'ouse I am stopping at - and that poor Mme Colbert— '

'Eh,' said the marquis, 'and who is Madame Colbert?'

It was Mrs Harris's turn to look surprised. ''Ow, surely you know Madame Colbert - the manageress - the one who tells you whether you can come in or not. She's a real love. Imagine putting Ada 'Arris right in with all the toffs.'

'Ah, yes,' said the marquis with renewed interest, 'that one. A rare person, a woman of courage and integrity. But why poor?'

Mrs Harris waggled her rear end more comfortably into the bench to enjoy a jolly good gossip. Why, this French gentleman was just like anybody else back home when it came to interest in titbits about other people's trouble and miseries. Her voice became happily confidential as she tapped him on the arm and answered: ''Ow, but of course you wouldn't know about her poor 'usband.'

'Oh,' said the Marquis, 'she has a husband then? What is the difficulty, is he ill?'

'Not exactly,' replied Mrs Harris. 'Madame Colbert wouldn't dream of telling anybody about it but, of course, she's told me. A woman who's buried a husband as I 'ave can understand things. Twenty-five years in the same office 'e was— '

'Your husband?' asked the marquis.

'No, no, Madame Colbert's, the brains of his office he is. But every time he comes up for a big job they give it to some count or some rich man's son until his 'eart is near broken and Madame Colbert's too.'

The marquis felt a curious tingling at the base of his scalp as a faint glimmer of light began to dawn. Mrs Harris's voice for a moment mimicked some of the bitterness contained in that of Mme Colbert's as she said: 'There's another chance for him now and no one to speak up for him or give him a 'and. Madame Colbert's crying her poor dear eyes out.'

A little smile that was almost boyish illuminated the stern mouth of the old marquis. 'Would Madame Colbert's husband by any chance have the name of Jules?'

Mrs Harris stared at him in blank amazement, as though he were a magician. 'Go on!' she cried, ''ow did *you* know? That's 'is name, Jules, do you know him? Madame Colbert says 'e's got more brains in his little finger than all the rest of them in their striped pants.'

The marquis suppressed a chuckle and said: 'Madame Colbert may be right. There can be no question as to the intelligence of a man who has the good sense to marry such a woman.' He sat in silent thought for a moment and then fishing into an inside pocket produced a card case from which he extracted a finely-engraved card and wrote on the back a brief message with an old-fashioned fountain pen. He waved the card dry and then presented it to Mrs Harris. 'Will you remember to give this to Madame Colbert the next time you see her.'

Mrs Harris inspected the card with unabashed interest. The engraved portion read 'Le Marquis Hypolite de Chassagne, Conseiller Extraordinaire au Ministère des Affaires Étrangères, Quai d'Orsay,' which meant nothing to her except that her friend was a nob with a title. She turned it over, but the message thereon was scribbled in French and she did not understand that either. 'Right-o,' she said, 'I've got a 'ead like a sieve, but I won't forget.'

A church clock struck eleven. 'Lor'!' she exclaimed, 'I 'aven't been watching the time. I'll be lyte for me fitting.' She leaped up from the bench, cried: 'So long, ducks, don't forget to put the penny in the jug for the flowers,' and was off. The marquis remained sitting on the bench in the sun looking after her, an expression of rapt and total admiration on his face.

During Mrs Harris's fitting that morning Mme Colbert dropped into the cubicle to see how things were going and assisted the seamstress with a hint here and a suggestion there when Mrs Harris suddenly gave a little shriek. 'Lumme! I almost forgot. 'Ere 'e said I was to give you this.' She secured her ancient handbag, rummaged in it and finally produced the card and handed it to Mme Colbert.

The manageress turned first red and then deathly pale as she examined the paste-board and the message on the reverse. The fingers holding the card began to shake. 'Where did you get this?' she whispered. 'Who gave it to you?'

Mrs Harris looked concerned 'The old gent. The one that was sitting next to me with the red thing in 'is button'ole that day at the collection. I met 'im in the Flower Market and 'ad a bit of a chat with 'im. It ain't bad news, is it?'

'Oh, no, no,' murmured Mme Colbert, her voice trembling with emotion and hardly able to hold back the tears. Suddenly and inexplicably she went to Mrs Harris, took her in her arms and held her tightly for a moment. 'Oh, you wonderful, wonderful woman,' she cried, and then turned and fled from the cubicle. She went into another booth, an empty one, where she could be alone to put her head down upon her arms and cry unashamedly with the joy of the message which had read: 'Please ask your husband to come to see me tomorrow. I may be able to help him - Chassagne.'

ON the last night of Mrs Harris's magical stay in Paris,
M. Fauvel had planned a wonderful party for her and
Natasha, an evening out with dinner at the famous restaurant 'Pré Catalan' in the Bois de Boulogne. Here in the most
romantic setting in the world, seated in the open-air beneath
the spreading boughs of a venerable hundred-and-sixty-
year-old beech tree, illuminated by fairy lights strung
between the leafy branches, and with gay music in the
background, they were to feast on the most delicious and
luxurious of foods and drink the finest wines that M. Fauvel
could procure.

And yet, what should have been the happiest of times for
the three started out as an evening of peculiar and penetrating sadness.

M. Fauvel looked distinguished and handsome in dinner
jacket in the lapel of which was the ribbon of the military
medal he had won. Natasha had never looked more ravishing in an evening dress of pink, grey, and black, cut to show
off her sweet shoulders and exquisite back. Mrs Harris came
as she was except for a fresh, somewhat daringly peek-a-boo

lace blouse she had bought with some of her remaining English pounds.

Her sadness was only an overlay on the delight and excitement of the place and the hour, and the most thrilling thing of all that was to happen tomorrow. It was due to the fact that all good things must come to an end and that she must be leaving these people of whom in a short time she had grown so extraordinarily fond.

But the unhappiness that gripped M. Fauvel and Mlle Petitpierre was of heavier, gloomier, and thicker stuff. Each had reached the conclusion that once Mrs Harris departed, this idyll which had brought them together and thrown them for a week into one another's company, would be at an end.

Natasha was no stranger to the 'Pré Catalan'. Countless times she had been taken there to dine and dance by wealthy admirers who meant nothing to her, who held her clutched to them in close embrace upon the dance floor and who talked interminably of themselves over their food. There was only one person now she wished to dance with ever again, whom she desired to hold her close, and this was the unhappy-looking young man who sat opposite her and did not offer to do so.

Ordinarily in any country two young people have little difficulty in exchanging signals, messages, and eventually finding one another, but when in France they have emerged, so to speak, from the same class and yet are still constrained by the echoes of this class strange obstacles can put themselves in the way of an understanding. For all of the night, the lights, the stars, and the music, M. Fauvel and Mlle Petitpierre were in danger of passing one another by.

For as he gazed upon the girl, his eyes misty with love, M. Fauvel knew that this was the proper setting for

Natasha - here she belonged amidst the light-hearted and the wealthy. She was not for him. He had never been to this colourful restaurant before in the course of the modest life he led and he was now more than ever convinced that it was only because of Madame Harris that Natasha endured him. He was aware that a curious affection had grown up between that glamorous creature, Dior's star model, and the little cleaning woman. But then he had grown very fond of Mrs Harris himself. There was something about this Englishwoman that seemed to drive straight to the heart.

As for Natasha, she felt herself pushed out of André Fauvel's life by the very thing for which she so much yearned, his middle-class respectability. He would never dream of marrying one such as her, presumably spoiled, flighty, steeped in publicity, dowerless. No, never. He would choose some good, simple, middle-class daughter of a friend, or acquaintance, or perhaps his absent sister would choose her for him. He would settle down to the tranquillity of an unexciting married life and raise many children. How she wished that she could be that wife and lead that tranquil life by his side and bear for him those children.

The band beat out a tingling Cha-cha-cha. A bottle of champagne stood opened on the table. They were between courses awaiting the arrival of a super Châteaubriand. All about them voices were raised in merriment and laughter, and the three sat enveloped in thick silence.

Shaking off the shadow that had fallen athwart her and feeling the wonderful excitement of life and beauty that was all about them, Mrs Harris suddenly became aware of the condition of her two companions and tried to do something about it. 'Ain't you two going to dance?' she asked.

M. Fauvel blushed and mumbled something about not having danced for a long time. He would have loved nothing better, but he had no wish to compel Natasha to endure an embrace that must be repulsive to her.

'I do not feel like dancing,' said Mlle Petitpierre. She would have given anything to have been on the floor with him at that moment, but would not embarrass him after his obvious reluctance to have anything to do with her beyond the normal requirements of duty and politeness.

But Mrs Harris's keen ears had already caught the hollowness of their voices with the unmistakable note of misery contained therein, and her shrewd eyes darted from one to the other appraising them.

'Look 'ere,' she said, 'wot's the matter wiv you two?'

'But nothing.'

'Of course, nothing.'

In their efforts to prove this M. Fauvel and Mlle Petitpierre simultaneously broke into bright and brittle chatter aimed at Mrs Harris while they avoided one another's eyes and which they kept up for a minute until it suddenly petered out and the silence resettled itself more thickly.

'Blimey,' said Mrs Harris, 'of all the fools, me. I thought you two 'ad it settled between you long ago.' She turned to M. Fauvel and asked: 'Ain't you got no tongue in your 'ead? What are you waitin' for?'

M. Fauvel flushed as brightly crimson as the electric light bulb above his head 'But - but - I - I—' he stammered, 'she would never.'

Mrs Harris turned to Natasha. 'Can't you 'elp 'im a bit? In my day when a young lydy had her 'eart set on a fellow she'd let him know soon enough. 'Ow do you think I got me own 'usband?'

There was a white light above the beautiful dark, glossy head of the girl, and now she turned as pale as its incandescence.

'But André does not— ' she whispered.

'Garn,' said Mrs Harris, ''E does too - and so do you. I've got eyes in me 'ead. You're both in love. What's keepin' you apart?'

Simultaneously M. Fauvel and Mlle Petitpierre began:

'He wouldn't— '

'She couldn't— '

Mrs Harris chuckled wickedly. 'You're in love, ain't you? 'Oo can't do wot?'

For the first time the two young people looked one another directly in the eyes and saw what lay there. Caught up in one another's gaze, which they could not relinquish, into their faces at last came the clarifying expressions of hope and love. Two tears formed at the corners of Natasha's exquisite eyes and glistened there.

'And now, if you'll excuse me for a minute,' Mrs Harris announced significantly, 'I'll just go and pay a little visit to me aunt.' She rose and went off in the direction of the pavilion.

When she returned a good fifteen minutes later, Natasha was locked in M. Fauvel's arms on the dance floor, her head pillowed on his chest and her face was wet with tears. But when they saw she had returned to the table, they came running to her and threw their arms about her. M. Fauvel kissed one withered-apple cheek, Natasha the other, and then the girl put both arms around Mrs Harris's neck and wept there for a moment murmuring: 'My dear, I am so happy, André and I are going to— '

'Go on,' said Mrs Harris, 'what a surprise ! 'Ow about a bit of bubbly to celebrate?'

They all lifted their glasses and thereafter it was the gayest, brightest, happiest night that Mrs Harris had ever known in her whole life.

AND so the day dawned at last when 'Temptation' was finished and it came time for Mrs Harris to take possession of her treasure swathed in reams of tissue paper and packed in a glamorous cardboard box with the name 'DIOR' printed on it in golden letters as large as life.

There was quite a little gathering for her in the Salon of Dior's in the late morning - she was leaving on an afternoon plane - and from somewhere a bottle of champagne had appeared. Mme Colbert was there, Natasha and M. Fauvel, and all of the fitters, cutters, and seamstresses who had worked so hard and faithfully to finish her dress in record time.

They drank her health and safe journey, and there were gifts for her, a genuine crocodile leather handbag from a grateful Mme Colbert, a wrist watch from an equally grateful M. Fauvel, and gloves and perfume from the more than grateful Natasha.

The manageress took Mrs Harris in her arms, held her closely for a moment, kissed her, and whispered in her ear: 'You have been very very lucky for me, my dear. Soon perhaps I shall be able to write to you of a big announcement concerning my husband.'

Natasha hugged her too and said: 'I shall never forget you, or that I shall owe all my happiness to you. André and I will marry in the autumn. I shall make you godmother to our first child.'

M. André Fauvel kissed her on the cheek and fussed over her, advising her to take good care of herself on the return trip, and then with the true concern of a man whose business is with cash asked: 'You are sure now that you have your money to pay the duty in a safe place? You have it well hidden away, no? It is better you have it not in the purse where it might be snatched.'

Mrs Harris grinned her wonderfully jagged and impish grin. Well fed for the first time in her life, rested, and happy, she looked younger by decades. She opened her new crocodile bag to show the air-ticket and passport therein, with one single green pound note, a five hundred franc note, and a few left-over French coins to see her to the airport. 'That's the lot,' she said. 'But it's plenty to get me back to me duties. There's nuffink for no one to snatch.'

'Oh la la! But no!' cried M. Fauvel, his voice shaken by sudden anguish while a fearful silence fell upon the group in the salon as the shadow of impending disaster made itself felt. 'I mean the customs duty at the British *douane*. Mon Dieu! Have you not provided? At six shillings in the pound' - he made a swift calculation - 'that would be one hundred and fifty pounds. Did you not know you must pay this?'

Mrs Harris looked at him stunned - and aged twenty years. 'Gor,' she croaked, 'hundred and fifty quid. I couldn't raise a bob to me nyme! - 'Ow, why didn't somebody tell me? 'Ow was I to know?'

Mme Colbert reacted fiercely. 'La, what nonsense are you talking, André? Who pays duty any more to customs? You think those titled ladies and rich Americans do? All, all is smuggle, and you too, my little Ada, shall smuggle yours—'

The little blue eyes of Mrs Harris became filled with fear, alarm, suspicion. 'That would be telling a lie, wouldn't it?' she said, looking helplessly from one to the other - 'I don't mind telling a fib or two, but I don't tell lies. That would be bryking the law. I could go to jail for that.' Then as the true and ghastly import of what M. Fauvel said dawned upon her she quite suddenly sank down into the pile of the grey carpet, covered her face with her workworn hands and sent up a wail of despair that penetrated through the establishment so that the *Great Patron* himself came running in. 'I can't 'ave it. It ain't for such as me. I should 'ave known me place. Tyke it away - give it away, do anything. I'll go 'ome and forget about it.'

The story of the dilemma ran like wildfire through the building. Experts appeared from all sides to give advice, including that there be a petition directed to the British Ambassador, until it was pointed out that so stern was the British regard for the law that not even the Ambassador or the Queen herself could intervene to have them set aside, even in so worthy a cause—

It was the *Patron* himself, familiar with Mrs Harris's story who solved the dilemma, severing the Gordian knot with one swift, generous stroke - or thought he had. 'Reduce the price of the dress to this good woman,' he ordered accountant Fauvel, 'and give her the balance in cash to pay the duty.'

'But sir,' protested the horrified Fauvel, who now for the first time himself saw the trap into which his benefactress had fallen, 'it is impossible!'

They all stared at him as though he were a poisonous reptile. 'Do you not see? Madame had already unwittingly broken British law by exporting the one thousand four hundred dollars, illegally exchanged by her American friend in the United Kingdom. If now she, poor woman, appears at the British customs at the airport declaring a dress worth five hundred pounds and offered a further hundred and fifty pounds in cash to pay the duty, there would be inquiries how she, a British subject, had come by these monies: there would be a scandal—'

They continued to look at the unfortunate accountant as though he were a king cobra, but they also knew that he was right. 'Let me go 'ome and die,' wailed Mrs Harris.

Natasha was at her side, her arms about her. Voices rose in a babel of sympathy. Mme Colbert had an inspiration. 'Wait,' she cried, 'I have it.' She, too, dropped to her knees at Mrs Harris's side - 'My dear, will you listen to me? I can help you. I shall be lucky for you, as you have been for me—'

Mrs Harris removed her hands to reveal the face of an old and frightened Capucin monkey. 'I won't do nuffink dishonest - or tell no lies.'

'No, no. Trust me. You shall say nothing but the absolute truth. But you must do exactly how and what I say for, my dear, we ALL wish you to have your beautiful dress to take home. Now listen.' And Mme Colbert, placing her lips close to Mrs Harris's monkey ear so that no one else might hear, whispered her instructions.

As she stood in the customs hall of London Airport, Mrs Harris felt sure that her thumping heart must be audible to all, yet by the time the pleasant-looking young customs officer reached her, her native-born courage and cheerfulness buoyed her up, and her naughty eyes were even twinkling with an odd kind of anticipatory pleasure.

On the counter before her rested, not the glamorous Dior box, but a large and well-worn plastic suitcase of the cheapest kind. The officer handed her a card on which was printed the list of dutiable articles purchased abroad.

'You read it to me, duckie,' Mrs Harris grinned impudently, 'I left me specs at 'ome.'

The inspector glanced at her sharply once to see whether he was being had; the pink rose on the green hat bobbed at him; he recognised the breed at once. 'Hullo,' he smiled. 'What have *you* been doing over in Paris?'

''Aving a bit of a 'oliday on me own.'

The customs man grinned. This was a new one on him. The British char abroad. The mop and broom business must be good, he reflected, then inquired routinely: 'Bring anything back with you?'

Mrs Harris grinned at him. ''Aven't I just? A genuine Dior dress called "Temptytion" in me bag 'ere. Five 'undred quid it cost. 'Ow's that?'

The inspector laughed. It was not the first time he had encountered the London char's sense of humour. 'You'll be the belle of the ball with it, I'll wager,' he said, and made a mark with a piece of chalk on the side of the case. Then he sauntered off and presented his card to the next passenger whose luggage was ready.

Mrs Harris picked up her bag and walked - not ran, though it was a great effort not to bolt - to the exit and down the escalator to freedom. She was filled not only with a sense of relief, but righteousness as well. She had told the truth. If, as Mme Colbert had said, the customs officer chose not to believe her, that was not her fault.

THUS it was that at four o'clock in the afternoon of a lovely London spring day, the last obstacle hurdled, and with 'Temptation' safe and sound in her possession, Mrs Harris found herself standing outside Waterloo Air Station, home at last. And but one thing was troubling her conscience. It was the little matter of Miss Pamela Penrose, the actress, and her flat.

Her other clients were all wealthy, but Miss Penrose was poor and struggling. What if Mrs Butterfield hadn't coped properly? It was yet early. The keys to the flat were in her new crocodile handbag, now emerged from the suitcase. Mrs Harris said to herself: 'Lord love the poor dear. It's early yet. Maybe she's got to entertyne some nobs. I'll just drop by 'er flat and surprise 'er by tidying up a bit.' She caught the proper bus and shortly afterwards was in the mews, inserting her key in the door.

No sooner had she the street door open, when the sound of the girl's sobs reached to her, causing Mrs Harris to hurry up the stairs and into the tiny living room, where she came upon Miss Penrose lying face down upon her couch crying her eyes out.

Mrs Harris went to her, laid a sympathetic hand upon a shaking shoulder and said: 'Now, now, dearie, what's the matter? It can't be as bad as all that. If you're in trouble maybe I can help you.'

Miss Penrose sat up. 'YOU help me!' she repeated, looking through tear-swollen eyes. Then in a more kindly tone she said: 'Oh, it's you, Mrs Harris. Nobody in the whole world could help me. Oh, I could die. If you must know, I've been invited to dine at the Caprice with Mr Korngold the producer. It's my one and only chance to impress him and get ahead. Nearly ALL of Mr Korngold's girls - I mean friends - have become stars—'

'Well, now I don't see anything to cry about there,' declared Mrs Harris. 'You ought to be a star, I'm sure.'

Miss Penrose's heartrending grief turned momentarily to rage: 'Oh, don't be STUPID!' she stormed. 'Don't you see? I can't go. I haven't anything to wear. My one good dress is at the cleaners and my other one has a stain. Mr Korngold is frightfully particular about what the girls he takes out wear.'

Could you, had you been Mrs Harris, with what she had in her plastic suitcase on the landing, have been able to resist the temptation to play fairy godmother? Particularly if you were still under the spell of the sweet gentleness and simplicity of Natasha, and the crusted kindness of Mme Colbert and all their people, and knew what it was like to want something dreadfully, something you did not think you were ever going to get?

Before Mrs Harris quite realised what she was saying, the words popped out - 'See 'ere. Maybe I can 'elp you after all. I could lend you me Dior dress.'

'Your WHAT? Oh, you - you odious creature. How DARE you make fun of me?' Miss Penrose's small mouth was twisted and her eyes cloudy with rage.

'But I ain't. 'Strewth, so 'elp me, I've just come back from Paris where I bought me a Dior dress. I'd let you wear it tonight if it would 'elp you with Mr Korngold.'

Somehow Miss Penrose, *née* Snite, brought herself under control as some guardian instinct warned her that with these charwomen one never really knew what to expect. She said: 'I'm sorry. I didn't mean - but of course you couldn't - where is it?'

''Ere,' said Mrs Harris, and opened the suitcase. The intense gasp of wonder and excitement and the joy that came into the girl's eyes made it worth the gesture. 'Oh - oh - oh!' she cried, 'I can't *believe* it.' In an instant she had the dress out of its tissue wrappings, holding it up, then hugging it to her she searched out the label with greedy fingers - 'Oh! It really IS a Dior. May I try it on right away, Mrs Harris? We are about the same size, aren't we? Oh, I could die with excitement.'

In a moment she was stripping off her clothes, Mrs Harris was helping her into the dress, and a few minutes later it was again fulfilling the destiny for which it had been designed. With her lovely bare shoulders and blonde head rising from the chiffon and tulle, Miss Penrose was both Venus appearing from the sea and Miss Snite emerging from the bedclothes.

Mrs Harris and the girl gazed raptly at the image reflected from the full-length mirror in the closet door. The actress said: 'Oh, you are a dear to let me wear it. I'll be ever so careful. You don't KNOW what it means to me.'

But Mrs Harris knew very well. And it seemed almost as though fate wished this beautiful creation to be worn and shown off and not hung away in a closet. This perhaps being so, she had a request: 'Would you mind very much if I came to the restaurant where you are 'aving dinner and stood outside to watch you go in? Of course, I wouldn't speak to you or anything—'

Miss Penrose said graciously: 'Of course I wouldn't mind. If you'll be standing at the right side of the door as I get out of Mr Korngold's Rolls-Royce, I can sort of turn to you so that you can see me better.'

'Oh,' said Mrs Harris. 'You *are* kind, dearie.' And meant it.

Miss Penrose kept her promise, or half of it, for a storm came up and suddenly it was a thundery, blustery, rain-swept night when at half-past nine Mr Korngold's Rolls-Royce drew up at the entrance to the Caprice. Mrs Harris was standing to the right of the door, somewhat protected from the rain by the canopy.

A rumble of thunder and a swooping wind accompanied the arrival; Miss Penrose paused for one instant, turning towards Mrs Harris, her head graciously inclined, her evening wrap parted. Then with a toss of her golden hair she ran swiftly into the doorway. Mrs Harris had had no more than a glimpse of jet beads beneath an evening wrap, a flash of foamy-pink, white, cream, chiffon, and tulle, and then it was over.

But she was quite happy and remained there a little longer, contented and lost in imaginings. For now the head waiter would be bowing low to *her* dress and leading IT to a favoured and conspicuous table. Every woman in the room would recognise it at once as one from Dior; all heads would be turning as the creation moved through the aisles of tables, the velvet skirt, heavy with jet beads swinging enticingly, while above, the sweet, young bosom, shoulders, arms, and pink and white face emerged from the lovely bodice. Mr Korngold would be pleased and proud and would surely decide to give so well dressed and beautiful a girl an important part in his next production.

And no one there, not a single, solitary soul outside the girl herself would know that the exquisite gown which had done it all and had made every eye brighten with envy or admiration was the sole and exclusive property of Mrs Ada Harris, char, of Number 5 Willis Gardens, Battersea.

And thither she went now smiling to herself all the way during the long bus ride home. There remained only the problem of Mrs Butterfield, who would be anxiously awaiting her, to be dealt with. She would wish to see the dress, of course, and hear all about it. For some reason she could not fathom, Mrs Harris felt that she did not care for Mrs Butterfield to know that she had loaned her dress to the actress.

But by the time she had arrived at her destination she had the solution. A little fib and the fatigue that had collected in her bones would serve to put her off.

'Lor'!' she said from the depths of Mrs Butterfield's billowy bosom where she found herself enveloped, 'I'm that fagged I've got to 'old me eyelids open with me fingers. It's so late, I won't even stay for a cup o' tea.'

'You poor dear,' sympathised Mrs Butterfield, 'I won't Keep you. You can show me the dress—'

It's coming tomorrow,' Mrs Harris demi-fibbed. 'I'll tell you all about it then.'

Once more in her own bed, she gave herself up to the sweet, delicious sense of accomplishment and with not so much as a single foreboding as to what the morrow might bring was soon fast asleep.

THE hour that Mrs Harris devoted to Miss Penrose was from five to six, and all the next day, as she worked in the various homes and made her peace with her clients who were too happy to see her back to grouse about her prolonged absence, she lived in tingling anticipation of that moment. At last it came and she hurried to the little flat that had once been a stable behind the great house in the square and opening the door stood for a moment at the foot of the narrow staircase.

At first it was only disappointment that she experienced for the place was dark and silent. Mrs Harris would have liked to have heard from the girl's own lips the story of the triumph scored by the Dior dress and its effect upon Mr Korngold.

But it was the strange, unfamiliar smell that assailed her nostrils that turned her cold with alarm and set the skin of her scalp to pricking with terror. And yet, on second thought the smell was *not* unfamiliar. Why did it awaken memories of the war she had lived through in London - the rain of high explosives and the deluge of fire— ?

At the top of the stairs, Mrs Harris turned on the lights in the vestibule and the living room and went in. The next instant she was staring down, frozen with horror at the ruins of her dress. And then she knew what the odour was that had assailed her nostrils and made her think of the nights when the incendiaries had poured down upon London.

The Dior dress had been tossed carelessly upon the disordered couch with the burned-out velvet panel where the fire had eaten into it showing shockingly in a fearful gap of melted beadwork, burned and singed cloth.

Beside it lay a pound and a hastily scrawled note. Mrs Harris's fingers were trembling so that she could hardly read it at first, but at last its contents became clear.

Dear Mrs Harris, I am terribly sorry I could not stay to explain in person, but I have to go away for a little while. I am most awfully sorry about what happened to the dress, but it wasn't my fault and if Mr Korngold had not been so quick I might have burned to death. He said I had a very narrow escape. After dinner we went to the '30' Club where I stopped to comb my hair in front of a mirror and there was an electric fire right underneath, and all of a sudden I was burning - I mean the dress, and I could have burned to death. I am sure they will be able to repair it and your insurance will take care of the damage, which is not as bad as it looks as it is only the one panel. I am going away for the week. Please look after the flat as usual. I am leaving a pound for your wages in the meantime.

It was astonishing that when Mrs Harris had finished reading the letter she did not cry out, or even murmur, or say anything at all. Instead she took up the damaged garment and, folding it carefully, packed it once more into the old plastic suitcase Mme Colbert had given her and which she retrieved from the closet where she had stowed it the night before. She left the letter and the money lying on the couch, went downstairs and into the street.

When she had closed the outside door, she paused only long enough to remove the key to the flat from her chain, since she would not be needing it any more, and push it through the slot of the letter box. Then she walked the five minutes to Sloane Square where she caught a bus for home.

It was damp and chilly in her flat. She put the kettle on for tea and then, guided by habit, she did all of the things she was used to doing, even to eating, though she hardly knew what food she tasted. She washed up the dishes and put everything away. But there the mechanism ended and she turned to the unpacking of the ruins of the Dior dress.

She fingered the charred edges of the velvet and the burned and melted jet. She knew night clubs, for she had cleaned in them. She thought she could see it happening - the girl, half-drunk, coming down the stairs from without, on the arm of her escort, thoughtless, heedless of all but that which concerned herself, pausing before the first mirror to study herself and apply a comb.

Then the sudden ascent of smoke from her feet, the little shriek of fright, perhaps an orange line of fire in the dress and the man beating at it with his hands until it was extinguished and only the smouldering wreck of the most beautiful and expensive frock in the world remained.

And here it was in her hands now, still with the stink of charred cloth rising from it and which all the perfume given to her by Natasha would not suffice to blot out. A thing, once as perfect and beautiful as human hands could make it, was destroyed.

She tried to tell herself that it was not the fault of the girl, that it had been an accident and that only she herself was to blame for trying to play fairy godmother to this spoiled brat of a bad actress who had not even the grace to be grateful to her for her foolish gesture.

Mrs Harris was a sensible person, a realist who had lived an unexciting life and was not given to self-delusion. Looking now upon this singed and tragic wreck of her desires she was well aware of her own foolish pride and vanity, not only involved in the possession of such a treasure, but in the displaying of it.

She had savoured the casual way she might say to her landlady, when queried as to where she had been: 'Oh, I was only over in Paris, dearie, to look at the collection and buy me a Dior dress. It's called "Temptytion".' And, of course, she had visualised a hundred times the reaction of Mrs Butterfield when she unveiled her prize. There would be no calling in of her friend now - or anyone else - for she would only croak: 'Didn't I tell yer something orful would 'appen? Things like that ain't for the likes of us! What was you going to do with it, anyway?'

What indeed had she been meaning to do with it? Hang it away in an old, stale cupboard next to her aprons, overalls, and one poor Sunday frock, secretly to gloat over when she came home at night? The dress had not been designed and created to languish in the dark of a cupboard. It was meant to be out where there was gaiety, lights, music, and admiring eyes.

Quite suddenly she could not bear to look upon it any longer. She was at the end of her resistance to grief. She reinterred it in the plastic suitcase, hurriedly blotting out the sight of it with the crumpled tissue paper and then flinging herself upon her bed, buried her face in her pillow and commenced to cry. She wept silently, inconsolably, and interminably, after the fashion of women whose hearts have been broken.

She wept for her own foolishness, and too for her self-acknowledged guilt of the sin of pride, and the swift, sure punishment that had followed upon its heels, but mostly she wept simply and miserably for her lost dress and the destruction of this so dear possession.

She might have wept thus into eternity, but for the insistent ringing of her doorbell which at last penetrated grief and into her consciousness. She raised her tear-swollen face momentarily and then decided to ignore it. It could be none other than Mrs Butterfield, eager to see and discuss her Paris dress and hear of her adventures amongst the heathen. What was there to show her now for the long wait, the hard work, the sacrifice, and the foolish determination? A burned-out rag. Worse than Mrs Butterfield's croakings of 'I told you so' would be the sympathy that would follow, the tuttings and cluckings and the warm but clumsy attempts to comfort her and which Mrs Harris felt she could not bear. She wanted only to get on with her crying - to be allowed to weep alone until she died.

She pulled the damp pillow about her ears to shut out the sound of the ringing, but now, somewhat to her alarm, heard it replaced by a loud knocking and thumping on the door, something rather more strenuous and imperative than she could connect with Mrs Butterfield. Perhaps there was something wrong somewhere, an emergency, and she was needed. She arose quickly, brushed the wisps of dishevelled hair out of her eyes and opened the door to reveal a BEA messenger standing there goggling at her as though he had seen a ghost.

He croaked forth a kind of bilious: 'Mrs 'Arris, is it?'

' 'Oo else did you expect? Princess Margaret? Bangin' and thumpin' like the 'ouse was afire ...'

'Phew!' he said, mopping his brow with relief, 'you didn't arf give me a turn, you did. I thought maybe you was dead. You not answering the doorbell, and these flowers to deliver. I thought they might be for the corpse.'

'Eh?' Mrs Harris asked. 'Wot flowers?'

The postman grinned. 'Flown over special from France, and express delivery. 'Ere now. Leave the door open while I bring 'em in.'

Swinging wide the rear doors of the van he began to produce them, white box, upon long white box marked: 'AIR EXPRESS - FRAGILE - PERISHABLE', looming shapes of objects packed first in straw, then in cartons, then in paper - it seemed to the mystified Mrs Harris that he would never end his trips from the van to her living room and that there must be some mistake.

But there was none. 'Sign 'ere,' he said, his task at last ended, and shoved his book under her nose. It was her name and address right enough - Madame Ada Harris, 5 Willis Gardens, Battersea.

He left and she was alone again. Then she turned to opening her boxes and packages and in an instant found herself transported back to Paris again, for the dingy little room suddenly vanished beneath the garden bower of flowers that overwhelmed it, dark, deep red roses by the dozen, cream white lilies, bunches of pink and yellow carnations, and sheaves of gladioli ready to burst into every colour from deep mauve to palest lemon. There were azaleas, salmon coloured, white, and crimson, geraniums, bundles of sweet-smelling freesias, and one great bouquet of violets a foot in span with six white gardenias centred.

In an instant, her dwelling seemed changed into a stall of the Marché aux Fleurs, for market fresh, the crisp, smooth petals were still dewed with pearls of water.

Was this coincidence, or some magic foresight that this sweet, healing gift should reach her in her moment of deepest anguish? She detached the cards from the blossoms and read the messages thereon. They were a welcome home, a simultaneous outpouring of remembrance and affection from her friends, laced with good news.

'Welcome home. We could not wait. André and I were married today. God bless you. Natasha.'

'I am the happiest man in the world thanks to you. André Fauvel.'

'A welcome back to the lady who loves geraniums. I have not forgotten the copper penny. Hypolite de Chassagne.'

'Compliments of M. Christian Dior' (this with the violets).

'Greetings on your return. The staff of Christian Dior.'

'Good luck to you. Cutters, Fitters, and Seamstresses, Maison Christian Dior.'

And finally: 'Jules was named First Secretary of the Department for Anglo-Saxon Relations at the Quai d'Orsay today. What can I say, my dear, but thank you. Claudine Colbert.'

Her knees trembling beneath her, Mrs Harris sank to the floor, leaned her cheek against the tight, smooth, cool, heavily fragrant petals of the roses Mme Colbert had sent her, tears filling her eyes again, her mind thrown into a turmoil of memories by the messages, the colours and the fragrance of the flowers that filled her little living room.

Once again she saw the understanding, womanly Mme Colbert, with her dark, glossy, perfectly groomed hair and pure skin, the lithe, exquisite, laughing Natasha and the blond, serious-minded, grave-faced and scarred M. Fauvel who overnight had changed from an adding machine into a boy and a lover.

All manner of memories and isolated pictures crowded into her thoughts. For an instant she saw the furrowed brows and concentrated expressions of the fitters kneeling before her, their mouths bristling with pins. She felt once more the pile of the thick grey carpet beneath her feet and smelled the sweet, thrilling scent of the interior of the House of Dior.

The hubbub and murmur of the voices of the audience and patrons in the grey and white salon seemed to come back to her, and immediately, blinking through her tears she was there again as each model more beautiful than the last clad in the loveliest frocks, suits, ensembles, gowns, and furs came thrusting, swaying, or gliding into the room - three steps and a twirl - three more steps and another twirl - then off with the pastel mink or dark marten coat to be dragged behind on the soft carpet, off with the jacket - a toss of the head, another twirl and she was gone to be replaced by yet another.

From there it was but a flash for her to be back in the hive of the cubicles, a part of the delicious atmosphere of woman world compounded of the rustle of silks and satins, the variegated perfumes carried thither by the clients, the murmuring voices of sales women and dressmakers like the droning of bees, and the sound of whispering from neighbouring booths, and smothered laughter.

Then she was sitting in the sunlight beneath a sky of a peculiar blue, on a bench in the Flower Market surrounded by nature's own fashion creations, flowers in their matchless shapes and colours and emanating perfumes of their own. And next to her was a handsome aristocratic old gentleman who had understood her and treated her as an equal.

But it was the people she had met who kept returning to her thoughts and she remembered the expressions on the faces of Fauvel and Natasha as they had embraced her the night of the 'Pré Catalan' and seemed to feel once again the warm pressure of Mme Colbert's arms about her as she had kissed her before her departure and whispered: 'You have been very lucky for me, my dear— '

Reflecting now upon Mme Colbert, Mrs Harris thought how the French woman had worked and schemed to help her to realize her vain, foolish wish to possess a Dior dress. Had it not been for her and her clever plan at the end it would never have reached England. And Mrs Harris thought that even the damage to 'Temptation' might not be irreparable. A letter to Mme Colbert would result in the immediate dispatch of another beaded panel such as had been destroyed. A clever seamstress could insert it so that the dress would be as good as new. And yet, would it ever be the same again?

This ephemeral question had a most curious effect upon Mrs Harris. It stopped the flow of tears from her eyes and brought her to her feet once more as she looked about the flower-laden room and the answer came to her in one shrewd, inspired burst of insight.

It would not. It would never be the same again. But then neither would she.

For it had not been a dress she had bought so much as an adventure and an experience that would last her to the end of her days. She would never again feel lonely, or unwanted. She had ventured into a foreign country and a foreign people whom she had been taught to suspect and despise. She had found them to be warm and human, men and women to whom human love and understanding was a mainspring of life. They had made her feel that they loved her for herself.

Mrs Harris opened the suitcase and took out 'Temptation'. Once more she fingered the burnt place and saw how easily the panel could be replaced and the damage repaired. But she would not have it so. She would keep it as it was, untouched by any other fingers but those which had expedited every stitch because of love and feeling for another woman's heart.

Mrs Harris hugged the dress to her thin bosom, hugged it hard as though it were alive and human, nestling her face to the soft folds of the material. Tears flowed again from the small, shrewd blue eyes and furrowed down the apple cheeks, but they were no longer tears of misery.

She stood there rocking back and forth, holding and embracing her dress, and with it she was hugging them all, Madame Colbert, Natasha, André Fauvel, down to the last anonymous worker, seamstress, and cutter, as well as the city that had bestowed upon her such a priceless memory, treasure of understanding, friendship, and humanity.

MRS HARRIS GOES TO NEW YORK

To Ginnie

The Marquis Hypolite de Chassagne is of course not the Ambassador of France to the United States. He is only the benevolent genie of a latter-day fairy tale. Nor will you find Mrs Harris, Mrs Butterfield, or the Schreibers at the addresses given, for every one and every thing in this story is fictitious. If, however, the characters herein do not resemble someone you have encountered somewhere sometime, then the author has failed to hold up a small mirror to life and extends his regrets to one and all.

P.W.G.

MRS ADA HARRIS and Mrs Violet Butterfield, of Numbers 5 and 9 Willis Gardens, Battersea, London, respectively, were having their nightly cup of tea in Mrs Harris's neat and flower-decorated little flat in the basement of number five.

Mrs Harris was a charwoman of that sturdy London breed that fares forth daily to tidy up the largest city in the world, and her lifelong friend and bosom companion, Mrs Butterfield, was a part-time cook and char as well. Both looked after a fashionable clientele in Belgravia, where they met varying adventures during the day, picking up stray and interesting pieces of gossip from the odd bods for whom they worked. At night they visited one another for a final cup of tea to exchange these titbits.

Mrs Harris was sixtyish, small and wiry, with cheeks like frosted apples, and naughty little eyes. She had a very efficient and practical side, was inclined to be romantic, an optimist, and see life in rather simplified divisions of either black or white. Mrs Butterfield, likewise sixtyish, was stout, billowy, a kindly, timorous woman, the complete pessimist, who visualised everyone, including herself, as living constantly on the brink of imminent disaster.

Both of these good ladies were widows of long standing. Mrs Butterfield had two married sons, neither of whom contributed to her support, which did not surprise her. It would have astonished her if they had. Mrs Harris had a married daughter who lived in Nottingham and wrote to her every Thursday night. The two women lived useful, busy, and interesting lives, supported one another physically and spiritually, and comforted one another in their loneliness. It had been Mrs Butterfield who by taking over Mrs Harris's clients temporarily had enabled her a year or so ago to make a flying trip to Paris for the exciting and romantic purpose of buying a Dior dress, which same trophy now hung in Mrs Harris's wardrobe as a daily reminder of how wonderful and adventurous life can be to one who has a little energy, stick-to-it-iveness, and imagination to make it so.

Snug and cosy in Mrs Harris's neat flat, by the glow of shaded lamplight, the teapot hot and fragrant beneath the yellow flowered tea-cosy Mrs Butterfield had knitted Mrs Harris for Christmas, the two women sat and exchanged the events of the day.

The wireless was turned on and from it issued a series of dismal sounds attributed to a recording made by one Kentucky Claiborne, an American hillbilly singer.

'So I sez to the Countess, "It's either a new 'Oover or me,"' recounted Mrs Harris. 'Stingy old frump. "Dear Mrs 'Arris," sez she, "cawn't we make it do another year?" Make do indeed! Every time I touch the flippin' thing I get a shock clear down to me toes. I gave 'er a ultimation. "If there ain't a new 'Oover on the premises tomorrow morning, the keys go through the door,"' Mrs Harris concluded. Keys to a flat dropped through the mail slot was the charwoman's classic notice of resignation from a job.

Mrs Butterfield sipped at her tea. 'There won't be one,' she said gloomily. 'I know that kind. They'll put every penny on their own back, and that's all they care.'

From within the speaker of the little table wireless Kentucky Claiborne moaned,

> 'Kiss me good-bye, ol' Cayuse.
> Kiss me ol' hoss, don' refuse.
> Bad men have shot me -
> Ah'm afeered they have got me,
> Kiss me good-bye, ol' Cayuse.'

'Ugh!' said Mrs Harris, 'I can't stand any more of that caterwauling. Turn it off, will you love.'

Mrs Butterfield obediently leaned over and switched off the radio, remarking, 'It's real sad 'im being shot and wanting 'is 'orse to kiss 'im. Now we'll never know if it did.'

This, however, was not the case, for the people next door apparently were devotees of the American balladeer, and the saga of tragedy and love in the Far West came seeping through the walls. Still another sound penetrated the kitchen in which the two women were sitting, a dim thud and then a wail of pain, which was followed immediately by the turning up of the wireless next door so that the twang of the guitar and Kentucky Claiborne's nasal groaning drowned out the cries.

The two women stiffened immediately, and their faces became grim and deeply concerned.

'The devils,' whispered Mrs Harris, 'they're 'avin' a go at little 'Enry again.'

'Ow, the poor lamb,' said Mrs Butterfield. And then, 'I can't 'ear 'im any more.'

'They've turned up the wireless so we carn't.' Mrs Harris went to a place in the wall between the houses where evidently at one time there had been a connecting hatchway and the partition was thinner, and pounded on it with her knuckles. An equal measure of pounding came back almost instantly.

Mrs Harris put her mouth close to the partition and shouted, ''Ere, you stop hitting that child. Do you want me to call the police?'

The return message from the other side of the partition was clear and succinct. A man's voice, 'Aw, go soak yer 'ead. 'Oo's 'itting anyone?'

The two women stood close to the wall listening anxiously, but no more sounds of distress came through, and soon the stridency of the wireless likewise diminished.

'The devils!' hissed Mrs Harris again. 'The trouble is they don't hit 'im 'ard enough so it shows, or we could call the N.S.P.C.C. I'll give them a piece of me mind in the morning.'

Mrs Butterfield said sorrowfully, 'It won't do no good, they'll only take it out on 'im. Yesterday I gave 'im a piece of cake left over from me tea. Cor', them Gusset brats was all over 'im, snatching it away from 'im before he ever got a mouthful.'

Two tears of frustration and rage suddenly appeared in Mrs Harris's blue eyes, and she delivered herself of a string of very naughty and unprintable words describing the Gusset family next door.

Mrs Butterfield patted her friend's shoulder and said, 'There, there, dear, don't excite yourself. It's a shyme, but what can we do?'

'Something!' Mrs Harris replied fiercely. Then repeated, 'Something. I can't stand it. 'E's such a dear little tyke.'

A gleam came into her eyes, 'I'll bet if I went to America I'd soon enough find his Dad. 'E's got to be somewhere, hasn't 'e? Eating his 'eart out for 'is little one, no doubt.'

A look of horror came into Mrs Butterfield's stout face, her duplicate chins began to quiver and her lips to tremble. 'Ada,' she quavered, 'you ain't thinkin' of goin' to America, are you?' Fresh in her memory was the fact that Mrs Harris once had made up her mind that the one thing she wanted more than anything else in the world was a Dior dress, and that she had thereupon scrimped and saved for two years, flown by herself to Paris, and returned triumphantly with the garment.

To Mrs Butterfield's great relief there apparently *were* limits to her friend's potentialities, for Mrs Harris wailed, ''Ow can I? But it's breaking me 'eart. I can't stand to see a child abused. 'E ain't got enough meat on 'is bones to sit down on.'

All Willis Gardens knew the story of little 'Enry Brown and the Gussets, a tragedy of the aftermath of the war and, alas, too often repeated.

In 1950, George Brown, a young American airman stationed at an American air base somewhere, had married a waitress from the near-by town, one Pansy Cott, and had a son by her named Henry.

When at the close of his tour of enlistment George Brown was posted for return to the United States, the woman refused to accompany him, remaining in England with the child and demanding support. Brown returned to the United States, mailing back the equivalent of two pounds a week for the care of the infant. He also divorced his wife.

Pansy and Henry moved to London, where Pansy got a job, and also met another man who was interested in marrying her. However, he wanted no part of the child, and the price of his making her an honest woman was that she get rid of it. Pansy promptly farmed out little Henry, then aged three, with a family by the name of Gusset, who lived in Willis Gardens and had six children of their own, married her lover, and moved to another town.

For three years the pound a week which Pansy had agreed to pay the Gussets for little Henry's keep (thus taking a clear pound of profit for herself) continued to come, and Henry, while not exactly overfed on this bounty, was not much worse off than the members of the Gusset brood. Then one day the pound did not arrive, and never again turned up thereafter. Pansy and her new husband had vanished and could not be traced. The Gussets had an address for the father, George Brown, somewhere in Alabama. A letter sent thither demanding funds was returned stamped 'Addressee not known here'. The Gussets realised they were stuck with the child, and after that things were not so good for Henry.

From then on it became evident to the neighbourhood that the Gussets, who anyway had a kind of Jukes-family reputation, were taking it out on the child. Little 'Enry had become a matter of deep concern to the two widows who lived on either side of the Gussets, but in particular to Mrs Harris, who found that the unhappy little orphan-by-law touched her heart, and his plight invaded her dreams of the day and of the night-time.

If the Gussets had been more brutally cruel to little Henry, Mrs Harris could have done something immediate and drastic in cooperation with the police. But Mr and Mrs Gusset were too smart for that. No one knew exactly what it was Mr Gusset did to eke out a living for his family, but it took place in Soho, sometimes during the night, and the general opinion held that it was something shady.

Whatever it may have been it was known that the Gussets were particularly anxious to avoid the attentions of the police, and therefore as far as little Henry was concerned, remained strictly within the law. They were well aware that the police were not able to take action with reference to a child except in cases of extreme and visible cruelty. No one could say exactly that the boy was starving or suffering from injuries. But Mrs Harris knew his life was made a constant hell of short rations, cuffs, slaps, pinches, and curses, as the Gussets revenged themselves upon him for the stoppage of the funds.

He was the drudge and the butt of the slatternly family, and any of their two girls and four boys ranging from the ages of three to twelve could tweak, kick, and abuse him with impunity. But worst of all was the fact of the child growing up without love or affection of any kind. On the contrary, he was hated, and this both Mrs Harris and Mrs Butterfield found the most painful of all.

Mrs Harris had had her share of hard knocks herself; in her world these were expected and accepted, but she had a warm and embracing nature, had successfully brought up a child of her own, and what she saw of the little boy next door and the treatment meted out to him began to assume the nature of a constant pain and worry, and something which was never too far or entirely out of her thoughts. Often when she was, as dictated by her nature, blithe, gay, light-hearted, and irrepressible about her work, her clients, and her friends, would come the sudden sobering thought of the plight of little 'Enry. Then Mrs Harris would indulge in one of her day-dreams, the kind that a year or so ago had sent her off to the great adventure of her life in Paris.

The new day-dream took on the quality of the romantic fiction of which Mrs Harris was a great devotee via magazines many of her clients sloughed off upon her when they were finished with them.

In Mrs Harris's opinion, and transferred to the dream, Pansy Cott, or whatever her new name now happened to be, was the villainess of the story, the missing airman Brown the hero, and little 'Enry the victim. For one thing, Mrs Harris was convinced that the father was continuing the support of his child, and that Pansy was simply pocketing the money. It was all Pansy's doing - Pansy who had refused to accompany her husband to America, as was her wifely duty; Pansy who had withheld the child from him; Pansy who, in order to satisfy a lover, had farmed out the little boy to this beastly family; and finally, Pansy who had vanished with the loot, leaving the boy to his awful fate.

George Brown, on the other hand, was one of nature's noblemen; in the intervening years in all likelihood he would have made his fortune, as Americans did. Perhaps be had remarried, perhaps not, but whatever and wherever, he would be pining for his lost 'Enry.

This estimate of George Brown was based upon her experience with American GIs in England, whom she had invariably found friendly, warm-hearted, generous, and particularly loving and kind to children. She remembered how during the war they had unfailingly shared their rations of sweets with the youngsters surrounding their bases. They were inclined to be loud, noisy, boastful, and spendthrift, but when one got to know them, underneath they were the salt of the earth.

They were, of course, the richest people in the world, and Mrs Harris reared a kind of fantasy palace where George Brown would now be living, and where little 'Enry too could be enjoying his birthright if only his Dad knew of his plight. She had no doubt but that if somehow

Mr Brown could be found and told of the situation, he would appear upon the scene, wafted on the wings of a faster-than-sound jet, to claim his child and remove him from the tyranny and thraldom of the nasty Gussets. It wanted only a fairy godmother to give the knobs of Fate a twist and set the machinery going in the right direction. It was not long before, so affected was she by the plight of little 'Enry, Mrs Harris began to see herself as that fairy godmother.

Somehow in the dream she was transplanted to the great United States of America, where by a combination of shrewdness and luck she turned up the missing George Brown almost at once. As she narrated the story of little 'Enry to him tears began to flow from his eyes, and when she had finished he was weeping unashamedly. 'My good woman,' he said, 'all my riches can never repay you for what you have done for me. Come, let us go at once to the aeroplane and set out to fetch my little boy home where he belongs.' It was a very satisfactory dream.

But, as has been noted before, Mrs Harris was not wholly given to spinning webs of fantasy. She was hard-headed, practical, and realistic about the situation of little Henry, the Gussets, and the knowledge that no one had been able to locate the father, coupled with the fact that no one had really attempted to do so. Underneath the dreams was a growing conviction that if only given an opportunity she could manage to find him, a conviction not at all diminished by the fact that all she knew of him was that his name had been George Brown, and he had been in the American Air Force.

DEEP in her heart, Mrs Harris was well aware that for her a trip to America was as remote as a trip to the moon. True, she had managed to cross the English Channel, and the aeroplane had made the Atlantic Ocean just another body of water over which to zoom, but the practical considerations of expense and living, etc., put such a journey well out of reach. Mrs Harris had achieved her Paris visit and heart's desire through two years of scrimping and saving, but this had been a kind of lifetime effort. It had taken a good deal out of her. She was older now and aware that she was no longer capable of making the attempt to amass the necessary number of pounds to finance such an expedition.

True, *l'affaire* Dior had been sparked by the winning of a hundred pounds in a football pool, without which Mrs Harris might never have undertaken the task of amassing another three hundred and fifty. She continued to play the pools, but without the blazing conviction which sometimes leads the face of fortune to smile. She knew very well that that kind of lightning never struck twice in the same place.

Yet, at the very moment that little Henry, under the cover of the abysmal gargling of Kentucky Claiborne, was being cuffed about in the kitchen of Number 7 Willis Gardens, and sent to bed yet another night insufficiently nourished, Fate was already laying the groundwork for an incredible change in the life not only of himself, but likewise of Ada Harris and Mrs Butterfield.

There was no miracle involved, nothing more supernatural than two sets of men facing one another either side of the directors' table in the board and conference room of a gigantic Hollywood film and television studio six thousand miles away, glaring at one another with all the venom that can be mustered by greedy men engaged in a battle for power.

Seven hours, one hundred and three cups of coffee, and forty-two Havana Perfectos later, the malevolence of the glares had not diminished, but the battle was over. A cablegram was dispatched which had consequences both direct and indirect in the lives of a strange assortment of people, some of whom had never even heard of North American Pictures and Television Company Inc.

Among the clients for whom Mrs Harris 'did' not only with regularity but enthusiasm, since she had her favourites, were Mr and Mrs Joel Schreiber, who had a six-roomed flat on the top floor of one of the reconditioned houses in Eaton Square. Joel and Henrietta Schreiber were a middle-aged, childless American couple who had made their home in London for the last three years, where Mr Schreiber had acted as European representative and distribution manager for North American Pictures and Television Company.

It was through the kindness of Henrietta Schreiber originally that Mrs Harris had been able to change her hard-earned pounds for the necessarily exportable dollars which had enabled her to pay for her Dior dress in Paris.

Neither of them had had any inkling that they were breaking the law in doing this. As Mrs Schreiber saw it, the pound notes were remaining with her in England, and not leaving the country, which was what the British wanted, wasn't it? But then Mrs Schreiber was one of those muddled people who never quite catch on to the way things operate, or are supposed to operate.

With the daily help and advice of Mrs Harris she had been able to accustom herself to keeping house in London, shopping in Elizabeth Street, and doing her own cooking, while Mrs Harris's energetic appearance for two hours a day kept her flat immaculate. Any sudden changes or problems turning up were likely to send Mrs Schreiber into a flutter. As one who before coming to England had been compelled to cope with the type of servants available in Hollywood and New York, Henrietta was a fervent admirer of Mrs Harris's speed, efficiency, skill at making the dust fly, and above all her ability to cope with almost any situation which arose.

Joel Schreiber, like Napoleon's every-man soldier who carried a marshal's baton in his knapsack, possessed an imaginary president's corporation seal in his briefcase. A hard-headed businessman who had worked his way up in North American Pictures from office boy to his present position, but always on the business side, he also had nourished dreams of arts and letters, and what he would do if he were president of North American, a contingency so remote that he never even so much as discussed it with his Henrietta. The kind of job Mr Schreiber had did not lead to presidencies, formations of policy, and conferences with the great and near-great stars of the film and television world.

Yet when the already-mentioned conference in Holly-wood was over and the cablegram dispatched, it was to none other than Joel Schreiber, with instructions to move his offices as well as his domicile to New York for the tenure of a five-year contract as President of North American Pictures and Television Company Inc. Two power combines battling for control of North American, neither strong enough to win, and facing exhaustion, had finally agreed upon Schreiber, a dark-horse outsider, as a compromise candidate and eventual President of North American.

Following upon the cablegram which reached Schreiber at his office that afternoon were long-distance telephone calls, miraculous 'conference' conversations spanning oceans and continents, in which five people - one in London, two in California, two in New York - sat at separate telephones and talked as though they were all in one room, and by the time Mr Schreiber, a stocky little man with clever eyes, returned home that early evening, he was simply bursting with excitement and news.

There was no holding it in, he spilled it all in one load upon the threshold as he entered his flat. 'Henrietta, I'm IT! I got news for you. Only it's real news. I'm President of North American Pictures, in charge of everything! They're moving the offices to New York. We've got to leave in two weeks. We're going to live there in a big apartment on Park Avenue. The Company found one for me already. It's a double penthouse. I'm the big squeeze now, Henrietta. What do you think of it?'

They were a loving and affectionate couple, and so they hugged one another first, and then Mr Schreiber danced Henrietta around the apartment a little, until she was breath-less and her comfortable, matronly figure was heaving.

She said, 'You deserve it, Joel. They should have done it long ago.' Then, to calm herself and collect her thoughts, she went to the window and looked out on to the quiet, leafy shade of Eaton Square, with its traffic artery running down the middle, and with a pang thought how used she had become to this placid way of life, how much she had loved it, and how she dreaded being plunged back into the hurly-burly and manic tempo of New York.

Schreiber was pacing up and down the flat with excitement, unable to sit down, as dozens of new thoughts, thrills, and ideas connected with his newly exalted position shot through his round head, and once he stopped and said, 'If we'd had a kid, Henrietta, wouldn't he have been proud of his old man at this minute?'

The sentence went straight to Henrietta's heart, where it struck and quivered like a dart thrown into a board. She knew that it was not meant as a reproach to her, since her husband was not that kind of man - it had welled simply from the need he had felt so long to be a father as well as a husband. And now that overnight he had become Somebody, she understood how the need had become intensified. When she turned away from the window there were tears brimming from the corners of her eyes and she could only say, 'Oh Joel, *I'm* so proud of you.'

He saw at once that he had hurt her, and going to her he put his arm around her shoulder and said, 'There, Henrietta, I didn't mean it like it sounded. You don't need to cry. We're a very lucky couple. We're important now. Think of the wonderful times we're going to have in New York, and the dinner parties you're going to give for all them famous people. You're really going to be the hostess with the mostes', like in the song.'

'Oh Joel,' Henrietta cried, 'it's been so long since we've lived in America, or New York - I'm frightened.'

'Psha,' comforted Mr Schreiber. 'What you got to be frightened of? It'll be a breeze for you. You'll do wonderful. We're rich now, and you can have all the servants you want.'

But that was just what Mrs Schreiber *was* worrying about, and which continued to worry her the following morning long after Mr Schreiber had floated away to his office on a pink cloud.

Her confused and excited imagination ranged over the whole monstrous gamut of international slatterns, bums, laggards, and good-for-nothings who sold their services as 'trained help'. Through her harassed mind marched the parade of Slovak, Lithuanian, Bosnian-Herzegovinian butlers or male servants with dirty fingernails, yellow, cigarette-stained fingers, who had worked for her at one time or another, trailing the ashes of their interminable cigarettes all over the rugs behind them. She had dealt with ox-like Swedes, equally bovine Finns, impudent Prussians, lazy Irish, lazier Italians, and inscrutable Orientals.

Fed up with foreigners, she had engaged American help, both coloured and white, live-in servants who drank her liquor and used her perfume, or daily women who came in the morning and departed at night usually with some article of her clothing or lingerie hidden upon their persons. They didn't know how to dust, polish, sweep, rinse out a glass, or clean a piece of silver, they left pedestal marks on the floor where, immobile like statues, they had leaned for hours on their brooms doing nothing. None of them had any pride of house or beautiful things. They smashed her good dishes, china, lamps, and bric-à-brac, ruined her slipcovers and linen, burnt cigarette holes in her carpets, and wrecked her property and peace of mind.

To this appalling crew she now added a long line of sour-faced cooks, each of whom had made her contribution to the grey hairs that were beginning to appear on her head. Some had been able to cook, others not. All of them had been unpleasant women with foul dispositions and unholy characters, embittered tyrants who had taken over and terrorized her home for whatever the length of their stay. Most of them had been only a little batty; some of them just one step from the loony bin. None of them had ever shown any sympathy or kindliness, or so much as a single thought beyond the rules they laid down for their own comfort and satisfaction.

A key rattled in the door, it swung open and in marched Mrs Harris carrying her usual rexine bag full of goodness-only knows - what that she always brought with her on her rounds, and wearing a too-long, last year's coat that someone had given her, with a truly ancient flowerpot hat, relic of a long-dead client, but which now by the rotation of styles had suddenly become fashionable again.

'Good morning, ma'am,' she said cheerily. 'I'm a bit early this morning, but since you said you was 'aving some friends for dinner tonight, I thought I'd do a real good tidying up and 'ave the plyce lookin' like apple pie.'

To Mrs Schreiber, her mind hardly cleared of the ghastly parade of remembered domestic slobs, Ada Harris looked like an angel, and before she knew what she was doing, she ran to the little char, threw her arms about her neck, hugged her, and cried, 'Oh Mrs Harris, you don't know how glad I am to see you - how very glad!'

And then unaccountably she began to cry. Perhaps it was the comfort of the return hug and pat that Mrs Harris gave her, or release from the emotional strain following the good news of her husband's promotion, but she sobbed, 'Oh Mrs Harris, something wonderful has happened to my husband. We're going to New York to live, but I'm so frightened - I'm so terribly afraid.'

Mrs Harris did not know what it was all about, but there was no doubt in her mind as to the cure: she put down her carry-all, patted Mrs Schreiber on the arm and said, 'There, there now, dear, don't you take on so. Just you let Ada 'Arris make you a cup of tea, and then you'll feel better.'

It was a comfort to Mrs Schreiber to let her do so, and she said, 'If you'll make yourself one too,' and as the two women sat in the kitchen of the flat sipping their brew, Mrs Schreiber poured it all forth to her sympathetic sister-under-the-skin, Mrs Harris - the great good fortune that had befallen her husband and herself, the change that would take place in their lives, the monstrous, gaping, two-storeyed penthouse apartment that awaited them in America, the departure in two weeks, and above all her qualms about the servant problem. With renewed gusto she narrated for Mrs Harris's appreciative ears all the domestic horrors and catastrophes that awaited her on the other side of the Atlantic. It relieved her to do so, and gave Mrs Harris a fine and satisfying sense of British superiority, so that she felt an even greater affection for Mrs Schreiber.

At the conclusion of her narrative she looked over at the little apple-cheeked char with a new warmth and tenderness in her own eyes and said, 'Oh, if only there were someone like you in New York to help me out, even if just for a little until I could get settled.'

There then fell a silence, during which time Henrietta Schreiber looked across the table at Ada Harris, and

Ada Harris over the empty teacups regarded Henrietta Schreiber. Neither said anything. It would not have been possible by any scientific precision instrument known to man to have measured any appreciable interval as to which of them was hit by the great idea first. If such a thing were possible, the two pennies dropped at one and the same moment. But neither said anything.

Mrs Harris arose, clearing the tea-things, and said, 'Well, I'd best be gettin' on with me work, 'adn't I?' and Mrs Schreiber said, 'I suppose I ought to look over the things I mean to take with me.' They both then turned to what they had to do. Usually when they were in the flat together they nattered, or rather, Mrs Harris did and Mrs Schreiber listened, but this time the little char worked in thoughtful silence, and so did Mrs Schreiber.

That night when Mrs Harris forgathered with Mrs Butterfield she said, ' 'Old on to your hair, Vi, I've got something to tell you. We're going to America!'

Mrs Butterfield's scream of alarm rang through the area with such violence that doors and windows were opened to check its source. After Mrs Harris had fanned her back to coherence she cried, ' 'Ave you gone out of yer mind? Did you say *we're* going?'

Mrs Harris nodded complacently. 'I told yer to 'ang on to yer hair,' she said. 'Mrs Schreiber's going to ask me to go along with her until she can get settled into 'er new plyce in New York. I'm going to tell 'er I will, but not unless she tykes you along as cook. Together we're going to find little 'Enry's father!'

That night when Mr Schreiber came home Henrietta broke a long period of taciturnity on her part by saying, 'Joel, don't be angry with me, but I have an absolutely hopelessly mad idea.'

In his present state of euphoria nothing was likely to anger Mr Schreiber. He said, 'Yes, dear, what is it?'

'I'm going to ask Mrs Harris to come to New York with us.'

Schreiber was not angry, but he was certainly startled. He said, 'What?'

'Only for a few months perhaps, until we get settled in and I can find someone. You don't know how wonderful she is, and how she keeps this place. She knows how I like things. Oh Joel, I'd feel so - secure.'

'But would she come?'

'I don't know,' Henrietta replied, 'but - but I think so. If I offered her a lot of money she'd have to come, wouldn't she? And I think she might just because she likes me, if I begged her.'

Mr Schreiber looked doubtful for a moment and said, 'A Cockney char in a Park Avenue penthouse?' But then he softened and said, 'If it'll make you feel better, Baby, go ahead. Anything you want now, I want you should have.'

EXACTLY fourteen and a half hours after Mrs Harris had told Mrs Butterfield she was about to be propositioned by Mrs Schreiber to go to America, it happened. Mrs Schreiber proposed the very next morning, shortly after Mrs Harris had arrived, and was enthusiastically accepted upon one condition - namely, that Mrs Butterfield be included in the party, and at a wage equal to that promised to Mrs Harris.

'She's me oldest friend,' explained Mrs Harris. 'I've never been away from London more than a week at a time in me life. If I 'ad 'er with me I wouldn't feel so lonely. Besides, she's a ruddy good cook - cooked for some of the best 'ouses before she retired from steady work. You ask old Sir Alfred Welby who he got 'is gout from.'

Mrs Schreiber was almost beside herself with joy at the prospect of not only having Mrs Harris to look after her during the first months of her return to the United States, but also at one and the same time acquiring a good cook who would get on well with the little char and keep her from getting too lonely. She knew Mrs Butterfield and liked

her, for she had subbed for Mrs Harris during the latter's
expedition to Paris to acquire her Dior dress. 'But do you
think she would come?' she asked of Mrs Harris anxiously.

'At the drop of a brick,' replied the latter. 'Adventurous,
that's what she is. Always wantin' to rush off into the
unknown. Sometimes I can 'ardly keep 'er back. Oh, she'll
come all right. Just you leave it to me to put it to 'er in the
right way.'

Mrs Schreiber was delighted to do so, and they began to
discuss details of departure - Mr Schreiber was planning
to sail in the French liner *Ville de Paris* from Southampton
within ten days - as though everything was all set and
arranged for the two of them.

Mrs Harris chose the psychological moment to move to
the attack upon her friend, namely, the witching hour
of that final mellow cup of tea they shared before retiring,
and this time in Mrs Butterfield's ample kitchen, well
stocked with cakes and biscuits, jams and jellies, for as her
figure indicated, Mrs Butterfield liked to eat well.

At first it seemed as though Mrs Harris had committed a
tactical error in approaching her friend on her own home
ground instead of getting her away from her familiar surroundings, for Mrs Butterfield was adamant in her refusal
to budge and appeared to have an answer to every argument
put forth by Mrs Harris.

'What?' she cried. 'Me go to America at my age, where
they do all that inflation and shooting and young people
killing one another with knives? Don't you read the papers?
And let me tell you something else, if you go it'll be the
death of you, Ada 'Arris - and don't say I didn't warn
you.'

Mrs Harris tried the financial offensive. 'But Violet,
look at the money she's offered to pay you - American

wages, a hundred quid a month and keep. You don't earn that much in three months 'ere. You could rent your flat while you was away, yer widow's pension'd be piling up, you'd have no expenses of any kind - why, you'd like as not have five hundred quid by the time you came 'ome. Look what a 'oliday you could 'ave with that. Or put it into Premium Bonds and win a thousand quid more. You'd never 'ave to do another stroke of work.'

'Money ain't everything,' Mrs Butterfield countered. 'You'd know that, Ada 'Arris, if you read your Bible more. The root of all evil, that's what it is. Who's got the most trouble in this world, who's always being dragged into Court and getting their nymes in the papers? Millionaires. I can make enough for me needs right 'ere, and that's where I'm stayin'. Anyway, I wouldn't go to that Soda and Gomorrow, what they say New York is, for five hundred quid a month.'

Mrs Harris moved up her inter-continental missile with megaton warhead. 'What about little 'Enry?' she said.

Mrs Butterfield regarded her friend with some alarm. 'What about 'im?' she asked, to gain time, for in the excitement and terror of Mrs Harris's proposition she had quite forgotten who and what lay behind it all.

'To find 'is dad and give the poor little tyke a decent life, that's what's all about 'im, Violet Butterfield, and I'm surprised and ashymed at you forgettin'. If you've 'eard it once, you 've 'eard me say a 'undred times, if I could only get to America I'd find 'is dad and tell 'im where 'is kid was and what was 'appening to 'im. Well now, 'ere's our chance to go and do just that, and you ask me what about little 'Enry! Don't you love 'im?'

This was almost attacking below the belt, and Mrs Butterfield let out a howl of protest. 'Ow, Ada, 'ow can you say such a thing? You know I do. Ain't I always feeding 'im up and cuddling 'im like a mother?'

'But don't you want to see 'im 'appy and safe with 'is father?'

'Of course I do,' said Mrs Butterfield, and then produced to her own great surprise out of her own locker an atomic-ray defence, which nullified Mrs Harris's attack. 'Oo's to look after 'im while you're away if I go too? What's the use of you turning up 'is old man only to 'ave 'im come over 'ere and find the poor little tyke starved to death? One of us 'as got to stay 'ere.'

There was intrinsically so much logic in this statement that for the moment Mrs Harris was nonplussed and could not think of an answer, and so with an extraordinary heaviness about her heart she looked down into her teacup and said simply, 'I do wish you'd come to America with me, Vi.'

It was now Mrs Butterfield's turn to look at her friend with astonishment. Sincerity brought forth an equal measure of sincerity in herself. Gone now were all the subterfuges and she replied, 'I don't want to go to America - I'm afraid to go.'

'So am I,' said Mrs Harris.

Mrs Butterfield's astonishment turned now to amazement. 'What!' she cried. 'You, Ada 'Arris, afraid! Why, I've known you for more than thirty-five years, and you've never been afraid of anything in your life.'

'I am now,' said Mrs Harris. 'It's a big step. It's a strange country. It's a long way off. Who's to look after me if anything happens? I wish you were coming with me. One never knows, does one?'

It might have sounded like irony, this sudden switch in the accustomed roles of the two women: Mrs Harris the adventurous optimist suddenly turned into a kind of Butterfield timorous pessimist. But the truth was that there was no irony whatsoever in her remark. It was just that the realization had suddenly come upon her of the enormity of the undertaking into which she had thrust herself so light-heartedly and with her usual sense of excitement and adventure. New York was not only a long way off, it would be totally different from anything she had ever experienced. True, Paris had been utterly foreign, but if you looked at a map, Paris was just across the street. America would be English-speaking, it was true, and yet in another sense more foreign than France, or perhaps even China. She was going to uproot herself from that wonderfully secure and comfortably-fitting London which had sheltered her for all her life and about whose streets and rhythm and noises and manifold moods she knew her way blindfolded. And she was no longer young. She knew of the many British wives who, having married Americans, had come running home, unable to adjust themselves to American life. She was sixty-one, a sixty-one that felt full of energy and brimming with life it is true, but one never did know, did one? Supposing she fell ill? Who in a strange land would provide the necessary link between herself and her beloved London? Yes, for that instant she was truly and genuinely afraid, and it showed in her eyes. Violet Butterfield saw it there.

'Oh dear,' said the fat woman, and her round chins began to quiver, 'do you mean it, Ada? Do you really need me?'

Mrs Harris eyed her friend, and knew that she really did want this big, bulky, helpless but comfortable woman to lean on a little. 'Yes, love,' said Mrs Harris, 'I do.'

'Then I'll come with you,' said Mrs Butterfield, and began to bawl. Mrs Harris started to cry too, and immediately the two women were locked in one another's arms, weeping together for the next few minutes, and having a most lovely time.

The die, however, had been cast, and the trip was on.

Anyone who knew the worth of Mrs Harris and Mrs Butterfield to their clients would not have been surprised had they come into Belgravia to have found large sections of this exclusive area decorated with black *crêpe* hung out after the two widows had notified their clients that within one week's time they were departing for the United States and would not be available for at least three months thereafter, and perhaps longer.

However, such is the toughness of the human spirit, as well as the frame, and likewise so stunning the news and excitement engendered by the fact that Mrs Harris and Mrs Butterfield were going out to what some of them still persisted in referring to as 'the colonies', that the blow was taken more or less in stride.

Had the two women merely announced a one- or two-day, or a week's hiatus, there would then have been such revolutions in the area as to shake every mews, crescent, square, and lane - but three months meant forever, and constituted one of the hazards of modern living. With a sigh most of them resigned themselves to renewed visits to the employment office, and a further period of trial and error until another such gem as Mrs Harris or Mrs Butterfield could be found.

EVER afterwards Mrs Harris swore that the thought of kidnapping little Henry from the disgusting Gussets, stowing him away aboard the *Ville de Paris*, and taking him bodily to his father in America would never have occurred to her but for the astonishing coincidence of the episode in the home of the Countess Wyszcinska, whose London *pied-à-terre* in Belgrave Street Mrs Harris brightened between the hours of five and six. It was that same Countess with whom she had had the *contretemps* over the new Hoover and who, contrary to the gloomy prognostications of Mrs Butterfield, had known what was good for her and produced one.

Thus, she was in the flat of the Countess when a parcel arrived for that august lady from her eighteen-year-old nephew in Milwaukee, Wisconsin. The contents of the parcel proved to be the most awful eyesore the Countess had ever beheld - a horribly encrusted beer stein with an imitation silver lid and 'Souvenir of Milwaukee' emblazoned on its side. Unfortunately, so thoroughly had this revolting *objet d'art* been wrapped in and stuffed out with old newspapers that it had arrived in unbroken condition.

The Countess with an expression of distaste about her aristocratic countenance said, 'Ugh! What in God's name?' And then, aware of Mrs Harris's interested presence, quickly corrected herself and said, 'Isn't it lovely? But I just don't know where to put it. There's so much in this little place already. Would you like to take it home with you, Mrs Harris?'

Mrs Harris said, 'Wouldn't I just. "Souvenir of Milwaukee" - I might be going there to visit when I'm in America.'

'Well, just get it out of here - I mean, I'm glad you like it. And throw all that trash away while you're at it,' pointing to the papers that had preserved its life. Thereupon the Countess departed, wondering what had got into chars nowadays that they seemed always to be travelling.

Left to herself, Mrs Harris then indulged in one of her favourite pastimes, which was the reading of old newspapers. One of her greatest pleasures when she went to the fishmonger's was to read two-year-old pages of the *Mirror* lying on the counter and used for wrapping.

Now she picked up a page of a newspaper called *The Milwaukee Sentinel*, eyed the headline 'Dominie Seduced Schoolgirl in Hayloft', enjoyed the story connected therewith, and thereafter leafed through the other pages of the same instrument of public service until she came to one labelled 'Society Page', on which she found many photographs of young brides, young grooms-to-be, and young married couples.

Always interested in weddings, Mrs Harris gave these announcements more undivided attention, until she came upon one which caused her little eyes almost to pop out of her head, and led her to emit a shriek, 'Ruddy gor'-blimey - it's 'im! It's 'appened! I felt it in me bones that something would.'

What she was looking at was the photograph of a handsome bridal couple over which was the caption, 'Brown-Tracy Nuptials', and underneath the story under the dateline of Sheboygan, Wisconsin, 23 January: 'The wedding was celebrated here today at the First Methodist Church on Maple Street, of Miss Georgina Tracey, daughter of Mr and Mrs Frank Tracey of 1327 Highland Avenue, to Mr George Brown, only son of Mr and Mrs Henry Brown of 892 Delaware Road, Madison, Wisconsin. It was the bride's first marriage, the groom's second.

'The bride, one of the most popular graduates of Eastlake High School, has been a leader in the social activities of the younger debutante set. The groom, aged 34, an electronics engineer, was formerly in the U.S. Air Force, stationed in England. The couple will make their home in Kenosha, Wisconsin.'

Clutching the paper fiercely between her thin, veined hands, Mrs Harris performed a little solo dance about the Countess's drawing room, shouting, 'It's 'im! It's 'im! I've found little 'Enry's father!' There was not the least shadow of doubt in her mind. He was handsome; he resembled little 'Enry in that he had two eyes, a nose, a mouth, and ears; he was of the right age; he was well-to-do, had a noble look about his eyes, as Mrs Harris had imagined him, and now he was married to a fine-looking girl, who would be just the mother for little 'Enry. Popular the paper said she was, but Mrs Harris also noted that she had a good, open countenance, and nice eyes. What clinched it and made it certs was the name of Mr Brown's father - Henry Brown: of course the grandchild would be named after him.

Mrs Harris ceased her dance, looked down upon the precious photograph and said, 'George Brown, you're going to get your baby back,' and at that moment, for the first time, the thought of abstracting little 'Enry from the Gussets and of taking him to his father immediately smote her between the eyes. True, she didn't have his address, but there would be no difficulty in locating him once she got herself and little 'Enry to Kenosha, Wisconsin. If this was not a sign from On High as to where her duty lay and what she ought to do about it, Mrs Harris did not know signs from Above, which she had been encountering and interpreting more or less successfully ever since she could remember.

Little Henry Brown was aged eight in terms of the tenure of his frail body, eighty in the light of the experience of the harsh and unhappy world into which that body had been ushered. In his brief sojourn he had learned all of the tricks of the persecuted - to lie, to evade, to steal, to hide - in short, to survive. Thrown on his own in the concrete desert of the endless pavements of London, he very early acquired the quickness of mind and the cunning needed to outwit the wicked.

Withal, he yet managed to retain a childish charm and innate goodness. He would never scupper a pal or do the dirty on someone who had been kind to him. Someone, for instance, like the two widow charladies, Mrs Ada Harris, and Mrs Violet Butterfield, in whose kitchen he was now momentarily concealed, involved in a thrilling and breathless conspiracy.

He sat there looking rather like a small gnome, gorging himself on tea and buns to the point of distension (since one of the things life had taught him was whenever he came across any food that appeared to be unattached, the thing to do was to eat it quickly, and as much of it as he could hold), while Mrs Harris unfolded the details of the plot.

One of Henry's assets was his taciturnity. Among other things he had learned to keep his mouth shut. He was eloquent rather by means of a pair of huge, dark, sad eyes, eyes filled with knowledge that no little boy of that age should have, and which missed nothing that went on about him.

Because he was thin and somewhat stunted in growth, his head had the appearance of being too large and old, rather an adult head, with a shock of darkish hair, underneath which was a pale and usually dirty face. It was to his eternal credit that there was still some youth and sweetness left in him - adversity had not made him either mean or vengeful.

Whatever the steps he took to make life as easy for himself as possible under the circumstances, they were dictated purely by necessity. He rarely spoke, but when he did it was to the point.

And now as Mrs Harris continued to unfold yet more details of the most fascinating scheme ever devised to free a small boy from hideous tyranny and guarantee him three square meals a day, he sat silently, his mouth stuffed full of bun, but nodding, his huge eyes filled with intelligence and understanding while Mrs Harris enumerated each point of what he was to do when, where, and under various circumstances. In these same eyes was contained also considerable worship of her.

It was true, he loved the occasional cuddle pillowed upon the pneumatic bosom of Mrs Butterfield, though he did not go for too much of that soft stuff, or would not let himself, but it was he and Mrs Harris who were kindred souls. They recognized something in one another, the independent spirit, the adventurous heart, the unquenchable soul, the ability to stand up to whatever had to be stood up to, and get on.

Mrs Harris was not one to fuss and gush over him, but she addressed him like an equal, for equal they were in that nether world of hard and unremitting toil to feed and clothe oneself, where life is all struggle and the helping hands are one's own.

In so many ways they were alike. For instance, no one had ever heard Henry complain. Whatever happened to him, that's how things were. No one had ever heard Mrs Harris complain either. Widowed at the age of thirty, she had raised, educated, and married off her daughter, and kept herself and her self-respect, and all on her hands and knees with a scrubbing brush, or bent over mop and duster, or sinks full of dirty dishes. She would have been the last person to have considered herself heroic, but the strain of simple heroism was in her, and Henry had it too. He also had that quick understanding that gets at the heart of the situation. Whereas Mrs Harris had to go into long and elaborate explanations of things to Mrs Butterfield, and she did so with great patience, little Henry usually got it in one, and would nod his acquiescence before Mrs Harris was half way through exposing what she had on her mind.

Now when Mrs Harris had finished rehearsing step by step how the plan was to work, Mrs Butterfield, who for the first time was hearing what seemed to her to be the concoction of a mad woman, threw her apron over her head and began to rock and moan.

'Ere, 'ere, love, what's wrong?' said Mrs Harris. 'Are you ill?'

'Ill,' cried Mrs Butterfield, 'I should think so! Whatever it's called, what you're doing, it's a jyle offence. You can't get away with it. It'll never work.'

Little Henry stuffed the last of a sugar bun into his mouth, washed it down with a swig of tea, wiped his lips with the back of his hand and turning his large eyes upon the quivering figure of Mrs Butterfield said simply, 'Garn, why not?'

Mrs Harris threw back her head and roared with laughter. 'Oh 'Enry,' she said, 'you're a man after me own 'eart.'

L IKE all great ideas and schemes born out of Genius by
Necessity, Mrs Harris's plan to smuggle little Henry
aboard the s.s. *Ville de Paris* at Southampton had the virtue
of simplicity, and one to which the routine of boarding the
ship with its attendant chaos, as Mr Schreiber had carefully
explained to her, lent itself beautifully.

Since the Schreibers were going First-Class and the two
women Tourist, they would not be able to travel together,
and he had rehearsed for her the details of exactly what
they would have to do - the departure by boat-train from
Waterloo, the arrival at the pier at Southampton where,
after passing through Customs and Immigration, they
would board the tender for the trip down the Solent, and
thus eventually would enter the side of the liner and be
shown to their cabin, and thereafter the French line would
take over.

To these instructions Mrs Harris added a vivid memory
of an instance when she had been at Waterloo to take a
suburban train, and at one of the gates had witnessed what
appeared to be a small-sized riot, with people milling and

crowding, children shrieking, etc., and inquiring into the nature of this disturbance had been informed that it was merely the departure of the boat-train at the height of the season.

As Mrs Harris's scheme was outlined to her, even that perpetual prophetess of doom, Mrs Butterfield, outdid herself with tremblings, groans, cries, quiverings, claspings of hands together, and callings upon heaven to witness that the only possible result could be that they would all spend the rest of their natural lives in a dungeon, and she, Mrs Violet Butterfield, would have no part of it. She had agreed to embark upon this hare-brained voyage across an ocean waiting to engulf them, to a land where death lurked at every corner, but not to make disaster doubly sure by beginning the trip with a kidnapping and a stowing away.

Mrs Harris who, once she had what she considered a feasible idea in her head, was not to be turned from it, said, 'Now, now, Violet - don't take on so. A stitch in time will help us to cross over those bridges.' And then with remarkable patience and perseverance managed to overcome practically all her friend's objections.

Her intrinsic plan was based upon recollections of childhood visits to Clacton-on-Sea with her Mum and Dad, and the outings they used to enjoy on the excursion steamers to Margate, a luxury they occasionally permitted themselves. Poor and thrifty, her folks could manage the price of two tickets, but not three. When time came to pass through the gates and encounter the ticket-taker, little Ada had been taught to detach herself from her parents and, seeking out a large family with five or more youngsters, join up with them until safely through the gates. Experience had taught them in the Sunday crush the harassed ticket-taker would not be able to distinguish whether it was five or six children who had passed him, and the equally harassed father of the family would not notice that he had suddenly acquired an extra little girl. Once they were inside, by the time paterfamilias, perhaps aware that something was a little unusual about his brood, instituted a nose count, little Ada would have detached herself from this group and joined up with her parents again.

Moreover, there was a reserve gambit in case a large enough family failed to turn up. Father and mother would pass through on their tickets, and a few seconds later little Ada would let forth a wail, 'I'm lost! I'm lost! I've lost my Mummie!' By the time this performance had reached its climax and she was restored to her frantic parents, nobody thought of collecting a ticket from her. The excursion proceeded happily.

Mrs Butterfield, who in her youth had had similar experiences, was forced to concede that neither of these devices had ever failed. She was further put off her prophetic stroke by Mrs Harris's superior knowledge as a world traveller.

'Don't forget, dearie,' said Mrs Harris, 'it's a *French* boat. Muddle, that's their middle name. They can't get nothing done without carrying on shouting and waving their arms. You'll see.'

Mrs Butterfield made one more attempt. 'But once 'e's in our room, won't they find 'im?' she quavered, her chins shaking.

Mrs Harris, now slightly impatient, snorted, 'Lor', love, use yer loaf. We've got a barfroom, 'aven't we?'

This was indeed true. So thrilled had Mrs Schreiber been with her luck in acquiring two servants whom she liked and trusted, that she had persuaded her husband to procure for them one of the better rooms available in Tourist-Class on the liner, one of a few with a bathroom connected, and intended for larger families. Mrs Harris had been shown the accommodations on a kind of skeleton plan of the ship, and while she did not exactly know what part the barfroom would play once aboard the lugger, it loomed large in her mind at least as a retreat into which parties could momentarily retire during alarm or crisis.

AS may be imagined, the departure of Mrs Harris and Mrs Butterfield for the United States was an event that shook the little street in Battersea known as Willis Gardens to its Roman foundations, and all of their friends and neighbours, including the unspeakable Gussets, turned out to bid them Godspeed. Such was the excitement engendered by the arrival of the taxicab at number five, and the piling of ancient trunks and valises on the roof and next the driver's seat, that no one thought about or noticed the absence of little Henry Brown.

Like all persons unused to travelling, the two women had taken far more with them than they would ever need, including photographs, ornaments, and little knick-knacks from their homes which meant something to them, and thus the inside of the cab was also stuffed with luggage, leaving, it seemed, barely room for the stout figure of Mrs Butterfield and the spare one of Mrs Harris to squeeze in.

Apprised that they were actually off to America, the cab driver was deeply impressed, and became most helpful and solicitous, and treated the two ladies with the deference one accords to royalty, lifting and fastening their boxes and suitcases, and playing to the crowd gathered for the farewell with a fine sense of the dramatic.

Mrs Harris accepted all of the deference done her and the interest and excitement of friends and neighbours with graciousness, mingling affectionate farewells with sharp directions to the cab driver to be careful of this or that piece of baggage, but poor Mrs Butterfield was able to do little more than palpitate, perspire, and fan herself, since she could not rid her mind of the enormity of what they were about to perpetrate, or cease to worry about the immediate future, beginning within the next few minutes, and whether it would come off.

The attitude of the Gussets was one of grudging interest, coupled with impudence, which bespoke their feeling of good riddance. Among other things, the departure of the two women meant to them an undisturbed period of abuse of the child who had been entrusted to their care.

It had actually to a great extent been Mrs Harris who had kept their cruelty within bounds, for they were a little afraid of her and knew that she would not hesitate to involve them with the police if there was a case. Now, with pairs of eyes and ears removed from either side of them, they could let themselves go. The Gusset children were going to have a field day, and Mr Gusset, when things had gone wrong with one of his shady deals in Soho and little Henry happened to fall foul of him, was not going to have to restrain himself. The child was in for a sticky time of it, and delight at the departure of his two protectresses was written all over the faces of the Gussets - mother, father, and offspring.

Finally the last valise had been stowed and secured, the taxi driver had taken his seat behind the wheel and animated the engine, perspiring Mrs Butterfield and sparkling

Mrs Harris took their places in the space left for them in the interior of the cab, each clutching a small nosegay of flowers tied with a bit of silver ribbon thrust into their hands at the last moment by friends, and they drove off to a cheer and individual cries of, 'Good luck!' - 'Tyke care of yerselves' - 'Send us a postcard' - 'Don't fergit to come back' - 'Give me regards to Broadway' - 'Don't forget to write' and 'May the Good Lord look after you.'

The cab gathered momentum, Mrs Butterfield and Mrs Harris turning and looking out through the rear window to see their friends waving and cheering still and gazing after them, with several of the Gusset children cocking a snook in their direction.

'Ow Ada,' quavered Mrs Butterfield, 'I'm so frightened. We oughtn't to be doing it. What if— ?'

But Mrs Harris who herself had been considerably nervous during the departure and had been playing something of a role, now indeed took command of the expedition and pulled herself together. 'Be quiet, Vi!' she commanded. 'Nuffink's going to happen. Blimey, dearie, if I didn't think you were going to give the show away. Now don't fergit when we get there - you keep your eye peeled out the back.' Therewith she tapped upon the window behind the driver with a penny, and when that individual cocked a large red ear in the direction of the opening she said, 'Go round the corner through Gifford Plyce to 'Ansbury Street - there's a greengrocer there on the corner, his nyme is Warbles.'

The cab driver chose a bad moment to joke. 'I thought you lydies said you was going to Hamerica,' and was surprised at the asperity of the reply he received from Mrs Harris.

'Do as you're told and you won't gather no flies,' she said, for she too was nervous approaching that moment when dreams which seem so easy of realisation are turned into action which very often is not.

The taxi drew up in front of the shop, where Mr Warbles was on the pavement tearing some tops off carrots for a customer.

Mrs Harris said, ''E would 'ave to be outside,' and added a naughty word. Just then the greengrocer was hailed from within and answered the call.

'Now!' Mrs Harris said fiercely to Mrs Butterfield, who was already peering anxiously out of the back window, 'Do you see anyone?'

'I don't know,' quavered Mrs Butterfield. 'I don't fink so. Leastways, nobody we know.'

Mrs Harris leaned forward to the opening in the window and whispered into the large red ear, ''Onk yer 'orn three times.'

Mystified and intimidated, the driver did so. From behind some stacked-up crates of cabbages the figure of a small, dark-haired boy came charging, looking neither right nor left, straight for the door of the cab which Mrs Harris now held open. With the combined speed and agility of a ferret, the boy wriggled his way beneath the luggage piled inside the cab and vanished.

The door slammed shut. 'Waterloo,' hissed Mrs Harris into the ear.

'Well I'm bowed,' said the taxi driver to himself at this curious performance, and put his machine into gear. That the two respectable charladies who were just departing for America from a respectable neighbourhood might be engaging in a casual bit of kidnapping never entered his head.

IT is a fact that nothing is quite as noticeable as a child that wants to be noticed, but the converse is likewise true, that there is nothing equally self-effacing as a child desiring to be vanished, and who in particular is permitted to operate in a crowd.

This was a technique known both to Mrs Harris and little Henry, and thus when the Schreibers were seen descending upon them along the bustling station platform at Waterloo, causing Mrs Butterfield to utter a little yelp of terror, it was no problem at all for Mrs Harris to vanish Henry. She gave him a slight pat on his bottom, which was the prearranged signal, at which he simply moved off from them and stood next to somebody else. Since the Schreibers had never seen him before, they now did not see him at all, except as some-body else's child, standing by a piece of luggage and gazing heavenward, apparently singing hymns to himself.

'Ah, there you are,' said Mrs Schreiber breathlessly. 'Is everything all right? I'm sure it will be. Have you ever seen so many people? I did give you your tickets, didn't I? Oh dear! It's all so confusing.'

Mrs Harris tried to soothe her mistress. 'Now there, dearie,' she said, 'don't you fret. Everything's right as rain. We'll be fine. I've got Violet here to look after me.' The sarcasm was lost on Mrs Butterfield, who only perspired more profusely and fanned herself more freely. It seemed to her that the Schreibers *must* ask, 'Who's that little boy with you?' even though at the moment he wasn't.

Mr Schreiber said, 'They're perfectly all right, Henrietta. You forget that Mrs Harris went to Paris and back all by herself, and stayed a week.'

'Of course,' Mrs Schreiber fluttered, 'I'm afraid you won't be allowed to visit us on the ship.' She blushed suddenly at the implication of the class distinction, both un-American and undemocratic, and then added quickly, 'You know how they are about letting anyone go from one part of the ship into the other. I mean - if there's anything you need, of course, you can send us a message - Oh dear— '

Mr Schreiber got his wife out of her embarrassment by saying, 'Sure, sure. They'll be all right. Come on, Henrietta, we'd better get back to our seats.'

Mrs Harris gave them the thumbs up as they departed. And as the Schreibers retreated, almost imperceptibly little Henry moved over and was with them again. 'That was fine, love,' applauded Mrs Harris. 'You're a sharp one. You'll do.'

All the while she was speaking her bright, buttony, wicked little eyes were taking in the people surrounding them, travellers as well as friends coming to see them off, and easily separated by the fact that the travellers looked nervous and worried, and the visitors gay and unencumbered.

Standing in front of an open carriage door several compartments away was a large family of Americans, a father, and mother surrounded by an immense pile of hand luggage, and an indeterminate number of offspring - that is to say, indeterminate between five and six, due to the fact that they were wriggling, jumping about, escaping, playing hide-and-seek, so that not even Mrs Harris was able successfully to count them. After observing them for an instant, Mrs Harris took little Henry by the arm, pointed the group out to him, and leaning down whispered into his ear, 'Them there'.

Little Henry did not reply, but only nodded gravely, and with his sad, wise eyes, studied the antics of the group in order that later he might blend the more perfectly with them.

It would be more suspenseful and dramatic to be able to report that Mrs Harris's plans were scuppered, or even scrambled by the usual malevolent fates, but the point is they simply were not.

Smoothly, efficiently, and without a hitch, they moved from Waterloo to Southampton, from Southampton to the tender, and from the tender to the great black, porthole studded wall crowned by cream superstructure and gay red funnel of the s.s. *Ville de Paris*. Whenever anyone remotely resembling a ticket collector, conductor, Immigration or Customs official appeared in the offing, quietly and inconspicuously little Henry became a temporary member of the family of a Professor Albert R. Wagstaff, teacher of medieval literature at Bonanza College, Bonanza, Wyoming. With her unerring instinct Mrs Harris had even managed to select an absent-minded professor for the deal.

If Dr Wagstaff was at times not quite certain whether his family consisted of six or seven members, he was also equally befuddled as to the number of pieces of luggage accompanying him. Each time he counted the articles they added up to a different sum, until his irritated wife shouted, 'Oh, for God's sakes, Albert, stop counting! It'll either be there or it won't.'

In his usual state of terror where Mrs Wagstaff was concerned, Dr Wagstaff said, 'Yes, dear,' and immediately stopped counting not only the luggage, but children, even though from time to time there did seem to be one extra. Thus little Henry's task was made comparatively simple, and as said before, there were no hitches.

One moment containing a slight measure of tension occurred when the three of them - Mrs Harris, Mrs Butterfield and little Henry - were safely ensconced in Tourist Cabin No. A.134, a roomy enough and rather charmingly decorated enclosure with two lower and upper berths, closet space, and a bathroom opening off, when heavy footsteps were heard pounding down the companionway and there came a sharp and peremptory knock upon the door.

Mrs Butterfield's florid countenance turned pink, which was the best she could do in the way of going pale. She gave a little shriek and sat down, perspiring and fanning. 'Lor',' she quavered, 'it's all up with us!'

'Shut up,' ordered Mrs Harris fiercely, and then whispered to little Henry, 'Just you go into that nice barfroom, dearie, and sit down on the seat, and be quiet as a mouse, while we see who's come to disturb two defenceless lydies travelling to America. You can do your duty if you like.'

When Henry had vanished into the bathroom in a matter of seconds, Mrs Harris opened the cabin door to be confronted by a sweating and frayed-looking steward in white coat with the collar unbuttoned. He said, 'Excuse me to disturb, I 'ave come to collect your steamship tickets.'

With one eye on Mrs Butterfield, who now had changed colour from pink to magenta, and appeared on the verge of apoplexy, Mrs Harris said, 'Of course you 'ave,' and diving into her reticule, produced them. "'Ot, ain't it?" she said pleasantly. 'My friend 'ere's in a proper sweat.'

'*Ah oui,*' the steward assented, 'I make it cooler for you,' and switched on the electric fan.

'Lots of people,' said Mrs Harris. This was like pushing a button releasing the steward's neurosis, and he suddenly shouted and waved his arms. '*Oui, oui, oui* - people, people, people. Everywhere people. They make you to be crazy.'

'It's the kids that's the worst, ain't it?' said Mrs Harris.

This appeared to be an even more potent button. '*Oh la, la,*' shouted the steward, and waved his arms some more. 'You 'ave seen? Keeds, keeds, keeds, everywhere keeds. I go crazy with keeds.'

'Ain't that the truth,' said Mrs Harris. 'I never seen so many. You never know where they are or where they ain't. I don't know how you keep track of 'em all.'

The steward said, '*C'est vrai.* Sometimes is not possible.' Having blown off steam, he recovered himself and said, 'Sank you, ladies. You wish for anything, ring for Antoine. Your stewardess's name is Arline. She look after you,' and he went away.

Mrs Harris opened the bathroom door, looked in and said, 'All done? That's a dear. You can come out now.'

Little Henry asked, 'Do I duck in there every time there's a knock?'

'No, pet,' Mrs Harris replied, 'not any more. From now on it will be all right.'

Which indeed it was, since Mrs Harris had planted her psychological seed at the right time and in the right soil. In the evening an Antoine even more frayed arrived to turn down the beds. There was little Henry with Mrs Butterfield and Mrs Harris. The steward looked at the child and said, "Ullo, 'oo's this?'

Mrs Harris now not gentle, friendly, and conversational as she had been before, said, "Ullo yourself. What do you mean, 'oo's this? This is little 'Enry, me sister's boy. I'm taking 'im to America to 'er. She's got a job as waitress in Texas.'

The steward still looked baffled. 'But he was not here before, was he?'

Mrs Harris bristled. "E wasn't what? 'Ow do you like that? The child's the happle of me eye and never been out of me sight since we left Battersea.'

The steward wavered. He said, '*Oui, madame*, but—'

'But nothing,' snapped Mrs Harris, attacking with asperity, 'it ain't our fault you Frenchies get excited over nothing and lose your 'eads, come in 'ere shouting about people and kids. You said yourself you couldn't remember all the kids. Well, don't you go forgetting little 'Enry 'ere, or we'll 'ave to 'ave a word with one of the officers.'

The steward capitulated. It had been an unusually trying sailing. Down the next hall there was an American family which still did not seem to be able to agree on the number of pieces of luggage and the number of children accompanying them. Besides which he had already turned in his tickets to the Purser. The women seemed like honest types, and obviously the child was with them and must have come through Immigration. Long years at sea and coping with passengers had taught him the philosophy of leaving well enough alone, and not bringing about investigations.

'*Oui, oui, oui, Madame*,' he soothed, 'of course I remember heem. 'Ow you call heem - little Henri? You try not to make a mess in the cabin for Antoine, we'll all have very 'appy voyage.'

He did the beds and went out. From then on little Henry was a full-fledged passenger of the s.s. *Ville de Paris*, with all the privileges and perquisites pertaining thereto. Nobody ever questioned his presence.

Back at number seven Willis Gardens, Battersea, the sole repercussion from Mrs Harris's tremendous *coup*, which saw little 'Enry removed for ever from the custody of the Gussets, and now afloat on the briny, took place upon the return of Mr Gusset from another of his slightly shady transactions in Soho. Mrs Gusset, who was sparing her feet with a session in the rocking chair while the elder Gusset children coped with dinner in the kitchen, lowered the *Evening News* as her better half appeared and said, ''Enry's been missing since this morning. I think maybe he's run away.'

''As 'e?' replied Mr Gusset. 'That's good.' Then snatching the paper from her fingers, he commanded, 'Up you get, old lady,' ensconced himself in the vacated rocker and applied himself to the early racing results in the newspaper.

'OH dear,' said Henrietta Schreiber suddenly, 'I wonder if I've done the right thing?' She was sitting in front of her mirror in her cabin, putting the final touches to her face. Beside her lay an engraved card of invitation which stated that Pierre René Dubois, Captain of the s.s. *Ville de Paris*, would be honoured by the company of Mr and Mrs Joel Schreiber for cocktails in his cabin at seven-thirty that evening. The ship's clock was already showing the hour seven thirty-five.

'What's that?' said her husband who, properly accoutred in black tie, had been waiting for ten minutes. 'Sure, sure. You look fine. I promise you, Momma, you never looked better. But I think we ought to go now. The French Ambassador's going to be there the steward said.'

'No, no,' said Henrietta, 'I don't mean me, I mean about Mrs Harris.'

'What about Mrs Harris? Is something the matter?'

'No - I'm just wondering if we've done right taking her and Mrs Butterfield out of their element. They're so very

London, you know. People over here understand about chars and their ways, but— '

'You mean they'll laugh at us because we've got a couple of Cockneys?'

'Oh no,' protested Mrs Schreiber. 'Why nobody would laugh at Mrs Harris.' She made another attempt upon her eyebrows. 'It's just I wouldn't want her to be frightened. Who could she talk to? Who could she have for friends? And you know what snobs people are.'

Waiting had made Mr Schreiber a little impatient. 'You should have thought of that before,' he said. 'She can talk to Mrs Butterfield, can't she?'

The corners of Mrs Schemer's mouth turned down. 'Don't be cross with me, Joel. I'm so proud you're president now of North American and I wanted to do everything to make things right for you in New York - and she's such a wonderful help. For all I know she may be back there crying her eyes out and frightened to death among a lot of strangers.'

Mr Schreiber went over and gave her an affectionate pat on the shoulders. He said, 'Well, it's too late now. But maybe tomorrow I'll take a walk back to Tourist and see how she's getting on. How about coming along now, baby? You couldn't look more beautiful if you worked for another hour. You'll be the best-looking woman there.'

Henrietta rested her cheek against his hand for a moment and said, 'Oh Joel, you're so good to me. I'm sorry I get into such a muddle.'

They emerged from their cabin, where their steward waited to guide them. He took them as far as the private stairway leading to the Captain's quarters, which they mounted, to be received by another steward who asked their names and then led them to the door of the huge cabin from which emerged that distinctive babble of sounds that denotes a cocktail party in full swing. Embedded in these sounds - the clink of glasses and the cross-currents of conversation - was an impossible sentence which smote the ear of Mrs Schreiber. 'Lor' love yer, the Marquis and I are old friends from Paris.'

It was impossible simply because it could not be so, and Mrs Schreiber said to herself, 'It's because I was *thinking* of Mrs Harris just before I came up here.'

The steward stepped through the doorway and announced, 'Mr and Mrs Joel Schreiber', which brought forth a drop in the conversation, and the bustle of all the men rising to their feet.

Entering thus late into a cocktail party there is a confusion of sight as well as sound - one sees everyone, and one sees no one. For an appalling moment Mrs Schreiber seemed to be aware of another impossibility, one even more unthinkable than the auditory one she had just experienced. It was Mrs Harris ensconced between the Captain and a distinguished-looking Frenchman with white hair and moustache - Mrs Harris wearing a very smart frock.

The Captain, a handsome man in dress uniform with gold braid, said, 'Ah, Mr and Mrs Schreiber. So delighted you could come,' and then with practised hand swung the circle of introductions - names that Mrs Schreiber only half heard until he came to the last two, and no mistake about those: ' - His Excellency the Marquis Hypolite de Chassagne, the new French Ambassador to your country, and Madame Harris.'

There was no doubt about it, it was true! Mrs Harris was there, apple-cheeked, beady-eyed, beaming, yet not at all conspicuous, and looking as quietly well-dressed as, if not better than, most of the women in the room. And somehow it was not the presence of Mrs Harris so much, but the matter of her appearance which bewildered Henrietta more than anything. All that went through her mind was, *Where have I seen that dress before?*

Mrs Harris nodded graciously and then said to the Marquis, 'That's 'er I been telling you about. Ain't she a dear? If it 'adn't been for 'er, I never could have got the dollars to go to Paris to buy me dress, and now she's tyking me with 'er to America.'

The Marquis went over to Henrietta Schreiber, took her hand in his and held it to his lips for a moment. 'Madame,' he said, 'I am enchanted to meet one with a warm heart that is able to recognize a warm heart and goodness in others. You must be a very kind person.'

This little speech, which established Mrs Schreiber socially for the rest of the voyage, also left her breathless, and she was still staggering under the impact of it all. 'But - but you *know* our Mrs Harris?'

'But of course,' replied the Marquis. 'We met at Dior in Paris, and are old friends.'

What had happened was that, having learned from his chauffeur of the presence of Mrs Harris on board in Tourist-Class, he had said to the Captain, who was a friend, 'Do you know, Pierre, that you have a most remarkable woman on board your ship?'

'You mean the Countess Touraine?' asked the Captain, whose business of course it was to study the passenger list. 'Yes, she is enormously talented, though if I might suggest, a trifle— '

'No, no,' said the Marquis, 'I am referring to a London scrubwoman - a char, as they call them - who all day long is on her knees scrubbing the floors of her clients in Belgravia, or having her hands in dirty dishwater washing-up after them - but if you looked into her wardrobe you would find hanging there the most exquisite creation from the house of

Christian Dior, a dress to the value of four hundred and fifty pounds, which she purchased for herself.'

The Captain was truly intrigued. 'What is that you say? But that is utterly astounding. You say this person is aboard my ship? But what is she doing? Where could she be going?'

'Goodness only knows,' replied the Marquis, 'what she is after now in America, what it has come into her head to possess. I can only tell you that when a woman such as this makes up her mind to something, nothing can stop her.' And thereupon he recounted to the Captain the story of Mrs Harris coming to Paris to buy herself a Dior dress, and how no one with whom she had come into contact had quite been the same thereafter.

When the Marquis had finished his tale the Captain, even more intrigued, and his curiosity aroused, had said, 'And this woman is aboard and you say is a friend of yours? Well then, we shall have her up for a drink. I should be honoured to meet her.'

And thus it was that Mrs Harris had received exactly the same kind of engraved invitation as had gone out to the Schreibers, except that on the card had been written: 'A steward will come for you to your cabin and lead you to the Captain's quarters.'

Before Mrs Schreiber was separated from her husband he found time to whisper to her, 'Looks like you can stop worrying about Mrs Harris, don't it?'

That composed and self-assured lady was now chattering away happily and unconcernedly with the Captain. It seemed that during her visit to Paris she had been taken to a little restaurant on the Seine which was also a favourite of the Captain's when he was ashore, and they were comparing notes.

Henrietta's next seated neighbour said to her, 'Are you enjoying the voyage, Mrs Schreiber?' and was somewhat astonished to receive the reply, 'Oh goodness gracious me! Why, it's one that I gave her!' He had, of course, no way of knowing that the dress encasing Mrs Harris was one that Mrs Schreiber had made her a present of several years ago after it had outlived its usefulness, and that she had just recognised it.

EVERYTHING went smoothly on the voyage, lulling Mrs Harris into self-congratulation and a false sense of security. Optimist though she was, life had taught her that frequently when things seem to be going too well, trouble lurked just around the corner. But the routine of the great ship was so wonderful, the food, the company, the entertainments so luxurious, that even Mrs Butterfield had begun to relax in this ambiance and concede that death and destruction might not be quite as imminent as she had imagined.

Three days of all the good things to eat he could stuff into himself, plus sunshine and the love and spoiling lavished on him by the two women, had already begun to work a change in little Henry, filling him out and somewhat relieving the pinched, pale look.

The s.s. *Ville de Paris* ploughed steadily without a tremor of motion through flat calm seas, and as Mrs Harris said to herself, everything was tickety-boo - yet disaster was no more than forty-eight hours away, and when she became aware of it, it loomed up as so appalling that she did not even take Mrs Butterfield into her confidence, for fear that in an excess of terror her friend might be tempted to leap overboard.

It all came about through a conversation which took place with the coterie of friends with whom Mrs Harris had surrounded herself, and at which, fortunately, Mrs Butterfield happened not to be present.

As usually occurred on these voyages, Mrs Harris soon found herself a member of a tight little British island which formed itself in the middle of the Atlantic Ocean aboard this floating hotel. It consisted of an elderly and elegant chauffeur, two mechanics from a British firm sent to America to study missile assembly, and a couple from Wolverhampton going over to visit their daughter who had married a GI, and their grandchild. Mrs Harris and Mrs Butterfield made up the set. They were all at the same table, and soon had their deck chairs next to one another. Basically they all spoke the same language and liked and understood one another.

If Mrs Harris was the life of this party - which indeed she was - the chauffeur, Mr John Bayswater '*of* Bayswater', as he himself would say, 'and no finer district in London,' was the unquestioned leader of the coterie, and looked up to by all.

To begin with, he was not only a chauffeur of long experience - thirty-five years - a small, sixtyish, grey-haired man whose clothes were well cut and in impeccable taste, but he was also a Rolls chauffeur. In all of his life he had never sat in or driven a car of any other make, he had not even so much as ever looked under the bonnet of one. They simply did not exist for him. There was only one car manufactured, and that was the Rolls. A bachelor, he had had a succession of these motor cars instead of wives or mistresses, and they took up his entire time and attention.

But if this were not sufficient *cachet*, he was also now going out to America as the chauffeur of the Marquis Hypolite de Chassagne, newly appointed Ambassador for France in the United States.

He was a happy and contented man, was Mr John Bayswater, for in the hold of the *Ville de Paris* there travelled the newest, the finest, the most modern and most gleaming Rolls-Royce in two tones of sky and smoke blue, body by Hooper, that he had ever driven. To celebrate the crowning of his diplomatic career by his appointment as Ambassador to the United States, the Marquis, who had been educated in England and had never got over his fondness for British cars, had treated himself to the finest Rolls that his independent wealth could buy.

When it came to the question of a chauffeur, the Rolls people had been able to secure for him the services of John Bayswater, who had once accompanied the British Ambassador to the United States on the same kind of job, one of the most respected and trusted of Rolls-trained drivers.

Mr Bayswater's estimate of a good or bad job was based not on the employer for whom he worked, but the nature, kind, and quality of the Rolls-Royce entrusted to his care. If the Marquis's appointment was the cap to his career, so was the new job to Mr Bayswater, since he had been commissioned by the Rolls-Royce Company to go into their factory and himself select the chassis and engine. That the Marquis had likewise turned out to be an all right chap and an understanding man as an employer was just so much money for jam.

But there was yet another reason why Mr Bayswater could assume and hold the leadership in his little group, and that was that of all of them he was the only one who had ever been out to America before. In fact he had made the trip twice - once with a '47 Silver Wraith, a sweet job he had loved dearly, and again with a '53 Silver Cloud, of which he was not quite so enamoured, but which he knew needed him, and all the more in the strange country.

And it was precisely this knowledge of Mr Bayswater's of the procedural ceremony upon entering the free and democratic United States of America which put the wind up Mrs Harris and indicated to her the extent of the trap into which she had led little Henry, Mrs Butterfield, and herself.

The conversation came about as indicated during the absence of Mrs Butterfield from the deck chairs, and the couple from Wolverhampton, Mr and Mrs Tidder, were expounding on the trials they had had to endure at the hands of American officials before a visitors' visa was granted them to set foot in America. Mrs Harris listened sympathetically, for she had been through the same routine: injections, fingerprints, names of references, financial situation, endless forms to be filled in, and seemingly equally endless interrogations.

'Goodness me,' said Mrs Tidder, whose husband was a retired Civil Servant, 'you would have thought we were going over to burgle a piece of the country.' Then she sighed, 'Oh well, I suppose one musn't complain. They gave us our visas, and it's all over now.'

Mr Bayswater put down a copy of the Rolls-Royce monthly bulletin he had been studying, but with half an ear cocked to the conversation, and snorted, 'Ho-ho, is that what you think? Wait until you come up against the American Immigration Inspectors - they'll put you through it. I'll never forget the first time I came over. It was after the war. They had me sweating. You ever heard of Ellis Island? It's a kind of a gaol where they can pop you if they don't like the look of your face. Wait till you sit down to have a chat with those lads. If there's so much as a bit of a blur on your passport, or a comma misplaced, you're for it.'

Mrs Tidder gave a little cry of dismay. 'Oh dear, is that really so?'

At the pit of Mrs Harris's stomach a small, cold stone was forming which she tried to ignore. She said to Mrs Tidder, 'Garn - I don't believe it. It's just people talking. It's a free country, ain't it?'

'Not when you're trying to get into it,' Mr Bayswater observed. 'Proper Spanish Inquisition, that's what it is. "Who are you? Where are you from? How much have you got? Who are you with? Where are you going? When? Why? For how long? Have you ever committed a crime? Are you a Communist? If not, then what are you? Why? Haven't you got a home in England - what are you coming over here for?" Then they start in on your papers. Heaven 'elp you if there's anything wrong with them. You can cool your heels behind bars on their ruddy Island until someone comes and fetches you out.'

The stone at the pit of Mrs Harris's tum grew a little larger, colder, and harder to ignore. She asked, trying to make her question sound casual, 'Are they like that with kids too? The Americans I knew in London were always good to kids.'

'Ha!' snorted Mr Bayswater again, 'not these chaps.' And then with another of his rare cultural lapses he said, 'They eats kids. A baby in arms is like a bomb to them. If they don't see the name and birth certificate and proper papers for them they don't get through. When the time comes they herd you into the main lounge, and there you are. Queue up until you sit at a desk with a chap in uniform like a prison warder on the other side, with eyes that look right through you, and you'd better give the right answers. I see one family held up for three hours because some clerk on the other side had made a mistake in one kid's papers. That's the kind of thing they *love* to catch you out on. And after that the Customs - they're almost as bad. Phew! I'll tell you.'

The stone was now as large as a melon and as cold as a lump of ice. 'Excuse me,' said Mrs Harris, 'I don't think I'm feeling quite well. I think I'll go down to my cabin for a bit of a lie-down.'

And so there it was. For twelve unhappy hours Mrs Harris kept the ghastly news and problem bottled up inside her, during which time she also managed to increase its scope and embroider its dangers. And Mr Bayswater's erudite reference to the Spanish Inquisition, which to Mrs Harris brought up pictures of dungeons, the rack, and tortures with hot pincers, did nothing to alleviate her uneasiness.

Anything British or even French she would have felt herself, as a London char, equipped to cope with, but Mr Bayswater had revealed an implacability about the American Immigration Service and the red tape surrounding entry into the country which, while it might have been somewhat exaggerated, nevertheless left her with a feeling of complete helplessness. There would be no hurly-burly such as had obtained on the station platform at Waterloo and the embarkation pier at Southampton, no friendly, easy-going British Immigration Officers with sympathy for a harassed family man, no attaching of himself by little Henry to the brood of pleasant and absent-minded Professor Wagstaff, no little tricks, no concealments. The fact was that little Henry, having no papers of any kind whatsoever, was going to be nabbed.

What appalled Mrs Harris was not so much the picture of Mrs Butterfield and herself languishing behind bars in that place of the dread name of Ellis Island, changed, it is true, since Bayswater's day to Staten Island and which appeared to be something in the nature of a German or Russian concentration camp, but rather the far more harrowing thought of little 'Enry being impounded and shipped back to London to the mercies of the Gusset family, while she and Mrs Butterfield would not be there to protect or comfort the youngster. She fretted herself into a state of near exhaustion trying to think of some way that little 'Enry might avoid the tight immigration net that Mr Bayswater had outlined, but could find none. The way Mr Bayswater had put it, not a mouse could get itself into the United States of America without proper credentials.

For herself she did not care, but it was not only little 'Enry who would be in dire trouble; she had likewise led her good friend, poor, timorous Mrs Butterfield, into a situation which might well result in her becoming dangerously ill with fright. And then there were likewise the Schreibers. What would Mrs Schreiber do when she, Ada Harris, was carried off to gaol at just the moment when Mrs Schreiber needed her the most?

There was no doubt but Ada Harris was for it, and needed help badly. But to whom to turn? Certainly not Mrs Butterfield, and she did not wish to alarm the Schreibers until it was absolutely necessary. Her mind then leaped to the one man of experience that she knew - Mr Bayswater - who, although he was the kind of bachelor she knew to be unalterably confirmed, had shown himself slightly partial to her and had already treated her to several ports and lemon in the cocktail lounge before dinner.

So that night when dinner was over and they were repairing up to the smoking room for coffee and a cigarette,

Mrs Harris whispered, 'Could I 'ave a word with you, Mr Bayswater? You being such a travelled man, I need your advice.'

'Of course, Mrs Harris,' Mr Bayswater replied courteously, 'I should be happy to give you the benefit of my experience. What was it you wished to know?'

'I think we'd better go up on deck, perhaps, where it's quiet and nobody's around,' she said.

Mr Bayswater looked a little startled at this, but detached himself from the group and followed Mrs Harris topside to the boat deck of the *Ville de Paris*, where in the starlit darkness, with the great ship leaving a phosphorescent trail behind her, they stood by the rail and looked out over the sea.

They were silent for a moment, and then Mrs Harris said, 'Lumme, now that I've got you 'ere, I don't know how to begin.'

Really alarmed, Mr Bayswater turned to look at the little char and steel himself. He had preserved his bachelorhood from numerous assaults for some forty-odd years, and did not consider surrendering it now. But all he saw on the face of the small, grey-haired woman standing next to him was concern and unhappiness. She said, 'I'm in trouble, Mr Bayswater.'

The chauffeur felt a sudden flood of relief, as well as warm, masculine protectiveness. He found that he was even enjoying being there and having her thus appeal to him. It was a most excellent feeling. He said to her, 'Supposing you tell me all about it, Mrs Harris.'

'You know the boy,' she said, 'little 'Enry, that is?'

Mr Bayswater nodded and replied, 'M - hm, good kid. Keeps his mouth shut.'

'Well,' Mrs Harris blurted, 'he isn't mine. He's not anybody's!' and then in a torrent the whole story came pouring forth from her - the Gusset family, the kindly Schreibers, the kidnapping and stowing-away of little 'Enry, and the plan to deliver him to his long-lost father.

When she had finished there was a silence. Then, 'Blimey,' said Mr Bayswater, lapsing once again, 'that's a nasty one, isn't it?'

'You've been to America before,' pleaded Mrs Harris, 'isn't there something we could do to hide him or get 'im through?'

'Not from those blokes,' said Mr Bayswater. 'You'll only make it worse if you do. It's ten times as bad if they catch you trying to evade them. Look here, what about the father? Couldn't we telegraph him to come to the pier, then at least he could stand up for the kid and claim him.'

Despite her worries Mrs Harris was not insensible that Mr Bayswater had used the word 'we' instead of 'you', thus including himself in her dilemma, and it gave her a sudden feeling of returning courage and warmth. 'But it receded almost immediately as she wailed. 'But I don't know 'is address yet. I just fink I know where he is going to live, but I've got to find him first, don't you see? It's a 'orrible mess.'

Now likewise stymied, Mr Bayswater nodded and agreed, 'It is that.'

A tear illuminated by starshine rolled down Mrs Harris's cheek. 'It's all my fault,' she said, 'I'm a stupid fool'ardy old woman. I should have known better.'

'Don't say that,' said Mr Bayswater, 'you were only trying to do your best for the kid.' He fell silent for a moment, thinking, and then said, 'Look here, Mrs Harris, I know you said you knew my boss, the Marquis - is it true what I heard, that you were invited by him up to the Captain's cabin for a drink?'

Mrs Harris gave the elegant-looking chauffeur an odd look, and wondered if he was going to go snobby on her. 'Certainly,' she replied, 'and why not? 'E's an old friend of mine from Paris.'

'Well then,' said Mr Bayswater, his idea growing within him to bursting point and the dropping of another aitch, 'if you know him that well, why don't you ask 'IM?'

' 'Im, the Marquis? Why, what good would that do? 'E's a pal of mine, I wouldn't want to get 'im sent off to Ellers Island or whatever it's called.'

'But don't you see,' said Mr Bayswater excitedly, 'he's just the very one who could do it. He's a diplomat.'

Unlike her, for an instant Mrs Harris was obtuse. She said, 'What's that got to do with it?'

'It means he travels on a special passport, but no one ever even looks at it, no questions asked - V.I.P. and red carpet. I'm telling you, last time I came over with the '53 Silver Cloud, the one with the weak number three cylinder gasket, it was with Sir Gerald Granby, the British Ambassador. We didn't half breeze through on the pier. No Immigration or Customs for him. It was "How do you do, Sir Gerald?" and "Welcome to the United States, Sir Gerald. Step this way, Sir Gerald," and "Never you mind about those bags, Sir Gerald. Is there anything we can do for you, Sir Gerald? Come right through, your car is waiting, Sir Gerald." That's how it went, smooth as silk when you've got a diplomatic passport and a title. Americans are awfully impressed by titles. Now just you think about my boss. He's not only the Ambassador himself, but a genuine French Marquis. Coo, they'll never even notice a kid, and if they do they won't ask any questions. You ask him. I'll bet he'd do it for you. He's a proper gent. Afterwards, when he's got the kid through and on to the pier, you can collect him easy as wink and no trouble to anyone. Well, what do you think?'

Mrs Harris was staring at him now with her mischievous little eyes shining - no longer from tears. 'Mr Bayswater,' she cried, 'I could kiss you.'

For an instant the hardened bachelor's fears returned to the dignified chauffeur, but in the light of Mrs Harris's relieved and merry countenance they were dispelled and he patted one of her hands on the rail gently and said, 'Save the smacker for later, old girl - until we see whether it's going to come off.'

THUS it was for the second time in twenty-four hours that Mrs Harris found herself narrating the story of little Henry, the missing father, and her escapade, this time into the attentive ear of the Marquis Hypolite de Chassagne, Ambassador and Plenipotentiary Extraordinary from the Republic of France to the United States of America, in the privacy of his First-Class suite aboard the liner.

The white-haired old diplomat listened to the tale without comment or interruption, occasionally pulling at the end of his moustache or stroking the feathers of his tufted eyebrows with the back of a finger. It was difficult to tell from his extraordinarily young-looking and lively blue eyes, or his mouth, often hidden behind his hand, whether he was amused or annoyed at her plea that he attach to his entourage one stateless and paperless British-American semi-orphan and smuggle him into an alien country as his first act as France's representative.

When Mrs Harris had finished with the tale of her misdeeds, concluding with the advice given her by Mr Bayswater, the Marquis reflected for a moment and then said, 'It was a kind and gallant thing for you to do - but a little fool-hardy, do you not think?'

Mrs Harris, sitting on the edge of a chair mentally as well as physically, clasped her hands together and said, 'Lor' love me, you're telling me! I suppose I ought to 'ave me bottom whacked, but, sir, if you'd heard 'is cries when they hit him, and 'im not getting enough to eat, what would you have done?'

The Marquis reflected and sighed. 'Ah, Madame, you flatter me into responding - the same, I suppose. But we have now all landed ourselves into a pretty pickle.' It was astonishing how anyone who even for the shortest time became associated with Mrs Harris's troubles, immediately took to using the pronoun 'we' and counting themselves in.

Mrs Harris said eagerly, 'Mr Bayswater said that diplomats like yourself 'ave special privileges. You'll get a special carpet to walk on and it'll be "Yes, Your Excellency. Step this way, Your Excellency. What a nice little boy, Your Excellency," and before you know it there you'll be on the pier with little 'Enry, and no questions asked. Then I'll come and collect the kid, and you'll 'ave 'is gratitude and mine and his father's for ever after.'

'Bayswater seems to know a great deal,' said the Marquis.

'Of course 'e does,' said Mrs Harris, ''e's done it before. He said the last time 'e came to America it was with somebody named Sir Gerald Granby, and it was "Yes, Sir Gerald. Step this way, Sir Gerald. Never mind about the passport, Sir Gerald— "'

'Yes, yes,' agreed the Marquis hastily, 'I know, I know.'

But the point was that he did not know in actual fact as much as he thought he did about what landing arrangements had been made for him. He was quite well aware that there might be some fuss and ceremony upon his arrival, but not to what extent, though he was also certain that no one would demand to see his credentials until officially and formally he presented them at the White House. The members of his entourage, his secretary, chauffeur, valet, etc., would receive equal consideration, and it was highly improbable that anyone would observe or question a small boy who seemed to be with him, particularly if he were well-behaved, as Mrs Harris had asserted, and given to keeping his mouth shut.

'Would yer?' pleaded Mrs Harris 'Don't you suppose you might? You'd take to little 'Enry once you saw him. 'E's a dear little lad.'

The Marquis made a gesture with his hand and said, 'Shhh - hush for a moment. I want to think.'

Mrs Harris immediately buttoned up her lips and sat with her hands folded, on the edge of the gilt chair, her feet barely touching the ground, and eyeing the Marquis anxiously out of her little eyes that now had lost their impudence and cunning, and were only anxious and pleading.

The august individual did exactly what he said he was going to do - he sat and thought, but he also felt.

It was a curious thing about Mrs Harris, that she had the power to make people feel the things that she was feeling. In Paris she had let him into the experience of her passion for flowers and beautiful things such as a Dior dress, and the excitement of loving and desiring them. Now here in her simple way she had made him feel her love for a lost child, and the distress that is experienced all too little at the thought of a child suffering. There were millions of children hungry, distressed, and abused throughout the world, and heaven forgive one, one never thought about them, and here *he* was thinking about a little starveling being cuffed on the side of the head by an individual named

Gusset, whom he had never seen and never would see. How did all this concern him? Looking at Mrs Harris sitting opposite him on the anxious seat, seeing the frosted apple cheeks, withered hair, and hands gnarled by toil, he felt that it concerned him very much.

In her own way, during her brief visit to Paris this London char had brought him some happy moments, and even, if one wanted to stretch a point, his ambassadorship might be laid partly at her feet, for she had been instrumental in causing him to aid the husband of a friend she had made in Paris, Monsieur Colbert, into an important post at the Quai d'Orsay, where within a year he had proved to be a sensational success. Credit for his discovery redounded to the Marquis, and might well have played a role in his selection for the coveted and honoured post of Ambassador to the United States. But even more, she had recalled to him the days of his youth, when he had been a student at Oxford and another charlady, one of her breed, had been kind to him in his loneliness.

The Marquis thought to himself, *What a good woman is Mrs Harris, and how fortunate I am to know her.* And he thought again, *What an astonishingly pleasant thing it is to have the power to help someone. How young it makes one feel!* and here his thoughts permitted themselves to digress to the change that had come over him since his promotion to this post. Prior to that he had been an old man, resigned to saying farewell to the world and engaged in re-examining and enjoying its beauties for the last time. Now he felt full of energy and bustle and had no thought of quitting this life.

And he had a final and highly satisfactory thought on the subject of what it means to be so old and dignified - namely, that people were a little afraid of you. It meant, he thought with an inward chuckle, and reverting to his British education, that you could do as you jolly well pleased in almost any situation, and no one would really dare to say anything. Thus he came to the final thought: what was the harm in helping this good person, and what in fact could go wrong with the simplicity of the scheme? He said to Mrs Harris, 'Very well, I will do as you ask.'

This time Mrs Harris did not indulge in any pyrotechnics of effusiveness of gratitude, but instead as her naughty sense of humour returned to her she grinned at him impishly and said, 'I knew you would. It ought to be a lark, what? I'll wash his 'ands and face good, and tell him exactly what 'e's got to do. You can rely on him - 'e's sharp as a new pin. 'E don't say much, but when he does it's right to the point.'

The Marquis had to smile too. 'Ah, you did, did you?' he said. 'Well, we shall see what kind of trouble I land myself in with this sentimental bit of foolishness.' Then he said, 'We are due to dock at ten o'clock in the morning; at nine o'clock there will be some kind of a deputation coming on board to greet me no doubt at Quarantine - the French Consul perhaps - and it would probably be best if the boy were here at that time so that the others became used to seeing him about. I will make arrangements to have you both conducted through to me from Tourist-Class at half past seven in the morning. I will advise my secretary and valet to be discreet.'

Mrs Harris got up and moved to the door. 'You're a love,' she said, and gave him the thumbs-up sign.

The Marquis returned it and said, 'You are too. It ought to be quite a lark, what?'

SOMEONE should have warned the Marquis about the American press, which was aware that the Marquis was the first new Ambassador appointed to the U.S. since de Gaulle came into power; someone likewise should have advised him of and prepared him for the landing arrangements that had been set up for his arrival. The former, however, was completely forgotten, and the latter, through one of those State Department muddles - surely-so-and-so-will-have-notified-the-Ambassador - totally neglected. Everyone thought the other fellow had done it, and nobody had.

The Marquis himself, a man of innate modesty, had never considered his own person of importance, and while he anticipated an official welcome and a facilitating of entry, he expected no more than that, and upon arriving in the morning meant to have Bayswater drive him to Washington as soon as his car was disembarked.

Thus he was wholly unprepared for the jostling horde of ship newsmen, feature writers, reporters, newspaper photographers, newsreel cameramen, radio and television interviewers, technical men, and operators of batteries of portable television equipment, who came streaming on board from a grimy tug that drew alongside in Quarantine, and came stamping down the companionways and pelting into his suite to demand his presence for an interview in the press conference room on the sun deck.

An equal surprise was the trim white Government cutter which also leeched itself to the side of the *Ville de Paris*, disgorging the official greeter of the City of New York and his henchmen, all wearing red, white, and blue rosettes in their buttonholes, the leaders of both political parties of that same city, along with the Deputy Mayor, the French Consuls of both New York and Washington, members of the permanent staff of the French Legation, half a dozen officials from the State Department, headed by an Under-Secretary of proper rank and protocol to receive an Ambassador, plus a member of the White House staff sent as a personal emissary to welcome him by President Eisenhower.

Most of these somehow managed to crowd into the suite, while a band on the cutter rendered the Marseillaise, and before little Henry could flee into the 'barfroom' where he had been warned by Mrs Harris to retire should anything untoward happen before the actual going ashore should take place.

He had been scrubbed and polished for the occasion, thrust into a clean shirt and shorts, which Mrs Harris had provided for him from Marks and Sparks before departure, and sitting on the edge of a chair with his feet likewise encased in new socks and shoes, he looked like quite a nice little boy, and one not out of place in his surroundings.

Before either the Marquis or little Henry knew what was what, or how it happened, they found themselves swept out of the cabin, up the grand staircase, and into the press conference room crowded to suffocation with inquisitors and facing an absolutely appalling battery of microphones, camera lenses - still, animated, and television - and barrages of questions flung at them like confetti.

'What about the Russians? Do you think there'll be peace? What is your opinion of American women? How about de Gaulle? What are you going to do about NATO? Do you wear the bottoms of your pyjamas when you sleep? Do the French want another loan? How old are you? Did you ever meet Khrushchev? Is your wife with you? What about the war in Algeria? What did you get the Legion of Honour for? What do you think about the hydrogen bomb? Is it true that Frenchmen are better lovers than Americans? Is France going to resign from the Monetary Fund? Do you know Maurice Chevalier? Is it true that the Communists are gaining ground in France? What do you think of *Gigi*?'

And amongst those questions shouted by male and female reporters and feature writers yet another: 'Who's the kid?'

Now it sometimes happens when a press conference is as unruly as this one was, chiefly because most of the press corps had had to get up very early in the morning to go down the Bay in a choppy sea to meet the ship, and many of them had hangovers, that in a barrage of shouted questions, none of which can be heard or answered, one of them will take place in a momentary lull, and thus stick out and, anxious to get *some* question answered, the reporters will temporarily abandon their own and pick up that particular one.

Thus it became: 'Who's the kid? Who's the kid? That's right - who's the kid, Your Excellency? Who's the boy, Mr Ambassador?' and then everybody quieted down to await the answer.

Seated together behind the conference table at the head of the room, the venerable statesman turned and looked down at the strange small boy with the somewhat too-large head and plaintive face, half as though he expected the explanation to come from him.

The small boy likewise turned and looked up into the august countenance of the venerable statesman out of his liquid, sad and knowing eyes, and buttoned up his lips. The Marquis saw them being firmly pressed together, remembered what Mrs Harris had told him about little Henry's disinclination for speech, and knew that there would be no help forthcoming there. Also, the wait between the asking of the question and the time when he had to reply was waxing heavy and intolerable; it was becoming absolutely necessary to say something.

The Marquis cleared his throat. 'He - he is my grandson,' he said.

For some unknown reason, but characteristic of some press conferences, this statement appeared to create a sensation. 'Say, it's his grandson! Did you hear that - it's his grandson? What do you know, it's his grandson!' Notebooks appeared, memos were scribbled, while the photographers now surged forward shouting their own war cries as their flash lamps began to go off in the faces of their victims, blinding the Marquis and confusing him even more. 'Hold it, Ambassador. Look this way, Marquis. Put your arm around the kid, Marquis. Hey kid, move up to your grandpa - closer, closer. Give us a smile now. That's it. Just one more! Just one more! Put your arm around his neck, son! Get up on his lap, bub. How about giving him a big kiss?'

Added to this bedlam were the further questions engendered by the revelation that the French Ambassador had a member of his family travelling with him. 'What's his name? Whose kid is he? Where's he going?'

The Marquis found himself caught up in them. 'His name is Henry.'

'Henry! Henry or Henri? Is he French or English?'

The Marquis was aware that sometime, somewhere, little Henry would have to open his mouth, and so he replied, 'English.'

The press conference now had settled down into some kind of semblance of order and a man in the rear of the room arose and, speaking with the British accent natural to the correspondent of the *Daily Mail*, asked, 'Would that be Lord Dartington's son, Your Excellency?' As a good English reporter, he was up on his Burke's Peerage and knew that one of the daughters of the Marquis de Chassagne had married Lord Dartington of Stowe.

Diplomats ordinarily are supposed never to become flustered, and in the conduct of his official life the Marquis had ice-water in his veins, but this time it was a little too much and too unexpected, and the disaster engulfing him too unforeseen and unprepared for.

To tell the truth was, of course, utterly unthinkable. To reply 'no' would lead to further embarrassing questions, and so without reflecting further the Marquis said, 'Yes, yes.' All he wished for now was to conclude this ordeal as quickly as possible and reach the friendly shelter of the shed on the pier, where Mrs Harris had promised to come and relieve him of the now embarrassing presence of little Henry.

But this latest revelation caused even a greater sensation, and once again the photographers surged forward, their flash lamps winking and flaring, while the shouts of the cameramen rose to a new pitch: 'What did he say? He's the son of a Lord? That makes him a Dook, don't it?'

'Brother, are you a square! That makes him a Sir. Only relations of the Queen are Dooks.'

'What's that?' somebody said. 'He's related to the Queen? Hey, Dook, look this way! Give us a smile, Lord. What's his name - Bedlington? How about you giving the Marquis the high sign?'

Beneath his dignified exterior the Marquis broke into a cold sweat at the horror of the thought that now that the press had him indissolubly linked by blood with little Henry it was not going to be quite so simple for these ties to be severed on the pier when Mrs Harris came to collect him.

The reporters and radio men now crowded about urging, 'OK, Henry, how about saying something? Are you going to go to school here? Are you going to learn to play base-ball? Have you got a message for American youth? Give us your impressions of America. Where does your Daddy live - in a castle?'

To this barrage little Henry remained mute and kept intact his reputation for taciturnity. The interviewers became more and more urgent, and little Henry's silence thicker and thicker. Finally one impatient inquisitor said facetiously, 'What's the matter - has the cat got your tongue? I don't believe the Marquis is your grand-daddy at all.'

Thereupon little Henry unbuttoned his lips. The veracity of his benefactor was being impugned. The nice bloke with the white hair and kind eyes had told a whopping big lie for him, and now corroboration was being demanded for that lie. As Mrs Harris had said, little Henry was always one to back up a pal.

From the unbuttoned lips, in the expected childish treble, came the words, 'You're bloody well right 'e's me grandfather.'

In the back of the room, the eyebrows of the correspondent of the *Daily Mail* were elevated clear up to the ceiling.

The Marquis felt himself engulfed by a wave of horror. He did not know that the catastrophe was just beginning to warm up.

BACK in Tourist-Class, all packed and dolled up in their best clothes, their passports and vaccination certificates clutched in their hands, Ada Harris and Mrs Butterfield stood on deck by the rail, thrilled with their first real look at this new and exciting land, and gazed down upon the bustle of tugs, cutters, and small boats crowding around the gangways of the *Ville de Paris*.

Earlier in the morning little Henry had been escorted forward to the cabin of the Marquis, his head filled with instructions to cover every possible contingency should Mrs Harris be delayed, etc.

Mrs Harris was triumphant, Mrs Butterfield nervous and perspiring now that action was again demanded of them and another crisis to be faced. She said, 'Ow Ada, are you sure it'll be all right? I've got a feeling in me bones somefink 'orrible is going to 'appen.'

Even if Mrs Harris had been able to avail herself of the prophetic nature of Mrs Butterfield's skeleton, it was anyway too late now to alter the plan, and whilst she was not entirely at her ease with little Henry away from her side - during the five days on the ship she had become more than ever attached to him - she refused to be depressed. Nevertheless, just to make sure she went over the planned routine.

She said to her friend, 'Come on love, buck up and keep your hair on - what's to go wrong?' She ticked off the sequence on each finger of her hand: ''E goes through with the Marquis, no questions asked. Once he's on the pier 'e goes and stands under the letter "B" - "B" for Brown - where we collect him. There'll be a taxi for us. 'Enry plays the standing-next-to-somebody-else game until the Schreibers have gone off. Then 'e gets in with us. We 've got the address. When we get there he waits down on the pavement until we 'ave a look about. When the coast's clear we'll have 'im upstairs with us as quick as wink. Didn't Mrs Schreiber say there was enough room in the flat for a regiment to get lost in? It'll only be a couple of days 'til we find 'is dad, and then Bob's yer uncle. Garn now and forget it, and enjoy yerself. What's to go wrong?'

'Somefink,' said Mrs Butterfield firmly.

Looking down over the side and a little before them they could see a gleaming white and grey U.S. Government cutter with a three-inch gun mounted forward, radar mast, and huge American flag. She was connected by a gangway to an opening low in the side of the ocean liner, and as the two women watched, obviously something of importance was about to take place, for the musicians aft pulled themselves together at the behest of their leader, a guard of sailors, and marines ranged themselves at the gangway in charge of a much beribboned officer, the bandleader raised his arms, the officer shouted a command, rifle bolts clicked, arms were presented, the bandleader's baton descended, the band crashed into 'The Star Spangled Banner', to be followed by the stirring strain of 'The Stars and Stripes Forever'.

To this rousing Sousa march there appeared a procession of gold-braided and uniformed *aides* provided by the Army, the Navy, and the Air Force, followed by dignitaries in striped trousers, frock coats and top hats, all emerging from the hole in the side of the *Ville de Paris* and marching down the gangplank on to the cutter. Then came a momentary pause, the bandleader again raised his arms and brought them down violently and his musicians dutifully and loudly went into a rendition of 'La Marseillaise'. The figure of a handsome, erect, and elegant old man likewise in striped trousers, grey frock coat, and grey top hat - an old man with white hair and moustache and piercing blue eyes under tufted eyebrows, the rosette of a Chevalier of the Legion of Honour in his buttonhole - appeared at the exit and stood there for a moment, removing his hat and holding it against his shoulder during the playing of the French anthem.

'It's me friend - it's the Marquis!' said Mrs Harris, not yet aware of what was happening.

Not so Mrs Butterfield, for as the anthem ended and to the strains of another tune the Marquis marched down the gangway, the stout woman uttered a piercing scream and pointed a fat and shaking finger, 'Look,' she cried, 'it's little 'Enry - 'e's going wiv 'im!'

He was, too. His hand clutched firmly in that of the immaculately uniformed Bayswater, and followed by secretary and valet and lesser members of the Embassy entourage, little Henry was following the Marquis down the incline and on to the cutter, where he likewise graciously accepted the presented arms of the marines' guard of honour.

With a sinking sensation in her stomach, Mrs Harris, began to twig what was happening. Just before they stepped on to the cutter, Mrs Harris saw the grey, refined face of Bayswater looking up and anxiously scanning the topside of the ship. By one of those minor miracles of communication he spotted Mrs Harris, and for an instant their eyes met, at which point Mr Bayswater delivered himself of a shrug which told Mrs Harris plainer than words that he was in the grip of something bigger than himself, and was messaging his regrets.

It was indeed so. What had enmeshed Bayswater, little Henry, and the Marquis was not only the high esteem in which the Marquis Hypolite de Chassagne was held personally in Washington, but the fact that the Administration had thought it a good idea to butter up de Gaulle, who had been acting somewhat peculiar of late, by according extra honours to his Ambassador and disembarking him and his entourage at Quarantine.

The Marquis, his luggage, and all those with him were taken off the ship and sailed in state through the Narrows and into New York Harbour, where another guard of honour awaited them at the Battery, along with a fleet of Cadillacs. They were then rolled uptown through the awesome chasm of Lower Broadway, where a small ticker-tape welcome had been organised, and bits of torn telephone books and festoons of paper ribbon covered with figures testifying to America's financial grandeur floated down upon little Henry's head. The cavalcade thereupon proceeded across the Queensboro Bridge and out to Idlewild Field, where the President's private aircraft, the *Columbia*, waited, and the Marquis and all those connected with him with the exception of Bayswater, who remained behind to drive the Rolls down - were flown to Washington.

Little Henry went too. He had never had such a wonderful time in all his life. This was a bit of all right.

Little Henry was gone, but one could hardly say that he was forgotten, for the afternoon papers and those of the morning following gave full coverage to the arrival of the new French Ambassador and his grandson, complete with pictures of same in the various artful poses into which he had been enticed by the veteran ship news photographers - hugging his grandfather, kissing his grandfather, sitting on his grandfather's lap, or staring solemnly with his large, disturbing eyes directly into the camera.

The austere *Times* reported Henry's presence with a single line in which it said that the Marquis was accompanied by his grandson, the Honourable Henry Dartington, youngest son of Lord Dartington of Stowe, but the other newspapers, particularly those employing female feature writers, did some embroidery upon the story: 'The handsome, white-haired, still virile French Ambassador, who caused many feminine hearts to beat faster during the voyage, brought along his little grandson, Lord Henry Partington, who is related to the Queen of England.

'Lord Partington, who is on holiday here from Eton, where he is reported to be an Honour Student, said, "I have brought a message from the youth of England to the youth of America - us kids must stick together. If we do not swim together we will sink. Everyone ought to learn to swim." He said the thing he wanted to see most in America was a baseball game, and will attend the Yankee-Red Sox game at the Yankee Stadium this afternoon.'

In the penthouse at number 650 Park Avenue, Mrs Schreiber (and in the kitchen Mrs Harris and Mrs Butterfield too) looked at these photographs and read the stories with her eyes popping.

'My goodness,' she said, 'so young, and a real Lord already. And it says here he's a relation of the Queen. And we were on the same ship. What a nice-looking little boy - and what beautiful eyes. He's a real little gentleman, isn't he? You can take one look and tell he's an aristocrat. When the family's good, everything's good.' Then her eyes met those of her husband, and they were caught there for a moment, and each knew of what the other was thinking.

To break the spell Mr Schreiber said quickly, 'I don't remember seeing him on the ship. That's a good picture of you, Henrietta - but I look like my own grandfather,' for they too had been photographed by the press and appeared among the arrivals of importance in the s.s. *Ville de Paris*.

And in the vast kitchen of the penthouse, surrounded by the newspapers, from the front pages of which the promoted little Henry stared up at them, Mrs Butterfield dithered and blubbered. 'What are you going to do now? I told yer somefink was going to 'appen.'

For once Mrs Harris did not have an answer. She said, 'I'm blowed if I know, Vi. And you might as well know, I forgot to give Mr Bayswater our address.'

650 Park Avenue, New York 21, N.Y.
15 April

DEAR MARQUIS,

I hope this letter reaches you, as I forgot to give our address to Mr Bayswater, and so you could not know where we are.

Mrs Butterfield and I saw you going on to the little boat that took you off our steamer, which neither you nor I thought of and did not expect. We waved to you, but I do not think you saw us, but Mr Bayswater and little Henry did.

We were very sorry we got you into this trouble with Henry. It was very good of you to say he was your grandson. I suppose you could not say anything else, and the pictures in the paper look very good. Ha ha, I guess it was not such a lark after all, and we are very sorry if we caused you any trouble.

You are a very kind man and I will come and get little Henry on Saturday when Mrs Schreiber has given me the day off. I will come on the train in the morning.

Mrs Schreiber has a very large flat and our rooms at the back are very nice. There are five of them with two bathrooms, and we will have no trouble in keeping little Henry out of sight when I bring him back, so you do not need to worry.

I have not had much time for sightseeing yet, though I have managed to visit Woodlawn Cemetery and it is a very nice one, with very many people buried there. Mrs Butterfield is still very nervous crossing the streets with the traffic all going the wrong side, and policemen blowing whistles at her, but the other day she went to a supermarket on Lexington Avenue to buy a few things for dinner and before she came away she had spent $187 of Mrs Schreiber's money, for she had never been in one before and she could not stop putting things in the little basket and wheeling them away.

Mrs Butterfield joins me in sending you her kindest regards and thanking you for your kindness and wishes me to say how sorry she is you have had all this trouble and hopes that little Henry has behaved himself like a little gentleman.

If Saturday is alright, I will be there to collect him at 1 o'clock.

Please give my regards to Mr Bayswater and tell him I will write to him and thank him myself.

How are you getting on in the new job?

Hoping this leaves you in the pink as it does me,

Yours sincerely,
A. HARRIS

French Embassy, 18 G. Street, Washington N 10, D.C.
17 April

DEAR MRS HARRIS,

Your welcome letter arrived here this morning, and although nothing would give me greater pleasure than seeing you again next Saturday, I am afraid that collecting little Henry, unfortunately, now that I have been compelled to claim him as a blood relative, will not be quite that simple or instantaneous. The fact is that Henry has been an immediate success here, not only due to the social position with which I was led to endow him when questioned by reporters on board the ship, but also because of his own personal magnetism. He has charmed an ever-growing circle of acquaintances in the Corps Diplomatique by not only his ability to hold his tongue, but the quaint expressions which emerge when he loosens it. He is also, I am happy to note, extremely handy with his mitts, as the British would say, and has already endeared himself to our little community by hitting the son of the Krasnodarian Minister - a child quite as unattractive as his father - one on the nose for making disparaging remarks about Great Britain, France, and the United States.

The truth is that little Henry has been the recipient of so many invitations which we have been compelled to accept due to the identity which he has assumed, that he will not be free to return to you until a week from Thursday, or possibly the following Monday. I shall write and let you know. In the meantime, this will leave you free to pursue your search for the boy's father, and perhaps bring this little adventure of yours to a rapid and happy conclusion.

I must confess that I await with some trepidation word from my son-in-law about this newest addition to his family. I have not heard from him as yet, but have no doubt that I shall.

As for myself, I am surely not as important as I am being made to feel by the hospitable Americans, but the sensation is a pleasant one. Is this not a wonderful and warm-hearted people? We English and French must cement an enduring friendship with them if the world is not to be lost.

As soon as I can extricate Henry from the social whirl into which circumstances have forced him I will notify you. In the meantime, let me know how the search for his father proceeds.

Yours,

CHASSAGNE

NIGHT LETTER TELEGRAM FROM STOWE-ON-DART, DEVONSHIRE.
18 April

MY DEAR HYPOLITE HAVE JUST SEEN WIRE PHOTO AND STORIES IN AMERICAN PRESS ON CHILD YOU HAVE SO BLITHELY KISSED OFF AS MINE STOP ARE YOU NOT A LITTLE ASHAMED AT YOUR AGE QUESTION MARK NEVER MIND THOUGH THESE WORDS ARE DICTATED OUT OF ENVY IN THE HOPE WHEN I REACH YOUR YEARS I SHALL BE ABLE TO ACHIEVE THE SAME STOP THE AMERICAN PRESS HAS OUTDONE ITSELF AND SOCIAL CIRCLES HERE ARE STIRRED BY THIS NEW CANDIDATE FOR THE PEERAGE STOP STILL HE LOOKS A PROPER LAD AND I AM GLAD TO HAVE HIM IN THE FAMILY STOP IF QUESTIONED I WILL CORROBORATE YOUR UNBLUSHING WHOPPER BY SAYING HE IS ONE OF MINE ON HOLIDAY IN THE U.S. STOP MARIETTE JOINS ME IN SENDING CONGRATULATIONS AND THANKS FOR A MOST PAINLESS BIRTH STOP YOURS AFFECTIONATELY DARTINGTON

650 Park Avenue, New York 21, N.Y.
19 April

DEAR MR BAYSWATER,

Well here I am at last, and hope you had no trouble getting to Washington with the Rolls and everything is going well.

I guess you are surprised what happened to little Henry. But it was not your fault, and I wish to thank you for your kindness in suggesting it. I have not written to say thanks before because there is a great deal of work to do in Mrs Schreiber's flat. The last person to live here, or whoever cleaned up, was a proper pig, or did not know anything, and what it needs is a thorough scrubbing, which we are doing.

New York is a most interesting city once you get used to the tall buildings and everyone rushing about, and they have the most wonderful cleansers in the supermarket. One is called Zip. You only put a few drops in water and it will take the paint off anything. They also have a most superior dish powder, it is called Swoosh and is better than anything we have over there. They also have a very good floor polish. It is called Swizz. You just put it on and then everything is like a skating rink. Mrs Butterfield nearly went A. over tip after I had put some on the kitchen floor and does not think much of it.

Everything is done by electricity here, but if you want to clean a house good and proper there is nothing like bucket and soap and getting down on your hands and knees, which we are doing.

I think America is very interesting, but I am working hard and sometimes wish I was back with you all having a port and lemon on the good old *Ville de Paris*. Have you heard from the Tidders? I had a postcard from them from Dayton, Ohio, and have written to them to keep an eye out for George Brown, little Henry's father. The Marquis says

Henry is fine, but I am glad that you are there to keep an eye on him too until I come to get him.

Well cheerio and hoping this leaves you in the pink as it does me.

I am your friend,
A. HARRIS

French Embassy, 18 G. Street, Washington, N 10, D.C.
22 April

DEAR MRS HARRIS,

I thank you for yours of 19th inst. and hasten to assure you that I encountered no difficulties whatsoever on the trip down from New York to Washington, nor, might I add, had I anticipated any in a Rolls of my own selection. I am, however, not quite certain that American air is quite as salubrious for the carburettors as British air, for which they were intended, and I may have to make some adjustments later to compensate for this. You will be interested to learn, however, as I was, that the engine thermostat has not been at all affected by the American atmosphere and maintains its proper minimum coolant temperature of approximately 78 degrees centigrade. I am forced to confess that American road surfaces are far superior to ours, and I am wondering whether the front suspension springs and rear hydraulic shock dampers cannot be somewhat released.

As it deserves, the car attracts a good deal of attention on the road, and when I stopped for petrol in the vicinity of Baltimore, a large crowd gathered to admire it and there were many exclamations of admiration. One gentleman stepped up to the car, thumped its side and exclaimed in the American vernacular 'Boy, they know how to build 'em over there.' Outside of finger-marks the car came to no harm through this, and it was encouraging to me to find at least one American aware of the superiority of British craftsmanship.

I have indeed heard from Mr and Mrs Tidder - a letter in fact containing a photograph of their grandchild, an infant whose finer points are bound to escape one who has been a bachelor all his life.

The days aboard the s.s. *Ville de Paris* were, as you say, most pleasant, and I look back upon them with pleasure.

I regret the unexpected turn taken by our little scheme, but can assure you that the boy is flourishing. He has made many friends among the younger members of the diplomatic colony here and I will add that so far, for reasons which we will not discuss, but which are known to us both, I have managed to keep him away from the children of the British Embassy, thus preserving his incognito.

Please remember me kindly to Mrs Butterfield, and with regards to your goodself,

I remain,
Yours faithfully,
JOHN BAYSWATER

Hotel Slade, Kenosha, Wisconsin.
1 May

DEAR MARQUIS,

I guess you will be surprised to receive a letter from me here where I have come to find the father of little Henry.

Kenosha is a beautiful city with many factories of all kinds and many parks and nice streets and houses on the shore of Lake Michigan. Mrs Schreiber was very kind and advanced me the money to fly here when I told her I had a relative, which is only half a fib because it almost would have been wouldn't it?

I had no trouble finding Mr George Brown and his wife here, the one from the newspaper cutting I told you about, and they were very nice to me and gave me tea, which Mr Brown learned to drink when he was in England stationed quite close to London, and was glad when I showed him how to make it the proper English way. He had some friends who lived in Battersea so we had a good time talking over all the old places. He and his wife very kindly showed me around Kenosha in their car.

Kenosha seems to have almost as many factories as London, but Mr Brown said it was only a small city compared to some others like Chicago and Milwaukee. The Captain of the aeroplane pointed out those cities when we flew over them. They are very large.

Well, I have saved my piece of news for the last. Mr George Brown of Kenosha, Wisconsin is not the George Brown who is the father of little Henry. He is someone else. But he was very kind about it and seemed to be very sorry he could not help me. He did not know the other George Brown, but said there were a great many in the Air Force, and he personally was acquainted with two but they were not married.

However, never you mind whether it was the right Mr Brown or not, that is my worry and I will find him very soon or my name is not Ada Harris. In the meantime thank you for telling me I may collect him on Sunday next. I will tell Mrs Schreiber I have a relative at Washington too. Ha ha. Having been with little Henry so long you almost are.

Now I must close as Mr and Mrs Brown are very kindly taking me to the airport in their car and I will go back to

New York, but next Sunday I will come and collect little
Henry and thank you for your kindness.

Hoping this finds you in good spirits.

Yours faithfully,
ADA HARRIS

French Embassy, 18 G. Street, Washington, N 10, D.C.
4 May

DEAR MRS HARRIS,

Thank you so very much for your letter from Kenosha,
Wisconsin, and I sympathise with you in your disappoint-
ment that the George Brown you were so certain was little
Henry's father turned out to be someone else.

Nothing would have given me greater pleasure than to
have received you next Sunday and to have heard personally
from you your impressions of the Middle West, but alas, I
fear that Fate has taken an unexpected hand and your visit
must be once more postponed. It appears that little Henry
has suddenly contracted a disease called the chicken-pox,
to which I understand children of his age are frequently
addicted, and he is compelled to remain in bed, where I
assure you he is receiving the very best of care, and the
doctor informs me that his recovery is not far distant.

You need not be alarmed over the fact that I myself have
acquired a mild attack of the disease from little Henry, who,
I suspect, received it as a gift from the son of the ambassador of Persia, and thus am sharing the quarantine. It seems
the illness skipped me when I was a child. I have no com-
plaint to make about this state of affairs, since it has given
me some necessary solitude and time to reflect upon the
grandeur of this vast nation and the responsibilities of my
position. It will also provide you with the necessary leeway

to pursue your inquiries and discover the father of this child, a task to which I have no doubt you are entirely equal.

As soon as little Henry's period of confinement is at an end I will advise you. At that time, too, I shall spread the word that the Easter holidays of my little grandson have come to an end and I have had to return him to his family in England. He will be greatly missed by the many friends he has made during his brief stay here, but by none more than the estimable Bayswater and myself. To avoid putting you to further expense in this unselfish and charitable enterprise of yours, I have commissioned Bayswater to drive you and the boy back to New York from Washington. It will also give you an opportunity to see a little more of this magnificent country.

If there is anything further I can do to aid you in your quest, do not hesitate to let me know. However, knowing you, your energy and intelligence, I have no doubt but that you will discover the right Mr Brown.

With kind regards and wishes for good luck,

I am yours, as ever,

CHASSAGNE

BUT if the Marquis had no doubts about Mrs Harris's
ability to locate the missing father, Mrs Harris, now
that she was there, was beginning to entertain some herself, since the one man upon whom she had banked so
heavily proved to be the wrong one.

Using her Cockney shrewdness and wit, she had had no
difficulty locating a particular Mr George Brown of Kenosha, Wisconsin, referred to in the newspaper cutting, and
who had turned out to be the wrong one; to find the right
one amidst the teeming millions who inhabited this vast land
mass, so great that not even the fastest jet planes could reduce
it appreciably in size, was a very different matter. She discovered for instance, to her horror, that there were no less
than thirty-seven George Brown's in the Manhattan telephone book alone, with an equal number in Brooklyn, and
further specimens crowding the other three boroughs. Just
to name a few of the large cities with whose names
she was now becoming familiar, there would be as many in
Chicago, Detroit, Los Angeles, San Francisco, Philadelphia,
and New Orleans, besides which she had no assurance

whatsoever that George Brown lived in any of these cities; he might be a wealthy tobacco planter in the South, a textile merchant in New England, or a mine owner in the Far West. A letter written to the Air Force brought the reply that there had been some 453 George Browns on its roster at one time or another, and which one did she mean, where had he been stationed when, and what had been his serial number?

For the first time Mrs Harris became fully aware of the enormity of her task, as well as the realisation that she had let her romantic nature betray her into doing something not at all characteristic of a sensible London char, and that was to go off half-cocked, saddling herself in a strange land - or at least she would be saddled when she collected him from the Marquis - with a small boy whom she would be forced to conceal from her kindly employers.

The almost fortuitous visitation of the chicken-pox it was true would give her more time and breathing space before she had to face the problem of how to conceal little Henry in a penthouse apartment day and night, but for the first time Mrs Harris felt the cold wind of discouragement.

Yet she did not give way to despondency, but remained her cheerful self and did her work as well. Under her aegis the running-in of the Schreiber penthouse was prospering, Mrs Butterfield, relieved of her fears and tremors by the continued absence of little Henry, was cooking like an angel, other servants were being added to the staff, with Mrs Harris inculcating into them her own ideas of how a house ought to be kept clean, and Mrs Schreiber, given confidence by the presence of Mrs Harris, was beginning to lose her trepidation and commence those rounds of dinner parties and entertainments expected of a man in her husband's position.

In the course of the social duties connected with business and the eminence of their position at the head of one of the largest film and television studios in America, the Schreibers were called upon to cater for and entertain some genuinely appalling people, including newspaper columnists who wielded a make or break power over entertainment properties with multi-million dollar investments, rock 'n' roll and hillbilly singers, crooked labour leaders who could shut down the studio unless properly buttered and kow-towed to, mad television directors whose frenetic profession kept them just one barely discernible step away from the booby-hatch, morbid and neurotic authors who had to be pampered in order to produce a daily output of grist for the mills to grind, and an assortment of male and female actors, stars, glamour girls and boys.

Many of these were faces with which Mrs Harris had long been familiar and admired only in their enlargements in the film theatres or their diminutions on the television screens, and who now sat living and in the flesh, close enough to touch, around the Schreibers' groaning board, devouring Mrs Butterfield's roast beef and Yorkshire pud, and accepting service from Mrs Ada Harris, imported from five Willis Gardens, Battersea, London, S.W.11.

Not all of them were as dreadful as one might imagine, but the house-broken ones would appear to have been definitely in the minority.

Mrs Harris, elegant in the black dress and white apron which Mrs Schreiber had bought her, acted as third server upon these occasions, removing plates and passing the gravy, salad dressing, and cheese biscuits, while the temporary butler and first waitress took on the more serious work of getting the food to the ravenous maws of the illustrious free-loaders.

If Mrs Harris could be said to have a weakness besides her romanticism, it was her affection and admiration for the people in the world of theatre, film, and television. She bought and cherished the illusions they made for her lock, stock, and barrel.

Ada Harris was a moral woman, with her own rigid code of ethics and behaviour, and one who would stand for no nonsense or misbehaviour on the part of others. To show people, however, this strict code simply did not apply, and she acknowledged that they lived in a world of their own and were entitled to different standards. Thus, Mrs Schreiber's Friday night dinner parties were as near heaven socially as Mrs Harris ever expected to come. To view Gerald Gaylord, North American's great film star, on a Thursday afternoon off, his beautiful head the size of a two-storey building on the Radio City Music Hall screen, and then the following Friday to see that same glamorous bean close up, and gaze upon him engulfing six Martinis one after the other, was a bliss she had never expected to attain.

There was Bobby Toms, the teenage rock 'n' roller with the curly hair and sweet face, and she closed her eyes to the fact that he got drunk early in the evening and used very bad language in the presence of ladies, language that was only surpassed by that issuing from the exquisite lips of Marcella Morell, the film *ingénue*, but who was so beautiful that even the most dreadful words when she used them somehow seemed beautiful too - if one had the same feeling towards show people as Mrs Harris. There was a hillbilly singer by the name of Kentucky Claiborne who came to dine in unwashed jeans, black leather jacket, and fingernails in deep mourning, a famous comic who actually was funny in real life as well, dancers, heavies, beautiful actresses who dressed glamorously - in short, a veritable paradise for Mrs Harris and Mrs Butterfield as well, who tasted the thrills of high life in the theatrical world via the reports of her friend.

However, broadminded as she was and extraordinarily tolerant in her approach to the people of the wonderful world of entertainment, Mrs Harris soon found the fly in this ointment namely - the hillbilly singer - who made himself so disagreeable that it was not long before he was loathed by everyone with whom he came in contact, including Mrs Harris.

Before his first appearance at a Schreiber dinner party Mrs Schreiber had given her something of a warning of what to expect, since the good-hearted American woman was certain that Mrs Harris would not have encountered such a specimen in London, and did not wish her to be too greatly shocked by his appearance and comportment. 'Mr Claiborne is a kind of a genius,' she explained. 'I mean, he's the idol of the teenagers and inclined to be a little unusual, but he is very important to my husband, who is signing him for North American Pictures and Television, and it is a great feather in his cap - everyone is after Kentucky Claiborne.'

The name had already awakened memories of curiously unpleasant feelings within Mrs Harris, recollections of emotions which eluded her until she suddenly had a moment of recall to the time when her adventure in a sense had begun; this was the night back in her little flat in London when the Gussets next door had used the caterwauling of an American hillbilly singer by that name on the wireless to cover up the beating of little Henry.

By that osmosis through which servants pick up what is going on about them, not only through their ears and the gossip of pantry, kitchen, and servants' quarters, but also somehow through the pores of their skin, Mrs Harris acquired the information and imparted it to Mrs Butterfield that this same Kentucky Claiborne, emerging from nowhere in the southern portion of the United States, had had a meteoric rise as a hillbilly singer, due to the fact that his recordings of folk songs had suddenly caught on with the teenagers, instigating a competition of frantic bidding among the moving picture and television powers to sign him up.

Mr Schreiber, who in a short time had metamorphosed into a genuinely brilliant cine-mogul, had not been afraid to gamble and was far out in front in the race. His lawyers and the lawyers of Claiborne's agent, a Mr Hyman, were in the process of hammering out a contract in which the singer would be paid the sum of ten million dollars over five years - a sum so vast that not only Mrs Harris, but all the entertainment world, were staggered.

In the meantime it was necessary to keep Mr Claiborne in an amiable frame of mind, which was difficult, for it was obvious even to Mrs Harris that, celebrity or not, Kentucky Claiborne was vain, shallow, selfish, self-centred, loud, rude, insulting, a bore, and a boor. As his agent, Mr Hyman, put it to Mr Schreiber: 'So what d'you want? He's a jerk - but he's a jerk with talent. The kids are nuts about him.'

This was true, as it is of many of the repellent characters who work their way to the top in the entertainment world. Now a thirty-five-year-old man with already thinning hair, deep-set eyes, and blue jowls, Kentucky Claiborne had suddenly emerged from the Deep South, where he had been moaning his hinterland folk songs in honky-tonks and cheap night clubs to the accompaniment of his guitar, to become a national sensation. His eyes, his voice, his demeanour, his delivery, apparently evoked the loneliness and melancholy of the pioneer woodsmen of America's past.

While his background and origins remained undisclosed, he must have been a poor boy - not to mention poor white trash - for the sudden access of fame, wealth, and adulation made him drunker even than he was wont to become on his favourite tipple of Bourbon and Branch. Added to these charms was the fact that he chewed tobacco, had grimy fingernails, and apparently did not wash either himself or his hillbilly uniform too often.

The Schreibers put up with him because they had to; their guests did because most of them were genuinely fond of the Schreibers, and many of them had come from equally humble origins and somehow had adjusted themselves.

It did not take Mrs Butterfield long to loathe Mr Claiborne with equal fervour, since his remarks about her cooking were delivered in a loud voice which, when the swinging doors opened, penetrated right into the kitchen, and on anything she missed Mrs Harris indignantly filled her in.

Mr Claiborne was vociferous and uninhibited on all subjects which in any way pertained to himself. For instance, one evening when Mrs Butterfield had concocted a really delectable cheese soufflé, the hillbilly singer rejected it out of hand after a sniff at it, saying, 'Pee-yew! That smells! What Ah wouldn't give for some real old-fashioned Southern cookin' - po'k fat back with turnip greens and pot liquor, or good old Southern fried chicken with hushpuppies. That's the kind of eatin' foh a man. Ah cain't put this foreign stuff in mah belly. Ah'll just hold off until you pass the meat an' potaters.'

At another meal he delivered an oration on his prejudices. 'Ah ain't got no time for niggers, nigger-lovers, or foreigners. Ah say, ship all the niggers back where they come from, and don't let no more foreigners in. Then we'll have God's own country here sure enough.'

Poor Mr Schreiber turned quite crimson at these remarks, and some of his guests looked as though they were about to explode. However, they had all been briefed that if Mr Claiborne were to be irritated he might suddenly break off the contract negotiations going on and take his fabulous popularity and box office value elsewhere.

Mrs Harris passed along her opinion of Mr Claiborne to Mrs Butterfield in good, solid Battersea terms, concluding more mildly, 'He looked right at me when 'e passed that remark about foreigners. It was all I could do to keep me tongue in me 'ead.'

When Mr Schreiber protested to Claiborne's agent, Mr Hyman, and asked whether he could not exert a civilising influence on him, at least so far as his personal appearance, tongue, and table-manners were concerned, that individual replied, 'What do you wanna do? He's a nature boy. That's why he's the idol of them millions of American kids. He's just like they are. Clean him up and put him in a monkey suit and you're gonna spoil him. He's gonna make plenty of dough for you, so why should you care?'

THE day dawned eventually when Mrs Harris, notified by the Marquis that little Henry was no longer catching, in fact was once more in the full flush of youthful health, boarded the Congressional Limited at Pennsylvania Station and took that train to Washington, where first, with her usual energy and initiative, she engaged a cab driver to take her for a quick swing around the nation's capital before depositing her at the French Embassy.

After a tour which embraced the Capitol, the Washington Monument, the Lincoln Memorial, the Pentagon Unit, and the White House, the driver, who had been in the Navy during the war and spent a good deal of time in British waters and British ports, leant back and asked, 'Well, Ma, what do you think of it? It ain't Buckingham Palace or Westminster Abbey - but it's our own.'

'Lor' love yer, ducks,' Mrs Harris replied, 'you can't have everything. It's even prettier than in the pictures.'

At the Embassy Mrs Harris was greeted by the Marquis de Chassagne with great warmth - compounded in part from the genuine affection he felt for her, and in part from relief that what might have turned into a very sticky business was now happily concluded at least so far as he was concerned.

A quite new Henry Brown came storming forth to throw his arms about the person of Mrs Harris; new in that, as with most children bedded with chicken-pox, he had grown an inch during the process, and through proper nourishment and lack of abuse had also filled out. The eyes and the large head were still wise and knowing, but had lost their sadness. Somehow he had even managed to acquire some manners by imitation, and during the luncheon treat that the Marquis provided for Mrs Harris he succeeded in refraining from bolting his food, eating with his knife, and other social misdemeanours.

Mrs Harris, herself a great stickler for etiquette and the gracefully lifted little finger, was not insensitive to these improvements and remarked, 'Lor' love yer, dearie, your father will be proud of you.'

'Ah,' said the Marquis, 'I was coming to that. Have you found him yet?'

Mrs Harris had the grace to blush. 'Blimey, no,' she said, 'and I ain't 'arf ashamed of meself - boasting to Mrs Butterfield how I'd find him in half a jiffy if I ever got to America. Me and my big mouth! But I will.' She turned and promised little Henry: 'Don't you worry, 'Enry, I will find your dad for you, or me nyme's not Ada 'Arris.'

Little Henry accepted this pledge with no particular alteration of expression or change in his taciturnity. At that moment, truth to tell, he was not especially concerned whether she did or not. Things had never been so good with him, and he was not inclined to be greedy.

The Marquis accompanied them to the front door of the Embassy, where the blue Rolls-Royce waited, its figurehead and chrome-work gleaming, with the handsome and immaculate Bayswater behind the wheel.

'Can I ride up front, Uncle Hypolite?'

'If Bayswater will permit it.' The chauffeur nodded gracious acquiescence.

'Both of us - Auntie Ada too?'

To his surprise Mr Bayswater found himself involved in a second acquiescence. Never before had anyone but a footman ridden beside him in the front seat of a Rolls.

'Goodbye, Uncle Hypolite,' said the boy, and went up and threw his arms about the neck of the Marquis and hugged him, 'you've been a real swell to me.'

The Marquis patted his shoulder and said, 'Goodbye, my little nephew and grandson. Good luck, and be a good boy.' To Mrs Harris he said, 'Goodbye, Madame, and good luck to you too - and when you find the father I hope he will be a good man who will love him.' He stood on the pavement watching them go until they turned the corner, and then went back into the Embassy. He was no longer feeling relieved, but only a little lonely and a little older.

Thus, driving up along the National Turnpike from Washington in the Marquis's elegant Rolls-Royce, Bayswater, little Henry, who in a new suit and shoes purchased for him by the Marquis looked more than ever like a young Lordling out of the pages of the *Tatler* or the *Queen*, and Mrs Harris sat all together up front in the chauffeur's compartment and chatted and compared notes.

Mrs Harris thought she had never seen anyone quite as elegant or attractive as Mr Bayswater in his grey whipcord uniform and the grey cap with the badge of the Marquis above the peak. Mr Bayswater found himself somewhat surprised by the pleasure he was taking in Mrs Harris's company. Ordinarily on such a trip he would have listened to nothing but the gentle, almost inaudible purring of the Rolls-Royce, the whine of the tyres, and the exquisite silence of the body bolts and springs. As it was now he lent half an ear to the questions and chatter of Mrs Harris, who was all settled into the comfortable leather seat for a proper chinwag.

He even deigned to talk to her, something he had not been known to do while driving since 1937, when he had had to speak sharply to Lord Boothey's footman sitting next to him to keep his eyes straight ahead instead of letting them wander all about. He said, 'I have driven through Madison, Wisconsin, a city of wide avenues and pleasant homes, but I have never been to Kenosha. What would you say was the most attractive feature of that city?'

'Something they had in the café of the 'otel there - North Country flapjacks with little pig sausages and genuine maple syrup. Coo! I never ate anything so good in me life. Four 'elpings of them, I 'ad. Afterwards I was sick. But blimey if it wasn't worth it.'

'Moderation is the signpost to health,' declared Mr Bayswater somewhat sententiously.

'Go on with you, John,' said Mrs Harris, using his Christian name for the first time. 'Did you ever eat a North Country flapjack?'

After he had got over the initial shock of hearing his first name thus falling from the lips of a female of the species, Mr Bayswater smiled a kind of a greyish, wintry smile, and said, 'Well, perhaps I haven't, Ada. But I'll tell you what we'll do, since you rather fancy your stomach; there's a Howard Johnson's about five miles ahead, and we'll stop there for a snack. Did you ever eat New England clam chowder? You'll be sick again, I'll warrant. It's the best in the world. And for the nipper there's ice cream. Howard Johnson's has thirty-seven different varieties of ice cream.'

'Lumme,' marvelled Mrs Harris, 'thirty-seven kinds! There ain't that many flavours to make ice cream of. Would you believe that 'Enry?'

Henry looked up at Mr Bayswater with great trust and confidence. 'If 'e says so,' he replied.

They pulled up to the red and white Howard Johnson restaurant at the edge of the Turnpike, where hundreds of cars were similarly lined up and nosed in like pigs at a trough, and there they sat and sampled Lucullan bits of American roadside gastronomy.

This time, however, it was not Mrs Harris, but little Henry, who was sick. He had got successfully through nine of the famous Howard Johnson flavours before the tenth - huckleberry liquorice - threw him. But after he had been cleaned up he was as good as new, and piling back into the Rolls-Royce they proceeded merrily northwards towards the great metropolis on the Hudson.

On the final lap Mr Bayswater regaled Mrs Harris with accounts of little Henry's popularity among the diplomatic set before the chicken-pox laid him low and curbed his activities, which seemed to include running faster and leaping and jumping further and higher than the scions of the ambassadors of Spain, Sweden, Indonesia, Ghana, Finland, and the Low Countries.

'My word,' said Mrs Harris. And then, throwing a wink over little Henry's head at Mr Bayswater, said, 'But 'ow come they didn't twig that little 'Enry wasn't - I mean— ?'

'Hoh!' scoffed Mr Bayswater, 'how would they? They can't speak the King's English any better themselves. A leader, that's what that boy's going to be.'

Little Henry here broke one of his long silences. 'I liked the Easter party on the lawn best,' he confided to Mrs Harris. 'We had to 'unt Easter eggs that was hidden, and we had egg races on a spoon. Uncle Ike said I was the best of anybody, and some day I'd be a champion.'

'Did 'e now?' said Mrs Harris. 'That was nice. 'Oo did you say said that - Uncle Ike? 'Oo's Uncle Ike?'

'I dunno,' replied little Henry. ''E was a kind of bald-headed bloke, and a bit of all right. 'E knew I was from London right away.'

'He is referring to the President of the United States and the annual Easter party for the children of the members of the Diplomatic Corps on the White House lawn,' explained Mr Bayswater just a trifle loftily. 'Mr Eisenhower conducted the ceremonies personally. I stood that close to him meself,' lapsing again at the mere memory of the event. 'We exchanged a few words.'

'Lor' love yer - the two of yer 'ob-nobbing with Presidents! I once was almost close enough to the Queen to touch - Christmas shopping at 'Arrods.'

The Rolls was purring - it seemed almost floating - over the steel and concrete tracery of the great Skyway over the Jersey marshes. In the distance, shining in the late afternoon spring sunshine, gleamed the turrets of Manhattan. The sun was caught by the finger tower atop the Empire State Building, glinted from the silvered steel spike terminating the Chrysler Building further uptown, more than a thousand feet above the street level, and sometimes was caught illuminating every window of the burnished walls of the R.C.A. and other buildings in mid-town New York, until they literally seemed on fire.

Mrs Harris feasted her eyes upon the distant spectacle before they plunged into the caverns of the Lincoln Tunnel and murmured, 'Coo, and I thought the Eiffel Tower was somefink!' She was thinking, *Who would ever have thought that Ada Harris of five Willis Gardens, Battersea, would be sitting in a Rolls-Royce next to such a kind and elegant gentleman, a real, proper gent - Mr John Bayswater - looking with her own eyes upon such a sight as New York?* And the greying little chauffeur was thinking, *Whoever would have thought that Mr John Bayswater, of Bayswater, would be watching the expression of delight and joy upon the face of a little transplanted London char as she gazed upon one of the grandest and most beautiful spectacles in the world, instead of keeping both eyes on the congested road, and his ears attuned only to the voices of his vehicle?*

Mrs Harris had the chauffeur drop them for safety's sake at the corner of Madison Avenue, and as they said good bye and she expressed her thanks for the ride and the meal, Mr Bayswater was surprised to hear himself say, 'I don't suppose we'll be seeing you again.' And then added, 'Good luck with the nipper. I hope you find his parent. You might let us know - the Marquis will be interested.'

Mrs Harris said blithely, 'If you're ever up this way again, get on the blower - Sacramento 9-9900. We might go to the flicks at the Music 'All. It's me fyvourite plyce. Mrs Butterfield and me go every Thursday.'

'If you're ever in Washington, look us up,' said Mr Bayswater, 'the Marquis will be glad to see you.'

'Righty-ho.' She and little Henry stood on the corner and watched him merge into the stream of traffic. In the Rolls

Mr Bayswater watched the two of them in his rear vision mirror until he came *that* close to touching fenders with a Yellow Taxi, and the exchange of pleasantries with the driver thereof, who called him 'a Limey so-and-so', brought him back to the world of realities and Rolls-Royces.

Mrs Harris nipped into a drugstore and telephoned Mrs Butterfield to notify her of their arrival and ascertain whether the coast was clear.

THE introducing of little Henry Brown into the servants' quarters of the Schreiber penthouse at 650 Park
Avenue presented no problems whatsoever. Mrs Harris
simply escorted him thither through the delivery entrance
on Sixty-ninth Street, up the service elevator, and through
the back door of the huge flat.

Nor would keeping him there have presented any insur-
mountable difficulties, trained as he was to self-effacement.
The Schreibers never entered the servants' quarters; they
never used the back way into the apartment. There was an
abundance of food at all times in the huge freezing units
and iceboxes into which a child would make no appreciable
dent, and since he was a silent little chap he might have gone
undetected there indefinitely, but for the unfortunate effect
that his presence had upon the nerves of Mrs Butterfield.

Well accustomed by now to the ways of American supermarkets and delivery men, no longer frightened by the
giantism of the city, delighted with the dollars she was
amassing, Mrs Butterfield had allowed herself to be lulled
into a sense of false security by the protracted absence of

little Henry among the diplomatic set in Washington. Now his return and physical presence on the premises put an end to that. All her fears, nervous tremors, worries, and prophecies of doom and disaster returned, and in double measure, for there now seemed no possible solution, happy ending or, for that matter, an ending of any kind but disaster to the impasse.

With the return of Mrs Harris from Kenosha, Wisconsin, bearing the ill tidings that this Brown was not the father of the boy, and her subsequent failure to make any progress in discovering him, Mrs Butterfield could see only execution or dungeons and durance vile staring them in the face. They had kidnapped a child in broad daylight in the streets of London, they had stowed him away on an ocean liner without paying his fare or keep, they had smuggled him into the United States of America - a capital crime, obviously, from all the precautions taken to prevent it - and now they were compounding all previous felonies by concealing him in the home of their employers. All of this could only end in a catastrophe of cataclysmic proportions.

Unhappily, it was in her cooking that the effects of strain began to show.

Salt and sugar were frequently interchanged; syrup and vinegar got themselves mysteriously mixed; soufflés either fell flat or blew up; sauces curdled; and roasts burned. Her delicate sense of timing went completely to pot so that she could no longer produce a four-minute egg that was not either raw or stone hard. Her coffee grew watery, her toast cindery - she could not even make an honest British cup of tea any more.

As for the State banquets she was called upon to prepare for the entertainment of Mr Schreiber's celebrated employees, they beggared description, and people who once were eager to be asked to one of the Schreiber evenings now invented every kind of excuse to absent themselves from the horrors that appeared from Mrs Butterfield's kitchen.

Nor was it any satisfaction to Mrs Schreiber, to Mrs Harris, or to Mrs Butterfield that the only one who now seemed contented was Kentucky Claiborne, who when a particularly charred roast accompanied by a quite appallingly over-salted and over-thickened gravy appeared on the table, dug into it with both elbows flying, and bawled, 'Say Henrietta, this is more like it. Ah reckon you must have fired that old bag you had in the kitchen and got yourself a hundred per cent American cook. Ah'll just have some more of that there spoon gravy.'

Naturally, all this did not happen at once. It was a more gradual deterioration than as narrated, but with a sudden acceleration as Mrs Butterfield, herself aware of her sins of omission and commission, grew only the more nervous and upset, and of course from then on things worsened rapidly, until Mr Schreiber felt called upon to ask his wife, 'See here, Henrietta, what's got into that pair you dragged over here from London? We ain't had a decent meal in two weeks. How am I going to ask anybody here for dinner any more?'

Mrs Schreiber said, 'But everything was going along so fine at first - and she seemed to be such a wonderful cook.'

'Well, she ain't now,' said Mr Schreiber, 'and if I were you I'd get her out of here before she poisons someone.'

Mrs Schreiber pressed Mrs Harris on the subject, and for the first time found the little charwoman, of whom she was genuinely fond, not entirely cooperative. When she asked, 'Tell me, Mrs Harris, is anything wrong with Mrs Butterfield?' she got only a curious look and a reply, ''Oo, Violet? Not 'er. Violet's one of the best.'

Mrs Harris herself was in a fearful dilemma, torn between affection for and loyalty to her kind employer, and love and even greater loyalty to her lifelong friend, who she knew was making a walloping failure of her job, and likewise why. What was she to do, besides what she had been doing, which was to implore Mrs Butterfield to pull herself together, only to be deluged by a flood of reproaches for the fix they were in, and predictions of swift retribution? She herself had not been blind to the deterioration in Mrs Butterfield's art, and the dissatisfaction at the table, and was aware now of a new danger that threatened them, namely that Mr Schreiber would order them both deported to London. If this happened before the finding of little Henry's father, then they were really for it, for Mrs Harris had no illusions about being able to smuggle him back as they had brought him over. Such a caper would work once, but never twice.

Mrs Harris knew that she had erred in not taking Mrs Schreiber into her confidence immediately, and it flustered her to the point where she did the wrong thing. On top of giving Mrs Schreiber a short and unsatisfactory answer, she then went out for a walk on Park Avenue to try to think things out and keep the situation from deteriorating still further.

Thus she was not present when for the first time Mrs Schreiber invaded the labyrinth of her own servants' quarters to have a heart-to-heart talk with Mrs Butterfield, and if possible ascertain the psychological causes for her difficulties, and discovered little Henry in the servants' sitting-room, silently and happily packing away his five o'clock tiffin.

Mild surprise turned into genuine shock when suddenly Mrs Schreiber recognised him from all the photographs she had seen in the newspapers, and cried, 'Great heavens, it's the Duke! I mean; the Marquis - I mean the grandson of the French Ambassador. What on earth is he doing here?'

Even though this catastrophic bolt of lightning had been long awaited by Mrs Butterfield, her reaction to it was what might have been expected: she fell upon her knees with her hands clasped, crying, 'Oh Lor', ma'am, don't send us to jyle! I'm only a poor widow with but a few more years to live.' And thereafter her sobs and weeping became so loud and uncontrollable that they penetrated into the front of the flat and brought Mr Schreiber hurrying to the scene.

For the first time, even little Henry lost some of his aplomb at seeing one of his protectresses reduced to a hysterical jelly, and he himself burst into wails of terror.

It was upon this tableau that Mrs Harris entered as she returned from her little promenade. She stood in the doorway for a moment contemplating the scene. 'Oh blimey,' she said, 'aren't we for it now.'

Mr Schreiber was likewise staggered at finding in a state bordering upon hysteria his Cockney cook, plus a young boy whose image not so long ago had decorated the front pages of the metropolitan press as the son of a lord and the grandson of the French Ambassador to the United States.

Somehow, perhaps because she was the only member of the drama who seemed to be all calm and collected, he had a feeling that Mrs Harris might be at the bottom of this. Actually, at this point, contemplating the scene and aware of all its implications, the little char was doing her best to suppress a giggle. Her eyes were shining with wicked merriment and inner mirth, for she was of the breed that never cries over spilt milk - to the contrary, is more likely to laugh at it if there is a joke to be found. She had always known that eventually they must be caught, and now that it had happened she had no intention of panicking.

'Can you explain this, Mrs Harris?' Mr Schreiber demanded. 'You seem to be the only one left here with any wits about her. What the devil is the grandson of the French Ambassador doing here? And what's got into Mrs Butterfield?'

'That's just what's the matter,' Mrs Harris replied, ''e ain't the grandson of the Marquis. That's what's got into 'er cooking. Poor thing, 'er nerves 'ave went.' She then addressed herself to the child and her friend saying, ''Ere, 'ere, 'Enry, stop yer bawling. Come on, Vi - pull yerself together.'

Thus admonished, both of them ceased their outcries instantly. Little Henry returned to his victuals, while Mrs Butterfield hauled herself to her feet and mopped her eyes with her apron.

'There now,' said Mrs Harris, 'that's better. Now maybe I'd better explain. This is little 'Enry Brown. He's a orphan, sort of. We brought 'im over with us from London to help 'im find 'is father.'

It was now Mr Schreiber's turn to look bewildered. 'Oh come on, Mrs Harris, this is the same kid whose picture was in the paper as the grandson of the Marquis.'

Mrs Schreiber said, 'I remarked at the time what a nice little boy he seemed to be.'

'That's because the Marquis took 'im through the Immigrytion for us,' elucidated Mrs Harris. 'Otherwise they wouldn't have let 'im in. The Marquis had to say something, so 'e used his nut. The Marquis is an old friend of mine - little 'Enry's been 'avin' the chicken-pox with him.'

Mr Schreiber's already slightly prominent eyes threatened to pop out of his head as he gasped, 'The Marquis smuggled him through for you? Do you mean to say— ?'

'Maybe I better explyne,' said Mrs Harris, and forthwith and with no further interruptions she launched into the story of little Henry, the lost GI father, the Gussets, and all that had taken place, including the abortive and unsuccessful visit to Kenosha, Wisconsin. 'And of course that's why poor Vi got so nervous 'er cooking went orf. There's none better than Vi when she's got nuffink on 'er mind.'

Mr Schreiber suddenly sat down in a chair and began to roar with laughter until the tears ran down his cheeks, while Mrs Schreiber went over, put her arms around little Henry and said, 'You poor dear. How very brave of you. You must have been terrified.'

In one of his rare moments of loquacity and warmth, and sparked by Mrs Schreiber's cuddle, little Henry said, 'Who - me? What of?'

Mr Schreiber recovered sufficiently to say, 'And if that ain't the damnedest thing I ever heard of! The French Ambassador stuck with the kid and has to say it's his grandson. You know you could have got into serious trouble with this, don't you? And still can if they find out about the kid.'

'That's what I've been lying awake nights thinking about,' confessed Mrs Harris. 'It would have been easy as wink if that Mr Brown at Kenosha had been 'is father - a father's got the right to have 'is own son in 'is own country, ain't 'e? But he wasn't.'

'Well, what are you going to do now?' asked Mr Schreiber.

Mrs Harris looked at him gloomily and did not reply, for the simple reason that she did not know.

'Why can't he stay here with us until Mrs Harris locates his father?' said Mrs Schreiber, and gave the child another hug, and received one in return - a sudden outburst of spontaneous affection which thrilled her heart. 'Nobody need know. He's such a dear little boy.'

Mrs Butterfield waddled over to Mrs Schreiber, twisting a corner of her apron. 'Oh ma'am, if you only could,' she said, 'I'd cook me 'eart out for yer.'

Mr Schreiber, whose face had been expressing considerable doubts as to the wisdom of such a course, brightened visibly as at least one solution to what had become a problem dawned, and said to Henry, 'Come here, sonny.' The boy arose, went over and stood in front of the seat of Mr Schreiber and looked him straight and unabashedly in the eye.

'How old are you, sonny?'

'Eight, sir.'

'Sir! That's a good beginning. Where did you learn that?'

'Auntie Ada taught me.'

'So you can learn? That's good. Are you glad Mrs Harris brought you away from London?'

With his large eyes bent upon Mrs Schreiber little Henry breathed a heartfelt sigh and replied, 'Not arf.'

'Would you like to live in America?'

Little Henry had the right answer here too. 'Cor,' he said, ''oo wouldn't?'

'Do you think you could learn to play baseball?'

Apparently little Henry had been experimenting in Washington. 'Ho,' he scoffed, 'anybody who can play cricket can 'it a baseball. I knocked one for six - only you call it a 'ome run 'ere.'

'Say,' said Mr Schreiber, now genuinely interested, 'that's good. Maybe we can make a ball player out of him.'

It had taken slightly longer, but there was that wonderful pronoun 'we' again. Mr Schreiber had become a member of the firm. He said to the boy, 'What about your father? I guess you're pretty anxious to find him, eh?'

To this little Henry did not reply, but stood there silently regarding Mr Schreiber out of eyes that only shortly before then had reflected little else than misery and unhappiness. Since he had never known a real father he could not genuinely form a concept of what one would be like, except that if it was anything like Mr Gusset he would rather not. Still, everybody was making such a fuss and trying so hard to find this parent that he felt he had best not be impolite on the subject, so instead of answering the question he said finally, 'You're OK, guv'ner, I like you.'

Mr Schreiber's round face flushed with pleasure and he patted the boy on the shoulder. 'Well, well,' he said, 'we'll have to see what we can do. In the meantime you can stay here with Mrs Harris and Mrs Butterfield.' He turned to Mrs Harris, 'Just how far have you got locating the boy's father?'

Mrs Harris told him how, foolishly, Mr Brown of Kenosha, Wisconsin, had been the only egg in her basket, and now that it had been broken she was at a loss as to how to continue. She showed him her official letter from the Air Force demanding to know which George Brown she referred to of the 453 who at one time or another had been in the Service, and asking to know his birthplace, birthday, serial number, date of enlistment, date of discharge, places of service abroad, at home, etc.

Mr Schreiber looked at the formidable document and scoffed, 'Huh, those guys couldn't find anyone if he was right under their noses. Just you leave it to me. I got a real organisation. We got distribution branches in every big city in the U.S.A. If we can't turn him up for you, nobody can. What did you say his name was? And have you got any other dope on him - where he was stationed, maybe, or how old he was at the time of his marriage, or any other thing that would help us?'

Mrs Harris shamefacedly had to admit that she could offer no more than that his name was George Brown, he had been an American airman stationed at an American air base in England sometime in 1951, and that he had married a waitress by the name of Pansy Cott, who had borne him little Henry, refused to accompany him to America, was divorced by Mr Brown, had remarried and vanished. As she revealed the paucity of these details, Mrs Harris became even more aware and further ashamed of the manner in which she had let her enthusiasm carry her away and handled the affair. 'Lumme,' she said, 'I've played the fool, 'aven't I? Wicked, that's what I've been. If I was you I'd send us all packing and 'ave done with it.'

Mrs Schreiber protested, 'I think what you've done is absolutely wonderful, Mrs Harris. Don't, you think so, Joel? Nobody else could have.'

Mr Schreiber made a small movement of his head and shoulders which indicated a doubtful but not antagonistic 'Well,' and then said, 'Sure ain't much to go on is there? But if anyone can find this feller, our organisation can.' To little Henry he said, 'OK, sonny. Tomorrow is Sunday. We'll get a baseball bat, ball, and glove and go in Central Park and see if you can hit a home run off me. I used to be a pretty good pitcher when I was a kid.'

IT was shortly before one of Mrs Schreiber's social-business dinners that Kentucky Claiborne definitely set the cap on to the loathing that Mrs Harris had come to entertain for him and made it an undying and implacable affair.

He had arrived, as usual, unkempt and unwashed in his blue jeans, cowboy boots, and too-fragrant leather jacket, but this time he had turned up an hour before the scheduled time, and for two reasons: one was that he liked to tank up early before the drinks were slowed down to being passed one at a time, and the other was that he wished to tune up his guitar at the Schreiber piano, for Mr Schreiber was entertaining some important distributors and heads of television networks and had persuaded Kentucky to sing after supper.

Kentucky was a 'Bourbon and Branch' man, and very little of the latter. After four tumblersful of 'Old Grand-pappy' that were more than half neat, he tuned up his instrument, twanging a half a dozen chords, and launched into a ballad of love and death among the feudin' Hatfields and McCoys. Halfway through he looked up to find himself being stared at by a small boy with a slightly too-large head and large, interested and intelligent eyes.

Kentucky paused in the midst of the blow-down of a whole passel of Hatfields at the hands of McCoys and their rifles and said, 'Beat it, bub.'

Little Henry, surprised rather than hurt, said, 'What for? Why can't I stay 'ere and listen?'

'Because I said beat it, bub, that's why.' And then, as his ear suddenly reminded him of something, said, 'Say, ain't that Limey talk? Are you a Limey?'

Little Henry knew well enough what a Limey was, and was proud of it. He looked Kentucky Claiborne in the eye and said, 'You're bloody well right I am - and what's it to you?'

'What's it to me?' said Kentucky Claiborne with what little Henry should have recognised as a dangerous amiability. 'Why, it's just that if there's anything I hate worse than nigger talk, it's Limey talk. And if there's anything I hate more than niggers, it's Limeys. I told you to beat it, bub,' and he thereupon leaned over and slapped little Henry on the side of the head hard, sending him spinning. Almost by reflex little Henry released his old-time Gusset wail, and instinctively, to drown out the sound, Kentucky launched into the next stanza in which avenging Hatfields now slaughtered McCoys.

And in the pantry where Mrs Harris was helping to lay out *canapés*, the little char could hardly believe her ears, and for a moment she thought that she was back in her own flat at number five Willis Gardens, Battersea, listening to the wireless and having tea with Mrs Butterfield, for penetrating to her ears had been the caterwauling of Kentucky Claiborne, then a thump and the sound of a blow, the wailing of a hurt child, followed by music up *forte crescendo.* Then she realised where she actually was, and what must have happened, though she could not believe it, and went charging out of the pantry and into the music room to find a weeping Henry with one side of his face scarlet from the blow, and a laughing Kentucky Claiborne twanging his guitar.

He stopped when he saw Mrs Harris and said, 'Ah tol' the little bastard to beat it, but he's got wax in his ears, so Ah had to clout him one. Git him out of here - Ah'm practisin'.'

'Bloody everything!' raged Mrs Harris. And then picturesquely added thereto, 'You filthy brute to strike an 'armless child. You touch 'im again and I'll scratch yer eyes out.'

Kentucky smiled his quiet, dangerous smile, and took hold of his instrument by the neck with both hands. 'Goddam,' he said, 'if this house just ain't filled with Limeys. Ah just tol' this kid if there's anything Ah hates worse'n a nigger it's a Limey. Git outta here before I bust this geetar over yoh' haid.'

Mrs Harris was no coward, but neither was she a fool. In her varied life in London she had come up against plenty of drunks, ruffians, and bad actors, and knew a dangerous man when she saw one. Therefore, she used her common sense, collected little Henry to her and went out.

Once in the safety of the servants' quarters she soothed him, bathed his face in cold water, and said, 'There, there, dearie, never you mind that brute. Ada 'Arris never forgets. It may take a week, it may take a month, it may take a year - but we'll pay 'im orf for that. 'Ittin' a defenceless child for being English!'

Had Mrs Harris kept a ledger on her vendettas it would have been noted that there were none that had not been liquidated long before the time she had allotted. Kentucky Claiborne had got himself into her black book, for, in Mrs Harris's opinion, the crime was unpardonable, and he was going to pay for it - somehow, sometime. His goose was as good as cooked.

UP to this time, due to business in hand, worry over little Henry and the Marquis, and the exigencies of her duties, namely to help Mrs Schreiber put her house in order and get it running properly, Mrs Harris's vista of New York after those two breathtaking approaches was limited to the broad valley of Park Avenue with its towering apartment houses on either side and the endless two-way stream of traffic obeying the stop and go of the red and green lights day and night. That, with the shops a block east on Lexington Avenue, and one trip to Radio City Music Hall with Mrs Butterfield, had been the extent of her contact with Manhattan.

Because she was busy and preoccupied, and everything was so changed and different from what she had been accustomed to, she had not yet had time to be overwhelmed by it. But now all this was to be altered. It was the George Browns who were to introduce Mrs Harris to that incredible Babylon and Metropolis known as Greater New York.

It came about through the fact that there was now an interim period of comparative peace, with little Henry integrated into the servants' quarters of the penthouse while the far-flung network of the branch offices of North American delved into the past of the George Browns of their community in an effort to locate the missing father.

Although he slept in the room with Mrs Harris and took his meals with her and Mrs Butterfield, little Henry was actually a good deal more at large in the Schreibers' apartment. He was allowed to browse in the library, and began to read omnivorously. Mrs Schreiber every so often would take him shopping with her or to an afternoon movie, while it became an invariable Sunday morning ritual that he and Mr Schreiber would repair to the Sheep Meadow in Central Park with ball, bat, and glove, where little Henry, who had an eye like an eagle and a superb sense of timing, would lash sucker pitches to all corners of the lot for Mr Schreiber to chase. This was excellent for Mr Schreiber's health, and very good for his disposition as well. Afterwards they might feed the monkeys in the Zoo or roam through the Rambles, or engage a rowboat on the lake and paddle about. Man and boy quickly formed an engaging friendship.

Thus relieved of most of the actual care of the boy, and with more time on her hands since she acted now more in an advisory capacity to the staff she had helped Mrs Schreiber carefully to select, Mrs Harris came to the sudden realisation that she was no longer pulling her weight in the search for the father of little Henry.

It was all very well for Mr Schreiber to say that if the man could be found his organisation would do the job, but after all the main reason for coming to America was to conduct this search herself, a search she had once somewhat pridefully stated she would bring to a successful conclusion.

She remembered the massive conviction she had felt that if only she could get to America she would solve little Henry's problems. Well, here she was in America, living off the fat of the land, and slacking while somebody else looked to the job that she herself had been so confident of doing. The least she could do was to investigate the Browns of New York.

'Go to work, Ada 'Arris,' she said to herself, and thereafter on her afternoons and evenings off, and in every moment of her spare time she initiated a systematic run-through of the Geo. and G. Browns listed in the telephone directories of Manhattan, Bronx, Brooklyn, Queens, and Richmond.

Although she might have done so and saved herself a lot of time and energy, Mrs Harris refused to descend to anything so crude as ringing up the scattered Browns on the telephone and asking them if they had ever served in the U.S. Air Force in Great Britain and married a waitress by the name of Pansy Cott. Instead, she paid them personal visits, sometimes managing to check off two and three in a day.

Familiar with the London tubes, the New York subway systems held no terrors for her, but the buses were something else again, and used to London civility, she soon found herself embroiled with one of the occupational neurotics at the helm of one of the north-bound monsters who, trying to make change, operate his money-gobbling gadget, open and close doors, shout out street numbers, and guide his vehicle through the tightly-packed lanes of Yellow Cabs, limousines, and two-toned cars, bawled at her to get to the rear of the bus or get the hell off, he didn't care which.

'Is that 'ow it is?' Mrs Harris snapped at him. 'You know what would happen to you if you spoke to me like that in

London? You'd find yerself on your bum sitting in the middle of the King's Road, that's what you would.'

The bus driver heard a not unfamiliar accent and turned around to look at Mrs Harris. 'Listen, lady,' he said, 'I been over there with the Seebees. All them guys over there gotta do is drive the bus.'

Injustice worked upon people of her own kind always touched Mrs Harris's sympathy. She patted the driver on the shoulder and said, 'Lor' love yer, it ain't no way to speak to a lydy, but it ain't human either for you to be doing all that - I'd blow up meself if I had to. We wouldn't stand for that in London either - trying to make a bloomin' machine out of a human being.'

The driver stopped his bus, turned around and regarded Mrs Harris with amazement. 'Say,' he said, 'you really think that? I'm sorry I spoke out of turn, but sometimes I just gotta blow my top. Come along, I'll see that you get a seat.' He left the wheel, quite oblivious to the fact that he was tying up traffic for twenty blocks behind him, took Mrs Harris by the hand, edged her through the crowded bus and said, 'OK one of you mugs, get up and give this little lady a seat. She's from London. Whaddayou want her to do - get a lousy impression of New York?'

There were three volunteers. Mrs Harris sat down and made herself comfortable. 'Thanks, ducks,' she grinned as the driver said, 'OK Ma?' and went forward to his wheel again. He felt warm inside, like a Boy Scout who had done his good deed for the day. This feeling lasted all of ten blocks.

In a short time Mrs Harris both saw and learned more about New York and New Yorkers and the environs of its five boroughs than most New Yorkers who had spent a lifetime in that city.

There was a George Brown who lived near Fort George in Upper Manhattan not far from the Hudson, and for the first time Mrs Harris came upon the magnificent view of that stately river, with the sheer walls of the Jersey Palisades rising opposite, and through another who dwelt near Spuyten Duyvel she learned something of this astonishing, meandering creek which joined the Hudson and East Rivers and actually and physically made an island of Manhattan.

A visit to another Brown at the exactly opposite end of Manhattan, Bowling Green, introduced her to the Battery, that incredible plaza overwhelmed by the skyscrapers of the financial district, at the end of which the two mighty arms of water - East and North Rivers as the Hudson is there called - merged into the expanse of the Upper Bay with such sea-going traffic of ocean liners, freighters, tugs, ferry boats, yachts, and whatnot afloat as Mrs Harris could not have imagined occupied one body of water. Not even through Limehouse Reach and the Wapping Docks back home was water traffic so thick.

For the first time in her life Mrs Harris felt dwarfed and overpowered. London was a great, grey, sprawling city, larger even than this one, but it did not make one feel so small, so insignificant, and so lost. One could get one's head up, somehow. Far up in the sky, so high that only an aeroplane could look down upon them, the matchless skyscrapers, each with a flag or a plume of steam or smoke at its peak, filled the eye and the mind to the point of utter bewilderment. What kind of a world was this? Who were these people who had reared these towers? Through the canyons rushed and rumbled the traffic of heavy drays, trucks, and gigantic double lorries with trailers, taxicabs beeped their horns, policemen's whistles shrilled, the shipping moaned and hooted - and, in the midst of this stood little Ada Harris of Battersea, alone, not quite undaunted.

In the district surrounding 135th Street and Lenox Avenue, known as Harlem, all the Browns were chocolate coloured, but nonetheless sympathetic to Mrs Harris's quest. Several of them had been to England with the Army or Air Force and welcomed Mrs Harris as a reminder of a time and place when all men were considered equal under Nazi bombs, and colour was no bar to bravery. One of them, out of sheer nostalgia, insisted upon her having a pink gin with him. None of them had married Pansy Cott.

Via several George Browns who lived in the Brighton district Mrs Harris became acquainted with the eastern boundary of the United States, or rather, at that point, New York - the shore with its long, curving, green combers rolling in to crash upon the beaches of that vast and raucous amusement park - Coney Island.

There the Brown she was tailing that day turned out to be a barker at a girlie sideshow. A tall fellow in a loud silk shirt and straw boater, with piercing eyes that held one transfixed, he stood on a platform outside a booth on which there were rather repulsive oleos of ladies with very little clothing on, and shouted down a précis of the attractions within to the passing throngs.

Mrs Harris's heart sank at the thought that such a one might be the father of little Henry. Yet in the vulgarity of the amusement park she felt not wholly out of place, for with the cries of the barkers, the snapping of rifles in the shooting gallery, the rushing roar of the thrill rides, and the tinny cacophony of the carousel music it reminded her of Battersea Festival Gardens, or any British funfair, doubled.

Between spiels George Brown, barker, listened to her story with attention and evident sympathy, for when she had finished he said, 'It ain't me, but I'd like to find the bastard and punch him one on the nose. If you ask me, he married the girl and took a powder. I know a lot of guys like that.'

Mrs Harris defended little Henry's father vigorously, but the barker remained sceptical. He said, 'Take my advice, ma'am, and don't trust none of them GIs. I know them.' Mr Brown had never been in England, but his grandmother had been English and this formed a bond between Mrs Harris and himself. He said, 'Would you like to come back and meet the girls? They're as nice a bunch of kids as you could want. I'll pass you into the show first.'

Mrs Harris spent a pleasant half hour watching Mr Brown's assortment of 'kids' doing bumps, grinds, hulas, and cooch dances, after which she was introduced to them and found, as Brown had said, that they were as described, good-natured, modest about their art, and far cleaner in speech than many of the celebrities who came to the Schreiber parties. She went home after an interesting evening, but no nearer finding the man she sought, though the barker promised to keep an eye out for him.

She learned to like many parts of Brooklyn, where her search took her, for the older and quieter portions of this borough on the other side of the East River, where the brownstone houses stuck against the side of one another, as like peas in a pod for block upon block, sometimes shaded by trees, reminded her somewhat of London far away across the sea.

Since she took the Browns as they came, one George she found was a ships' chandler who lived over his shop on the waterfront of the Lower East Side. Here again she was an infinitesimal speck in the grand canyons of the downtown skyscrapers, but standing on the cobbled pave by the docks that smelled of tar and spices, she looked up to the great arches and wondrous spiderweb tracery of the Brooklyn and Williamsburg Bridges, across which rumbled electric trains and heavy traffic with such a shattering roar that it seemed to be the voices of those vast spans themselves shouting down to her.

On a visit to the Staten Island George Browns via the Staten Island Ferry, Mrs Harris found one of them to be a tug-boat captain working for the Joseph P. O'Ryan Towing Company, in command of the twin diesel-engined tug *Siobhan O'Ryan*, who was just leaving to go on duty as Mrs Harris arrived.

Captain Brown was a pleasant, brawny man of some forty-odd years, with a pleasant wife half his size, who lived in a cheerful flat in St George not far from the ferry landing. They had once had something in common, for the *Siobhan O'Ryan* had been one of the tugs which had nursed the s.s. *Ville de Paris* into her berth the day of Mrs Harris's arrival, and the sharp-eyed little char had noted the unusual name painted on the pilot house of the tug, and had remembered it.

Those Browns too were fascinated by the saga of the deserted boy and Mrs Harris's quest for his father. The upshot was that Captain Brown invited Mrs Harris to come aboard his tug and he would take her for a waterborne ride around Manhattan Island. This she accepted with alacrity, and thereafter was sailed beneath the spans of the great East River bridges, past the glass-walled buildings of the United Nations to look with awe upon the triple span of the Triborongh Bridge, thence over into the Hudson River and down the Jersey side, passing beneath the George Washington Bridge and afforded the view unsurpassed of the cluster of mid-town skyscrapers - a mass of masonry so colossal it struck even Mrs Harris dumb, except for a whisper, 'Lor' lumme, yer carn't believe it even when you see it!'

This turned out to be one of the red letter days of her stay in America, but of course it was not the right Mr Brown either.

There was a George Brown in Washington Square who painted, another in the garment district of Seventh Avenue who specialised in 'Ladies Stylish Stouts', yet another in Yorkville who operated a delicatessen and urged Mrs Harris to try his pickles - free - and one who owned a house in the refined precincts of Gracie Square, an old gentleman who reminded her somewhat of the Marquis, and who, when he had heard her story, invited her in to tea. He was an American gentleman of the old school who had lived in London for many years in his youth, and wished Mrs Harris to tell him what changes had taken place there.

She found Browns who had been airmen in the war, and soldiers, and sailors, and marines, and many of course who had been too young or too old to fill the bill.

Not all were kind and patient with her. Some gave her a brusque New Yorkese brush-off, saying, 'Whaddaya trying to hand me about being married to some waitress in England? Get lost, willya? I got a wife and t'ree kids. Get outta here before you get me in trouble.'

Not all who had been to London were enamoured of that city, and learning that Mrs Harris came from there said that if they never saw that dump again it would be too soon.

She interviewed Browns who were plumbers, carpenters, electricians, taxi drivers, lawyers, actors, radio repairmen, laundrymen, stock-brokers, rich men, middle-class men, labouring men, for she had added the City Directory to her telephone list. She rang the door bells in every type and kind of home in every metropolitan neighbourhood, introducing herself with, 'I hope I ain't disturbin' you. My name's 'Arris - Ada 'Arris - I'm from London. I was looking for a Mr George Brown who was in the American Air Force over there and married an old friend of mine, a girl by the name of Pansy Cott. You wouldn't be 'im, would you?'

They never were the one she sought, but in most cases she had to tell the story of the desertion of little Henry, which almost invariably fell upon interested and sympathetic ears, due as much to her personality as anything else, so that when she departed she had the feeling of leaving another friend behind her, and people who begged to be kept in touch.

Few native New Yorkers ever penetrated so deeply into their city as did Mrs Harris, who ranged from the homes of the wealthy on the broad avenues neighbouring Central Park, where there was light and air and the indefinable smell of the rich, to the crooked down-town streets and the slums of the Bowery and Lower East Side.

She discovered those little city states within the city, sections devoted to one nationality - in Yorkville, Little Hungary, the Spanish section, and Little Italy down by Mulberry Street. There was even a George Brown who was a Chinaman and lived on Pell Street in the heart of New York's Chinatown.

Thus in a month of tireless searching the George Browns of the metropolitan district provided her with a cross-section of the American people, and one which confirmed the impression she had of them from the soldiers they had sent over to England during the war. By and large they were kind, friendly, warm-hearted, generous, and hospitable. They were all so eager to be helpful, and many a George Brown promised to alert all the known others of his clan in other cities in aid of Mrs Harris's search. So many of them had an appealing, childlike quality of wanting to be loved. She discovered about them a curious paradox: on their streets they were filled with such hurry and bustle that they had no time for anyone, not even to stop for a stranger inquiring the way - they simply hurried on unseeing, unhearing. Any who did stop turned out to be strangers themselves. But in their homes they were kind, charitable, neighbourly, and bountiful, and particularly generous hosts when they learned that Mrs Harris was a foreigner and British, and it was warming to her to discover that the Americans had never forgotten their admiration for the conduct of the English people during the bombing of London.

But there was yet something further that this involuntary exploration of New York did for Mrs Harris. Once she lost her awe of the great heights of the buildings to which she was frequently whisked sickeningly by express elevators that leapt thirty floors before the first stop, as well as the dark, roaring canyons they created of the streets, something of the extraordinary power and grandeur, and in particular the youth of this great city, and the myriad opportunities it granted its citizens to flourish and grow wealthy, impressed itself upon her.

This and her glimpses of other cities made her glad that she had brought little Henry to his country. In him, in his independence of spirit, his cleverness, resourcefulness, and determination, she saw the qualities of youth-not-to-be-denied visible on all sides about her in the great metropolis. For herself it was indeed all too much as scene piled upon scene - Mid-town, East Side, West Side, New Jersey, Long Island, Westchester - and experience upon experience with these friendly, overwhelming Americans, but it was not a life to which she could ever adapt herself. Little Henry, however, would grow into it, and perhaps even make his contribution to it, if he might only be given his chance.

And this, of course, was the continuing worry, for none of this brought her any closer to the conclusion of her search. None of the George Browns was the right one, or could even so much as give her a clue as to where or how he might be found.

And then one day it happened, but it was not she who succeeded - it was none other than Mr Schreiber. He came home one evening and summoned her to his study. His wife was already there, and they were both looking most queer and uneasy. Mr Schreiber cleared his throat several times ostentatiously, and then said, 'Sit down will you, Mrs Harris.' He cleared his throat again even more portentously. 'Well,' he said, 'I think we've got your man.'

A T this abrupt, and though not wholly unexpected, but still startling piece of news, Mrs Harris leapt from the edge of the seat she had taken as though propelled by the point of a tack, and cried, 'Blimey - 'ave you? 'Oo is he? Where is he?'

But Mr and Mrs Schreiber did not react to her excitement and enthusiasm. Nor did they smile. Mr Schreiber said, 'You'd better sit down again, Mrs Harris, it's a kind of a funny story. You'll want to take a grip on yourself.'

Something of the mood of her employers now communicated itself to the little charwoman. She peered at them anxiously. She asked, 'What's wrong? Is it something awful? Is 'e in jyle?'

Mr Schreiber played with a paper-cutter and looked down at some papers on his desk before him, and as Mrs Harris followed his gaze she saw that it was U.S. Air Force stationery similar to the kind she had received, plus a photostatic copy of something. Mr Schreiber then said gently, 'I think I'd better tell you, it's - ah - I'm afraid, someone we know. It's Kentucky Claiborne.'

Mrs Harris did not receive the immediate impact of this statement. She merely repeated, 'Kentucky Claiborne little 'Enry's dad?' And then as the implications of the communication hit her with the force of an Atlas missile she let out a howl, 'Ow! What's that you say? 'IM little 'Enry's dad? It can't be true!'

Mr Schreiber eyed her gravely and said, 'I'm sorry. I don't like it any better than you do. He's nothing but an ape. He'll ruin that swell kid.'

Waves of horror coursed through Mrs Harris as she too contemplated the prospect of this child who was just beginning to rise out of the mire falling into the hands of such a one. 'But are you sure?' she asked.

Mr Schreiber tapped the papers in front of him and said, 'It's all there in his Air Force record - Pansy Cott, little Henry, and everyone.'

'But 'ow did you know? 'Oo found out?' cried Mrs Harris, hoping that somewhere, somehow yet a mistake would have occurred which would nullify this dreadful news.

'I did,' said Mr Schreiber. 'I should have been a detective, I always said so - like Sherlock Holmes. I got a kind of a nose for funny business. It was while he was signing his contract.'

Mrs Schreiber said, 'It was really brilliant of Joel.' Then her feelings too got the better of her, and she cried, 'Oh poor dear Mrs Harris, and that poor, sweet child - I'm so sorry.'

'But I don't understand,' said Mrs Harris. 'What's it got to do with 'is contract?'

'When he signed it,' said Mr Schreiber, 'he used his real name, George Brown. Kentucky Claiborne is just his stage name.'

But there was a good deal more to it as Mr Schreiber told the story, and it appeared that he really had displayed acumen and intelligence which would have done credit to a trained investigator. It seemed that when all the final details were settled and Kentucky Claiborne, Mr Hyman, his agent, Mr Schreiber, and the battalions of lawyers for each side gathered together for the signing of the momentous contract and Mr Schreiber cast his experienced eye over it, he came upon the name 'George Brown', typed at the bottom and asked, 'Who's this George Brown feller?'

Mr Hyman spoke up and said, 'That's Kentucky's real name - the lawyers all say he should sign with his real name in case some trouble comes up later.'

Mr Schreiber said that he felt a queer feeling in his stomach - not that for a moment he suspected that Claiborne could possibly be the missing parent. The qualm, he said, was caused by the contemplation of how awful it would be if by some million-to-one chance it might be the case. They went on with the signing then, and when George Brown alias Kentucky Claiborne thrust his arm out of the sleeve of his greasy black leather jacket to wield the pen that would bring him in ten million dollars, Mr Schreiber noticed a number, AF28636794, tattooed on his wrist.

Mr Schreiber had asked, 'What's that there number you've got on your wrist, Kentucky?'

The hillbilly singer, smiling somewhat sheepishly, had replied, 'That's mah serial number when I was in the goddam Air Force. Ah could never remember it nohow, so Ah had it tattooed.'

With a quick wit and sangfroid that would have done credit to Bulldog Drummond, the Saint, James Bond, or any of the fictional international espionage agents, Mr Schreiber had committed the serial number to memory, written it down as soon as the ceremony was over and he was alone, and had his secretary send it on to Air Force Headquarters in the Pentagon Building in Washington. Three days later it was all over: back had come the photostat of the dossier from the Air Force records, and Mr Kentucky Claiborne was unquestionably the George Brown who had married Miss Pansy Amelia Cott at Tunbridge Wells on the 14th of April, 1950, and to whom on the 2nd of September a son was born, christened Henry Semple Brown. To make matters completely binding, a copy of the fingerprints was attached and a photograph of an irritable-looking GI who was incontrovertibly Mr Kentucky Claiborne ten years younger and minus his sideburns and guitar.

Mrs Harris inspected the evidence while her mind slowly opened to the nature and depth of the catastrophe that had suddenly overwhelmed them. The only worse thing that could befall little Henry than to be brought up in the poverty-stricken, loveless home of the Gussets was to be reared by this ignorant, selfish, self-centred boor who despised everything foreign, who had hated little Henry on sight, who hated everything and everyone but himself, who cared for nothing but his own career and appetites, and who now would have a vast sum of money to splash about and cater for them.

Mrs Harris in her romantic fancy had envisioned the unknown, faceless father of little Henry as a man of wealth who would be able to give the child every comfort and advantage; she was shrewd enough to realise that unlimited wealth in the hands of such a person as Claiborne would be deadlier than poison, not only to himself but to the boy. And it was smack into the fire of such a situation and into the hands of such a man that Mrs Harris was plunging little Henry after snatching him from the frying pan of the horrible Gussets. If only she had not given way to the absurd fancy of taking little Henry to America. With the ocean between, he might still have been saved.

Mrs Harris left off inspecting the document, went and sat down again because her legs felt so weak. She said, 'Oh dear - oh dear!' And then, 'Oh Lor', what are we going to do?' Then she asked hoarsely, ''Ave you told 'im yet?'

Mr Schreiber shook his head and said, 'No, I have not. I thought maybe you'd want to think about it a little. It is you brought the child over here. It's really not up to us. It is you must decide whether you will tell him.'

At least it was a breathing spell. Mrs Harris said, 'Thank you, sir. I'll have to fink,' got up off her chair and left the room.

When she entered the kitchen Mrs Butterfield looked up and gave a little scream. 'Lor' love us, Ada,' she yelped, 'you're whiter than yer own apron. Something awful 'appened?'

'That's right,' said Mrs Harris.

'They've found little 'Enry's father?'

'Yes,' said Mrs Harris.

'And 'e's dead?'

'No,' wailed Mrs Harris, and then followed it with a string of very naughty words. 'That's just it - 'e ain't. 'E's alive. It's that (further string of naughty words) Kentucky Claiborne.'

Into such depths of despair was Mrs Harris plunged by what seemed to be the utter irretrievability of the situation, the burdens that she had managed to inflict upon those who were kindest to her, and the mess she seemed to have made of things, and in particular the life of little Henry, that she did something she had not done for a long time - she resorted to the talisman of her most cherished possession, her Dior dress. She removed it from the cupboard, laid it out upon the bed and stood looking down upon it, pulling at her lip and waiting to absorb the message it had to give her.

Once it had seemed unattainable and the most desirable and longed-for thing on earth. It had been attained, for there it was beneath her eyes, almost as crisp and fresh and frothy as when it had been packed into her suitcase in Paris.

Once, too, the garment had involved her in a dilemma which had seemed insoluble, and yet in the end had been solved, for there it was in her possession.

And there, too, was the ugly and defiling scar of the burned out velvet panel and beading which she had never had repaired, as a reminder of that which she knew but often forgot, namely that the world and all of which it was composed - nature, the elements, humans - were inimical to perfection, and nothing really ever wholly came off. There appeared to be a limitless number of flies to get into peoples' ointment.

The message of the dress could have been read: want something hard enough and work for it, and you'll get it, but when you get it it will either prove to be not wholly what you wanted, or something will happen to spoil it.

But even as her eyes rested upon the garment which she had once struggled so valiantly to acquire, she knew in her heart that these were other values, and that they simply did not apply to the trouble in which she now found herself. In the dilemma which had arisen at the last moment and which had threatened collapse to the whole adventure of the Dior dress, she had been helped by someone else. In this dilemma which faced her now, whether to turn a child she had grown to love over to a man who was obviously unfit to be his father, or send him back to the horrors of his foster-parents, Mrs Harris knew that no one could help her - not die Schreibers, certainly not Mrs Butterfield, or even Mr Bayswater, or her friend the Marquis. She would have to make the decision herself, it would have to be made quickly, and whichever, she knew she would probably never have another moment's quiet peace in her own mind. That's what came of mixing into other people's lives.

For a moment as she looked down upon the mute and inanimate garment it appeared to her almost shoddy in the light of the work and energy it had cost her to acquire it. It was only she who had felt pain when the nasty little London actress to whom she had lent the gown in a fit of generosity one night, had returned it to her, its beauty destroyed by her own negligence and carelessness. The dress had felt nothing. But whichever she did with little Henry Brown, whether she revealed him to this monstrously boorish and selfish man as his son, or surrendered him to the hateful Gussets, little Henry would be feeling it for the rest of his life - and so would Ada Harris. There were many situations that a canny, bred-in-London char could by native wit and experience be expected to cope with, but this was not one of them. She did not know what to do, and her talisman provided no clue for her.

The dress broadcast superficial aphorisms: 'Never say die; don't give up the ship; if at first you don't succeed, try, try again; it's a long lane that has no turning; it is always darkest before dawn; the Lord helps those who help themselves.' None of them brought any real measure of solace, none of them solved the problem of a life that was still to be lived - that of little Henry.

She even saw clearly now that she had over-emphasised - others would have called it over-romanticised - the boy's position in the Gusset household. Had he actually been too unhappy? Many a boy had survived kicks and cuffs to become a great man, or at least a good man. Henry had had the toughness and the sweetness of nature to survive. Soon he would have grown too big for Mr Gusset to larrup any further, he would have had schooling, vocational perhaps, got a job, and lived happily enough in the environment into which he had been born, as had she and millions of others of her class and situation.

She became overwhelmed suddenly with a sense of her own futility and inadequacy and the enormity of what she had done, and sitting down upon the bed she put her hands before her face and wept. She cried not out of frustration or self-pity, but out of love and other-pity. She cried for a small boy who it seemed, whatever she did, was not to have his chance in the world. The tears seeped through her fingers and fell on to the Dior dress.

THEREAFTER, when she had recovered somewhat, she rejoined Mrs Butterfield and far, far into that night and long after little Henry had gone to sleep blissfully unconscious of the storm clouds gathering over his head, they debated his fate.

All through the twistings and turning of arguments, hopes, fears, alternating hare-brained plans, and down-to-earth common sense, Mrs Butterfield stuck to one theme which she boomed with a gloomy reiteration, like an African drum: 'But dearie, 'e's 'is father, after all,' until Mrs Harris, almost at her wits' end from the emotional strain brought on by the revelation cried, 'If you say that once more, Vi, I'll blow me top!' Mrs Butterfield subsided, but Mrs Harris could see her small mouth silently forming the sentence, 'But 'e is, you know.'

Mrs Harris had been involved in many crises in her life, but never one that had so many facets which tugged her in so many different directions, and which imposed such a strain upon the kind of person she was and all her various natures.

Taken as only a minor example of the kind of things that kept cropping up, she had sworn to get even with Kentucky Claiborne for striking little Henry; but now that Mr Claiborne - or rather, Mr Brown - was little Henry's father, he could hit him as much as he liked.

From the beginning Mrs Harris had set herself stonily against doing what she knew she ought to do, which was to turn little Henry over to his blood and legal father and wash her hands of the affair. The Schreibers had given her the way out. By not telling Claiborne and leaving the matter to her they had indicated their sympathy and that they would not talk - only they, she, and Mrs Butterfield would ever know the truth.

But what then would become of the boy? Bring him back to the Gussets? But how? Mrs Harris had lived too long in a world of identity cards, ration cards, passports, permits, licences, a world that in effect said you did not exist unless you had a piece of paper that said you did. Little Henry existed officially in a photostat of the American Air Force records, a London birth certificate, and nowhere else. He had been illegally removed from Britain, and had even more illegally entered the United States. She felt it in her bones that if they tried to get him back the same way they had brought him over they would get caught. She would not have cared for herself, but she could not do it to her already sorely tried friend Violet Butterfield.

Keep little Henry to themselves secretly? Even should they with Mr Schreiber's help succeed in getting him back to England - not very likely - the unspeakable Gussets were but one wall removed from them. True, they had not kicked up a fuss over the kidnapping. Obviously there had not been a peep out of them, or Mrs Harris would have heard via the police. But with little Henry back they would most certainly claim him, for he had his uses as a drudge.

She saw likewise how fatally wrong her fantasy had been about little Henry's parents. It was not Pansy Cott who was to blame, but George Brown - mean, ignorant, vengeful, and intrinsically bad. Pansy had simply used her nut and done the child a good turn when she refused to accompany her husband to America. Unquestionably Brown had just not sent her any money for the support of the child.

Yet a decision would have to be made and she, Ada Harris, must accept the responsibility of making it.

Most deeply painful and overriding every other consideration was the love - feminine, human, all-embracing - that she felt for the boy, and her deep-seated wish to see him happy. She had let her life become inextricably entangled with that of the child, and now there was no escaping from it. Like all people who play with fire, she knew that she was in the process of getting herself badly burned.

And through all her arguments, deliberations, and meditations, Mrs Butterfield boomed her theme: 'But love, after all, 'e is the father. You said how 'appy 'e'd be to 'ave 'is little son back, and 'ow 'e'd soon enough take 'im away from the Gussets. 'E's entitled to 'ave 'im, ain't 'e?'

This was the bald, staring, naked, unavoidable truth whichever way one twisted, squirmed or turned, and the documents in Mr Schreiber's hands put the seal on to it. George Brown and Henry Brown were united by the ties of blood. So now at four o'clock in the morning Mrs Harris gave in. She breathed a great sigh and said with a kind of humility that touched the other woman more than anything in their long friendship, 'I guess you're right, Vi. You've been more right through all of this all along than

I have. 'E's got to go to 'is father. We'll tell Mr Schreiber in the morning'.

And now Mrs Harris's battered, tired, and sorely tried mind played her a dirty trick, as so often minds will that have been driven to the limit of endurance. It held out a chimera to her, a wholly acceptable solace to one who was badly in need of it. Now that the decision was made, how did they not know that under the softening influence of a little child, George Brown-Kentucky Claiborne would not become another person? Immediately and before she was aware of it, Mrs Harris was back again in that fantasy land from which practically all her troubles had sprung.

Everything suddenly resolved itself: Claiborne-Brown had cuffed little Henry when he had thought him an interfering little beggar, but his own son he would take to his bosom. True, he had bellowed his scorn of Limeys - the boy was only half a Limey, the other at least fifty per cent of one hundred per cent American Brown.

All the old day-dreams returned - the grateful father overjoyed at being reunited with his long-lost son, and little Henry brought to a better life than he had ever known before, and certainly this would be true from a financial standpoint; he would never again be hungry, or ragged, or cold; he would be for ever out of the clutches of the unspeakable Gussets; he would be educated in this wonderful and glorious country, and would have his chance in life.

As for George Brown, he needed the softening influence of little Henry as much as the boy needed a father. He would succumb to the charm of the boy, give up his drinking, reform his ways in order to set his son a good example, and thus become twice the idol of American youth he already was.

The conviction grew upon Mrs Harris that she had fulfilled the role of fairy godmother after all. She had done what she had set out to do. She had said, 'If I could only get to America I would find little Henry's father.' Well, she *had* got to America, she *had* found the child's father - or at least had been instrumental in his finding - the father *was* a millionaire as she had always known he would be. 'Then dry your tears, Ada Harris, and still your worries, and write at the bottom of the page, "Mission accomplished", smile, and go to bed.'

It was thus the treacherous mind lulled her and let her go to sleep without ever so much as dreaming what awaited her on the morrow.

George-Kentucky-Claiborne-Brown was waiting uneasily in Mr Schreiber's study in the penthouse, whither he had been summoned, the next afternoon after lunch, and this uneasiness increased as Mr and Mrs Schreiber entered the room together, followed by Mrs Harris, Mrs Butterfield, and an eight-going-on-nine-year-old boy known as Little Henry.

Mr Schreiber motioned his own side to sit and said to the performer, 'Sit down, Kentucky. We have something rather important to talk to you about.'

The too-easily aroused ire began to shine in the singer's eyes. He knew what the meeting was all about all right, and he wasn't having any of it. He took up a kind of a defiant stand in a corner of the room and said, 'If you-all think you're going to come over me for givin' that kid a poke, you can guess again. The little bastard was annoyin' me at mah rehearsin'. I tol' him to beat it - he got fresh and Ah belted him one. And what's more, Ah'd do it again. Ah tol' you Ah didn't like foreigners any more'n Ah liked negras.

All they have to do is keep out of mah way, and then nobody is goin' to have any trouble.'

'Yes, yes,' said Mr Schreiber testily, 'we know all that.' But now that he had Kentucky safely under contract he was no longer compelled to be as patient or put up with as much. 'But that isn't what I've asked you to come here to talk about today. It's something quite different. Sit yourself down and let's get at it.'

Relieved somewhat that the purpose of the get-together was not to chew him out for slapping the child, Kentucky sat on a chair back-to-front and watched them all suspiciously out of his small, mean eyes.

Mr Schreiber said, 'Your right name is George Brown, and you did your military service in the U.S. Air Force from 1949 to 1952.'

Kentucky set his jaws. 'What if Ah am and what if Ah did?'

Mr Schreiber, who appeared to be enjoying himself - indeed, he now relinquished the role of detective and was seeing himself as Mr District Attorney - said, 'On the 14th of April, 1950, you married a Miss Pansy Amelia Cott in Tunbridge Wells, while you were still in the Air Force, and approximately five months or so later a son was born to you, christened Henry Brown.'

'What?' shouted Kentucky. 'Man oh man, are you real crazy? You're just nothin' but off. Ah never heard of any of those people.'

Mrs Harris felt as though she were taking part in a television play, and that soon she would be called upon to speak her lines, lines that in anticipation of this scene she had rehearsed to herself and thought rather effective - slightly paraphrased from films and stories she remembered. It was to go something like this: *Mr Claiborne, I have a great surprise for you, and one that may cause you some astonishment. In my neighbourhood in London there lived a lonely child, starved, beaten, and abused by cruel foster-parents, unbeknownst to his father in far off America. I - that is to say, we, Mrs Butterfield and I - have rescued this child from the clutches of the unfeeling monsters into whose hands he had fallen and brought him here to you. That child is little Henry here, none other than your own natural son. Henry, go over and give your Dad a great big hug and kiss.*

While Mrs Harris was going over this speech and clinging to her fancy to the last, Mr Schreiber uncovered the papers on his desk and Kentucky, attracted by the rustle, looked over and saw the photostatic copy of his Air Force record, plus the photograph of himself. It cooled him off considerably. 'Your serial number in the Air Force was AF28636794, like it's tattooed on your wrist,' said Mr Schreiber, 'and your record up to the date of your discharge is all here, including your marriage and the birth of your son.'

Kentucky glared at Mr Schreiber and said, 'So what? What if it is? What business is that of anyone? Ah deevo'ced the woman - she was a no-good slut. It was all done legal and proper in accordance with the laws in the State of Alabama, and Ah got the papers that say so. What's all this about?'

Mr Schreiber's interrogation continued as inexorably as his fancy told him it should. 'And the boy?' he asked. 'Have you any idea where he is or what has become of him?'

'What's it to you? And why don't you mind your own business?' Kentucky snarled. 'Ah signed a contract to sing for your lousy network, but that don't give you no right to be askin' no personal questions. Anyway, Ah deevo'ced the woman legal and proper and contributed to the support of the child. Last I heard of him he was bein' looked after by his mother and gittin' along fine.'

Mr Schreiber put down the papers, looked across his desk and said, 'Tell him, Mrs Harris.'

Thus taken by surprise and thrown an entrance cue entirely different from the one she had expected, Mrs Harris went completely up in her lines and blurted, 'It's a lie! 'E's 'ere - this is 'im right 'ere sitting next to me.'

Kentucky's jaw dropped and he stared over at the three, with the child in the middle, and yelled, 'What? That little bastard?'

Mrs Harris was on her feet in a flash, ready for battle, her blue eyes blazing with anger. ''E ain't no little bastard,' she retorted, ''e's your flesh and blood, legally married like it sez in those pypers, and I brought 'im to you all the way over 'ere from London.'

There was one of those silences during which father looked at son, and son looked at father, and between them passed a glance of implacable dislike. 'Who the hell asked you to?' Kentucky snarled.

How it happened Mrs Harris never would have known, but there she was, Samaritan and Fairy Godmother Extraordinary, suddenly forced upon the defensive. 'Nobody asked me,' she said. 'I did it on me own. The little tyke was bein' beaten and starved by them 'orrid Gussets. We could hear 'im through the walls. I said to Mrs Butterfield, "If his dad in America knew about this, 'e wouldn't stand for it, not for a minute"' - Mrs Butterfield here gave a corroborative nod - '"he'd want 'im out of there in a flash." So here we are. Now what 'ave you got to say to that?'

Before he could reply something that might have been unprintable, from the twist that his mouth had taken, Mrs Schreiber, who saw that Mrs Harris was floundering and things getting out of hand, interpolated quickly, 'Mrs Harris and Mrs Butterfield live right next door to these people - the Gussets - there were the foster-parents - that is to say, Henry's mother boarded the child with them after she remarried, and when the money stopped coming and they couldn't find her they began to abuse the child. Mrs Harris couldn't bear it and brought him over here to you. She is a good woman and had the best interests of the child at heart and—' here she suddenly realised that her explanations were sounding just as lame and flustered as Mrs Harris's had a moment ago, and she subsided in confusion, looking for help to her husband.

'That's about the way of it, Kentucky,' said Mr Schreiber, stepping into the breach, 'though I think maybe it could have been better put. When she brought him over here Mrs Harris didn't know who the father was, except she figured when she located him and he found out how much the kid needed him and what was happening to him, he'd take over.'

Kentucky clucked his tongue and snapped his knuckles in a curious kind of rhythm he sometimes used in a ballad, and when he had finished he said, 'Oh she did, did she?' He then looked over at Mrs Harris and Mrs Butterfield and said, 'Listen, you two interferin' old bitches, you know what you can do with that brat? You can take him right back where he come from, wherever that was. Ah didn't ask you to bring him over here, Ah don't want him, and Ah ain't goin' to have him. Ah'm just a little ol' country boy, but Ah'm smart enough to know man public don't want me hooked up with no deevo'ce and no kid, and if you try any funny business about tryin' to make me take him, Ah'll call the pack of you a bunch of dirty liars, tear up mah contract and then you can go whistlin' for Kentucky Claiborne - and Ah got ten million hundred per cent American kids that'll back me up.'

Having delivered himself of this homily, Claiborne let his glance wander around the little group, where it lingered not so much as a second upon his son, and then said, 'Well, folks, I guess that'll be about all. Reckon Ah'll be seein' you.' He got up and shambled out of the room.

Mr Schreiber gave vent to his feelings. 'That dirty low-life!' he said.

Mrs Butterfield threw her apron over her head and ran for the kitchen.

Mrs Harris stood, ashen-faced, and repeated, 'I'm an interferin' old bitch.' And then said, 'I've done it now, 'aven't I?'

But the loneliest figure was that of little Henry, who stood in the centre of the room, the large eyes and the too-large head now filled with more wisdom and sadness than had ever been collected there, while he said, 'Blimey, I wouldn't want 'im for a dad.'

Mrs Schreiber went over, took the child in her arms and wept over him.

But Mrs Harris, faced with the last and total collapse of all her dreams and illusions, was far too shattered even to weep.

MRS HARRIS'S mind, which previously had tricked her so naughtily into believing that Kentucky Claiborne would receive his child with open arms and from then on exude nothing but sweetness and light, now did her a kindness. It simply blanked out completely. It permitted her to get to her room, take off her clothes, don a nightdress, and get into bed, and thereafter draw a merciful curtain over all that had happened. Had it not done so, the fierce pride of Mrs Harris would not have been able to have borne the humiliation she had undergone and the collapse of the beautiful dreams of a good life for a little boy that she had nourished for so long, and to which she had given so much of herself. She lay with her eyes wide open, staring up at the ceiling, seeing, hearing, and saying nothing.

It was Mrs Butterfield's shrill scream of fear and anguish upon making the discovery that gave the alarm and brought Mrs Schreiber rushing into the kitchen.

'Oh Ma'am,' said Mrs Butterfield after she had been calmed somewhat, 'it's Ada. Something's wrong with 'er - something 'orrible. She just lies there kind of like she's 'arf dead and won't say a word.'

Mrs Schreiber took one look at the small, wispy figure tucked away in the bed, looking even smaller and wispier now that all the air of her ebullient ego had been let out of her, made one or two attempts to rouse her and when they failed, rushed to her husband, and telephoned to Dr Jonas, the family physician.

The doctor arrived and did those professional things he deemed necessary, and then came out to the Schreibers. 'This woman has had a severe shock of some kind,' he said. 'Do you know anything about her?'

'You're telling me,' said Mr Schreiber, and then launched into the story of what had happened, culminating with the scene with the unwilling father.

The doctor nodded and said, 'Yes, I can see. Well, we shall have to wait. Sometimes this is Nature's way of compensating for the unbearable. She seems to have a good deal of vitality, and in my opinion it will not be too long before she begins to come out of it.'

But it was a week before the fog which had descended upon Mrs Harris began to lift, and the impetus for its dispelling arose in a somewhat extraordinary manner.

The Schreibers were hardly able to endure waiting, because of what had taken place in the interim and the new state of affairs which they were dying to impart to Mrs Harris, certain that if once she returned to herself it would contribute to her rapid convalescence.

It began with a telephone call for Mrs Harris shortly before lunch one day, and which Mrs Schreiber answered. Mr Schreiber was likewise present, as his office was not far from his home and he liked to return for lunch. What seemed to be a most elegant and cultured English voice said, 'I beg your pardon, but might I have a word with Mrs Harris?'

Mrs Schreiber said, 'Oh dear, I am afraid not. You see, she's ill. Who is this, please?'

The voice echoed her, 'Oh dear,' and added, 'ill, you say? This is Bayswater speaking - John Bayswater of Bayswater, London. Nothing serious, I trust.'

Mrs Schreiber in an aside to her husband said, 'It's someone for Mrs Harris by the name of Bayswater,' then into the phone, 'Are you a friend of hers?'

Mr Bayswater replied, 'I believe I may count myself such. She requested me to telephone her on my next visit to New York, and certainly my employer, the Marquis de Chassagne, the French Ambassador, will be anxious about her. I am his chauffeur.'

Mrs Schreiber remembered now, and with her hand over the mouthpiece quickly transferred the information to her husband.

'Have him come up,' said Mr Schreiber. 'What harm can it do? And maybe it could do her some good - you never know.'

Twenty minutes later an anxious Mr Bayswater, elegant in his grey whipcord uniform, his smart chauffeur's cap in one hand, appeared at the door of the Schreiber apartment and was ushered by them into Mrs Harris's bedroom, with the worried and, since Mrs Harris's illness, perpetually snuffling Mrs Butterfield looming in the background.

Mrs Harris had been taking mild nourishment, tea and bread and butter or light biscuits, but otherwise had given no sign of recognition of anyone about her.

Mr Bayswater, it seemed, had been a very worried man over a period, and it was this worry which had brought him to New York. The most perfect Rolls to which he had ever been wedded had developed a mysterious noise in its innards, a noise barely audible to any but the trained ear of Mr Bayswater, to whom it sounded like the crackling of mid-summer thunder, and whom it was driving up the wall. It was unbearable to him that this should happen in a Rolls, and even more so in one he had had the honour to select and test himself.

All his skill, knowledge, acumen, and experience of years had not enabled him to locate the seat of this disturbance, and thereafter for him there had been no rest or solace, and he had brought the car to New York for a more thorough stripping down and examination at the Rolls Service Station there. He had delivered the machine to the garage and thought that in a chat with Mrs Harris he might relieve his mind of the burdens imposed upon it by this imperfection.

But now that he stood looking down upon this pale ghost of a woman, the apple cheeks shrunken and the heretofore naughty, snapping, and merry little eyes clouded over, all thoughts of the stricken Rolls were swept from his head and for the first time in many, many years he was conscious of a new kind of heartache. He went over to her bedside, sat down, took one of her hands in his, quite oblivious to the watching Schreibers and Mrs Butterfield, and lapsing as he was inclined to when under a great emotional strain, "Ere, 'ere Ada, this will never do. What's all this about?"

Something in his voice penetrated. Perhaps it was the two dropped aitches which turned the key in the lock and opened the door for Mrs Harris. She lifted her head and looked directly into the elegant and austere face of Mr Bayswater, noted the curly grey hair, almost patrician nose and thin lips, and said in a weak voice, "Ullo, John. What brings you up 'ere?"

'Business,' replied Mr Bayswater. 'You told me to get on the blower if I came this way. I did, and they told me you weren't too perky. What's it all about?'

They all thrust to the fore now, Mrs Butterfield yammering, 'Ow Ada, thank the Good Lord you're better,' Mrs Schreiber crying, 'Oh Mrs Harris, how wonderful! You're better, aren't you? We've been so worried,' and Mr Schreiber shouting, 'Mrs Harris! Mrs Harris, listen! Everything's all right - we've got the most wonderful news for you!'

The face and the voice of Mr Bayswater had indeed put Mrs Harris's cart back on the road by recalling the most delectable drive up from Washington with him, and an even more delectable stop at a famous roadside restaurant on the way, where she had had a most extraordinarily tasty soup of clams, leeks, potatoes, and cream, called New England clam chowder. It would have been better for her had she been able to live within these memories a little longer, but alas, the cries of the others soon broke the spell and brought her back to the realisation of the catastrophe she had precipitated. She covered her face with her hands and cried, 'No, no! Go away - I can't face anyone. I'm silly, interferin' old woman who spoils everything she lays her 'ands on. Please go away.'

But Mr Schreiber was not to be denied now. He pushed forward saying, 'But you don't understand, Mrs Harris - something terrific has happened since you've been - I mean since you haven't been well. Something absolutely stupendous! We're adopting little Henry! He's ours. He's going to stay with us, if you don't mind. You know we love the kid and he loves us. He'll have a good home with us and grow up into a fine man.'

Mrs Harris was yet very ill in her soul and thus only half heard what Mr Schreiber was saying, but since it seemed to have something to do with little Henry, and he sounded cheerful and happy about it, she took her hands from her face and gazed about her, looking greatly like an unhappy little monkey.

'It was Henrietta's idea,' Mr Schreiber explained, 'and right away the next day I got hold of Kentucky and had another talk with him. He ain't a bad guy when you get to know him more. It's just he don't like kids. He's got a thing about he'd lose his following if it came out he'd been married and divorced abroad and had a kid who was half English. So I said if he wouldn't have any objections we'd like to adopt the kid, Henrietta and I, and bring him up like our own son.'

'"You're an interferin' old bitch. Take the brat back to England," 'e sez to me,' quoted Mrs Harris. ''Is own father.'

'But you don't understand,' Mr Schreiber said. 'He isn't making any trouble. It all works out one hundred per cent for everybody. The kid's an American citizen, so he's got a right to be here. Kentucky's his legal father, and the evidence is right there in the Air Force files. We've written to England to get a birth certificate for the little fellow. There'll be no trouble with anybody because, as his father, Claiborne's got the right to have him here with him. The legal beagles are making out the adoption papers, and he's going to sign 'em as soon as they're ready.'

Some penetration had been achieved now, for Mrs Harris turned a slightly more cheerful countenance to Mr Schreiber and said, 'Are you sure? 'E'd 'ave a good 'ome with you.'

'Of course I'm sure,' cried Mr Schreiber, delighted that he had registered. 'I'm telling you, the guy was tickled to death to get rid - I mean, he's glad too that the kid's going to be with us.'

Mrs Schreiber thought that Mrs Harris had gone through enough for that particular period, nudged her husband and said, 'We can talk more about it later, Joel - maybe Mrs Harris would like to be alone with her friend for a bit now.' Mr Schreiber, film magnate, detective, and District Attorney, showed himself to be an exemplary husband as well by getting it in one and saying, 'Sure, sure. We'll run along now.'

When they had gone, Mrs Butterfield too having tactfully withdrawn, Mr Bayswater said, 'Well, there you are. It's turned out all right, hasn't it?'

A remnant of the black wave of disillusionment that had engulfed her swept over Mrs Harris again, for it had been such a beautiful dream, and she had steeped herself in it for so long. 'I'm a fool,' she said. 'An interferin' busy-body who ain't got the brynes to mind 'er own business. I've done nothink but cause everybody trouble. Me, who was so cocksure about turnin' up little 'Enry's father in America. Lor', what a bloody mess I've made of things.'

Mr Bayswater went to give her a little pat on her hand, and was surprised to find he was still holding it clutched in his, so he gave it a squeeze instead, and said, 'Go on with you. You shouldn't talk like that. It looks to me as though you managed to turn up not one but two fathers for little 'Enry. Two for the price of one isn't so bad.'

The merest whisper of a smile softened Mrs Harris's face for the first time, but she was not going to let go her megrims and guilt-feelings quite so easily. 'It could've turned out 'orrible,' she said, 'if it 'adn't been for Mr Schreiber. What would've become of the little fellow if it 'adn't been for 'im?'

'What would have become of the little fellow if it hadn't been for *you*?' said Mr Bayswater, and smiled down at her.

Mrs Harris smiled back and said, 'What brings you up to New York, John?'

Now his troubles came sweeping back over Mr Bayswater, and his elegant frame in the whipcord uniform gave a slight shudder, and he passed the back of his hand over his brow. 'It's the Rolls,' he said. 'She's developed a noise in her and I can't find it. I'm like to go out of me mind - that is to say, go out of my mind. I've been at it for over a week now and can't find it. It isn't in the gear-box, and it isn't in the silencer or the oil bath air cleaner. I've had the rear axle down, and it isn't there. I've looked through the hydraulic system, and taken down the engine. It isn't in the distributor head, and there's nothing the matter with the water pump. Sometimes you get a click in the fan belt, but it isn't that.'

'What's it like?' Mrs Harris asked, thus showing herself to be a woman who could be interested in a man's world as well.

'Well, it isn't exactly a tapping or a clicking, nor would I say it was exactly a knocking or a scraping - nor even a ticking or a pipping,' explained Mr Bayswater, 'but it's there. I can 'ear it. You shouldn't hear anything in a Rolls-Royce - not *my* Rolls-Royce. It's under the seat somewhere, but not exactly - rather more at the back, and it's driving me up the wall. It's somehow as if the Good Lord had said, "You there, so proud and stuck-up about your automobile - perfect you said it was. I'll show you perfect. Let's see you get around *this*, Mr Stuck-up." It ain't that I'm stuck-up,' explained Mr Bayswater, 'it's just that I love Rolls cars. All me life I've never loved anything else. All me life I've been looking for the perfect one, and this was it - until now.'

The distress on the handsome features of the elderly chauffeur touched Mrs Harris's heart and made her forget her own troubles, and she wished genuinely to be able to comfort him as he somehow had managed to comfort her. Some long-ago memory was nibbling at her newly awakened and refreshed mind, and it suddenly gave her a sharp nip. 'I 'ad a lady once I did for some years ago,' she said, 'a proper Mrs Rich-Bitch she was. She 'ad a Rolls and a chauffeur, and one day I heard 'er say, "James, there's something rattling in the back of the car. Find it before I 'as a nervous breakdown." Coo, 'e nearly went orf 'is loaf tryin' to locate it. 'Ad the car took apart and put together twice, and then come across it by accident. You know what it was?'

'No,' said Mr Bayswater. 'What was it?'

'One of 'er hairpins that fell out and slipped down be'ind the seat. But that couldn't be it, could it? The Marquis don't wear 'airpins.'

Mr Bayswater had a lapse, a real, fat, juicy lapse. 'Blimey,' he cried, 'Gaw bleedin' blimey!' and on his face was the look of the condemned who hears that he has been reprieved by the Governor. 'I think you've got it! The Marquis doesn't wear hairpins, but last week I drove Madame Mogahdjibh, the wife of the Syrian Ambassador, home after a party. She was loaded with them - big black ones. Ada, my girl, here's the smack you didn't get on the boat,' and he leaned down and kissed her brow, then leaped to his feet and said, 'I'm going to find out. I'll be seeing you,' and rushed from the room.

Left to herself Mrs Harris reflected upon this matter of perfection for which humans seem to strive, as exemplified by Mr Bayswater's distress over something that had come to shatter the perfection of the finest car in the world, and she thought that perhaps perfection belonged only to that Being on High who sometimes seemed friendly to humans, and sometimes less so, and at other times even a little jealous.

Had she been asking too much? 'Yes', something inside Mrs Harris answered vehemently, 'far too much.' It had not been only fairy godmother she had been trying to play, it had been almost God, and the punishment that had followed had been swift and sure. And then her thoughts turned back to her Dior dress which had been so exquisite and so perfect, and the ugly burnt-out panel that was in it to remind her that though the dress itself had been spoiled, out of the experience had come something even better in the shape of some wonderful friendships.

And from thence it was but a step to the comfort that if she had been less than successful in her avowed mission of reuniting little Henry with his father, it had not been wholly a failure. Nothing in life ever was a complete and one hundred per cent success, but often one could well afford to settle for less, and this would seem to be the greatest lesson one could learn in life. Little Henry was out of the hands of the unspeakable Gussets, he had acquired adoptive parents who loved him and would help him to grow into a good and fine man; she herself had experienced and learned to feel an affection for a new land and a new people. Thus to grouse and grumble and carry on in the face of such bounty now suddenly took on the colour of darkest ingratitude. The Schreibers so happy, little Henry equally so - how dare she not be happy herself because her ridiculous and vainglorious little dream had been exploded.

'Ada 'Arris,' she said to herself, 'you ought to be ashymed of yerself, lyin' about 'ere on yer back when there's work to be done.' She called out aloud, 'Violet.'

Mrs Butterfield came galumphing into the room like an overjoyed hippopotamus. 'Did you call me, dearie? Lor' bless us, but if you ain't lookin' like yer old self again.'

''Ow about making me a cuppa tea, love?' said Mrs Harris. 'I'm gettin' up.'

THE early summer enchantment of May and June in
New York, with girls out in their light summer dresses, the
parks in full bloom, and the skies clear and sunny, had given
way to the sweltering, uncomfortable humidity and heatwaves
of July. The Schreiber household was running like clockwork,
with a permanent staff now trained and disciplined by
Mrs Harris, the final formalities by which the Schreibers
became the adopted parents and guardians of Henry Brown
completed, and the child installed in his own quarters in the
Schreiber house. The passage of time was bringing nearer
two events about which something would have to be done.

One of them was the arrival of vacation time, the annual
exodus from the hot city to the more temperate climes of
mountains or seashore, and the other was the approaching
expiration on the 17th of July of the visitors' visas to the
United States of the dames Butterfield and Harris.

Mr and Mrs Schreiber held several conferences together
on the subject, and then one evening Mrs Butterfield and
Mrs Harris were called into Mr Schreiber's study, where
they found the couple seated, looking portentous.

'Dear Mrs Harris and dear Mrs Butterfield, don't stand, do sit down please,' said Mrs Schreiber. 'My husband and I have something to discuss with you.'

The two Englishwomen exchanged glances and then gingerly occupied the edges of two chairs, and Mrs Schreiber said, 'Mr Schreiber and I have taken a small cottage in Maine by the sea for little Henry and ourselves, where we intend to spend several months and rest quietly. Mr Schreiber is very tired after the work of reorganizing his company and we don't wish to do any entertaining. We can leave our flat here in the hands of our staff, but we were wondering whether you and Mrs Butterfield wouldn't accompany us to Forest Harbour and look after little Henry and myself while we are there. Nothing would make us happier.'

The two women exchanged looks again, and Mr Schreiber said, 'You don't have to worry about your visitors' visas - I got friends in Washington who can get you a six months' extension. I was going to do that anyway.'

'And afterwards in the fall when we come back, well, we rather hoped you'd stay with us too,' Mrs Schreiber continued. And then in a rush blurted, 'We hoped somehow we might persuade you to stay with us for always. You see, little Henry loves you both, and - so do we - I mean, we feel we owe you a debt of gratitude we can never repay. If it hadn't been for you we never should have had little Henry for our very own, and he already means more to us than my husband and I are able to say. We just don't ever want you to go. You won't have to work hard, and you can always make your home with us. Will you stay? Will you come with us this summer?'

In the silence that ensued after this plea the two Londoners exchanged looks for the third time, and Mrs Butterfield's chins began to quiver, but Mrs Harris as spokesman and captain of the crew remained more in control, though she too was visibly touched by the offer. 'Lor' bless you both for your kindness,' she said, 'Violet and I have been discussing nothing else for days. We're ever so sorry - we carn't.'

Mr Schreiber looked genuinely nonplussed. 'Discussing it for days?' he said. 'Why, we've only sprung it on you now. We haven't known about it ourselves until just recent—'

'We've seen it coming,' said Mrs Harris, and Mrs Butterfield, all her chins throbbing now, put a corner of her apron to one eye and said, 'Such dear, kind people.'

'You mean you knew all about the house we've taken in the country and that we'd want you and Mrs Butterfield to come with us there?' Mrs Schreiber asked in astonishment.

Mrs Harris was not at all abashed. She replied, 'One 'ears things about the 'ouse. Little pitchers have big ears, and rolling stones have bigger ones. What is there to talk about in servants' 'all except what goes on in the front of the 'ouse?'

'Then you won't stay?' said Mrs Schreiber, a note of unhappiness in her voice.

'Love,' said Mrs Harris, 'there's nuffink we wouldn't want to do for you to repay you for your kindness to us, and for giving little 'Enry a 'ome and a chance in life, but we've talked it over - we carn't, we just carn't.'

Mr Schreiber, who saw his wife's disappointment, said, 'What's the matter? Don't you like America?'

'Lor' love yer,' said Mrs Harris fervently, 'it ain't that. It's wonderful. There's nuffink like it anywhere else in the world. Ain't that so, Violet?'

Mrs Butterfield's emotions were such that she was able to do no more than nod acquiescence.

'Well then, what is it?' persisted Mr Schreiber. 'If it's more money you want, we could—'

'Money!' exclaimed Mrs Harris aghast. 'We've had too much already. We wouldn't take another penny off you. It's just - just that we're 'omesick.'

'Homesick,' Mr Schreiber echoed, 'with all you've got over here? Why, we've got everything.'

'That's just it,' said Mrs Harris. 'We've got too much of everything 'ere - we're 'omesick for less. Our time is up. We want to go back to London.' And suddenly, as though it came forth from the deep and hidden wells of her heart, she cried with a kind of anguish that touched Mrs Schreiber and penetrated even to her husband, 'Don't ask us to stay, please - or ask us why.'

For how could she explain, even to the Schreibers who knew and had lived in and loved London themselves, their longing for the quieter, softer tempo of that great, grey, sprawling city where they had been born and reared?

The tall, glittering skyscrapers of New York raised one's eyes into the heavens, the incredible crash and bustle and thunder of the never-still traffic, and the teeming canyons at the bottom of the mountainous buildings excited and stimulated the nerves and caused the blood to pump faster, the glorious shops and theatres, the wonders of the supermarkets, were sources of never-ending excitement to Mrs Harris. How, then, explain their yearning to be back where grey, drab buildings stretched for seemingly never-ending blocks, or turned to quaint, quiet, tree-lined squares, or streets where every house was painted a different colour?

How to make their friends understand that excitement too long sustained loses its pitch, that they yearned for the quiet and the comforting ugliness of Willis Gardens, where the hooves of the old horse pulling the flower vendor's dray in the spring sounded cloppety-cloppety-cloppety in the quiet, and the passage of a taxicab was almost an event?

What was there to compare, Mrs Harris and Mrs Butterfield had decided, in all this rush, scurry, litter, and hurry, this neon-lit, electricity-blazing city where they had indeed been thrilled to have been a part of it for a short time, with the quiet comfort of cups of tea that they drank together on alternate evenings in their little basement flats in their own particular little corner of London?

Nor could they, without hurting the feelings of these good people, tell them that they were desperately missing quite a different kind of excitement, and that was the daily thrill of their part-time work.

In London each day brought them something different, some new adventure, some new titbit of gossip, something good happened, something bad, some cause for mutual rejoicing or mutual indignation. They served not one but each a dozen or more clients of varying moods and temperaments. Each of these clients had a life, hopes, ambitions, worries, troubles, failures, and triumphs, and these Mrs Harris and Mrs Butterfield shared for an hour or two a day. Thus instead of one, each of them lived a dozen vicarious lives, lives rich and full, as their part-time mistresses and masters confided in them, as was the custom in London between employer and daily woman.

What would Major Wallace's new girl be like, the one he had carefully explained as his cousin just arrived from Rhodesia, but whom Mrs Harris knew he had encountered at the 'Antelope' two nights before? What new demands of service to be joyously, fiercely, and indignantly resisted would the Countess Wyszcinska present on the morrow? Did the *Express* have a juicy scandal story of how Lord Whosit had been caught by his wife canoodling with Pamela Whatsit among the potted palms at that gay Mayfair party? Mrs Fford Ffoulkes, she of the twin Fs and the social position of a witty and attractive divorcée, would have been there, and the next afternoon when Mrs Harris arrived to 'do' for her between the hours of three and five she would have the story of what really happened, and some of the riper details that the *Express* had been compelled by the laws of libel to forgo.

Then there was the excitement connected with her other bachelor client, Mr Alexander Hero, whose business it was to poke his nose into haunted houses, who maintained a mysterious laboratory at the back of his house in Eaton Mews, and whom she looked after and mothered, in spite of the fact that she was somewhat afraid of him. But there was a gruesome thrill in being connected with someone who was an associate of ghosts, and she revelled in it.

Even such minor items as whether Mr Pilkerton would have located his missing toupee, the progress of convalescence of the Wadhams' orange-coloured toy poodle, a dear little dog who was always ill, and whether Lady Dant's new dress would be ready in time for the Hunt Ball, made each day an interesting one for them.

And furthermore there was the excitement of the sudden decision to discard a client who had gone sour on them or overstepped some rule of deportment laid down by the chars' union, and the great adventure of selecting a new one to take his or her place; the call at the employment office or Universal Aunts, the interrogating of the would-be client, the final decision, and then the thrill of the first visit to the new flat, a veritable treasure palace of new things to be snooped at and gone over.

What was there in New York, even though it was the greatest city in the world, to compare with that?

The littlest things were dragging Mrs Harris and Mrs Butterfield homeward. Never had food been presented more enticingly yet, alas, more impersonally, than in the giant supermarket where they shopped. Every chop, every lettuce leaf, every gleaming, scrubbed carrot, had its cellophane envelope on its shining counter, washed, wrapped, packed, ticketed, priced, displayed, untouched by human hands. What both Mrs Butterfield and Mrs Harris longed for was the homeliness of Warbles', the corner grocer's shop with its display of tired greens, dispirited cabbages, and overblown sprouts, but smelling of spices and things well-remembered, and presided over by fat Mr Warbles himself. They wanted to see Mr Hagger, the butcher, slice off a chop, fling it on to the scales with a 'There you are, dear, as fine a bit of English lamb as ever you'll set your teeth in. One and tuppence-ha'penny, please,' wrap it in a piece of last month's newspaper and hand it over the counter with the air of one bestowing a great gift.

They had sampled all of the fabulous means of snacking in New York - the palatial Child's with their griddle cakes and maple syrup, to which Mrs Harris became passionately addicted, the automats where robots miraculously produced cups of coffee, and even the long drugstore counters where white-coated attendants squirted soda-water into chocolate syrup, and produced triple- and quadruple-tiered sandwiches of regal splendour. But the two women born within the sound of Bow Bells, and whom London fitted like a well-worn garment, found themselves yearning for the clatter of a Lyons' Corner House, or the warm redolency and pungent aroma of a fish and chip shop.

The bars and grills on Lexington and Third Avenues they sometimes visited for a nip were glittering places of mirror glass, mahogany, and gilt, each with a free television show included, but the Mesdames Harris and Butterfield longed for the drab mustiness of the 'Crown' close to their demesne, and the comfort of its public bar, where two ladies could sit quietly sipping beer or gin, indulging in refined conversation, or an occasional game of darts.

The police of New York were strong, handsome men, mostly Irish, but they just weren't Bobbies. Mrs Harris remembered with ever-increasing nostalgia the pauses for chats about local affairs with P.C. Hooter, who was both guardian and neighbourhood psychiatrist, of their street.

The sounds, the smells and rhythms, the skies, the sunsets, and the rains of London were all different from those of the fabulous city of New York, and she craved for all of them. She yearned even to be lost and gasping in a good old London pea-soup fog.

But how convey all this to the Schreibers?

Perhaps the Schreibers with their own memories of a beloved and happy stay in London were more sensitive than she had thought, for they heeded her cry and questioned her no more. Mr Schreiber only sighed and said, 'Well, I suppose when you gotta go, you gotta go. I'll fix it up for you.'

EVEN though it takes place almost weekly in New York, there is always something, exciting and dramatic about the sailing of a great liner, and in particular the departure of that hugest of all ships ever to sail the seven seas, the *Queen Elizabeth.*

Especially in the summertime, when Americans swarm to the Continent for their holidays, is the hubbub and hurly-burly at its peak, with the approaches to Pier 90 beneath the elevated highway at Fiftieth Street packed solid with Yellow Cabs and stately limousines delivering passengers and their luggage. The pier is a turmoil of travellers and porters, and aboard the colossal steamer there appears to be one huge party going on, cut into smaller ones only by the walls of the companionways and cabins, as in each room departing passengers entertain their friends with champagne, whisky, and *canapés.*

There is a particular, infectious gaiety about these farewell parties aboard ship, a true manifestation of a holiday spirit, and of all those taking place on the *Queen Elizabeth* on her scheduled summer sailing of the 16th of July, none was gayer, happier or more infectious than that which took place in Cabin A.59, the largest and best apartment in Tourist-Class, where at three o'clock in the afternoon prior to the five o'clock sailing, Mesdames Harris and Butterfield held court from amidst a welter of orchids and roses.

Reporters do not visit Tourist-Class on sailing day, reserving their attentions for the celebrities certain to be spotted in the luxury quarters. In this case they missed a bet, and just as well, for the guests collected at Mrs Harris's sailing party were not only celebrated but heterogeneous. There was, for instance, the French Ambassador to the United States, the Marquis Hypolite de Chassagne, accompanied by his chauffeur, Mr John Bayswater of Bayswater, London.

Then they would have come upon Mr Joel Schreiber, President of North American Pictures and Television Company Inc., recently celebrated for his signing of Kentucky Claiborne to a ten-million-dollar contract, accompanied by his wife, Henrietta, and their newly adopted son, Henry Brown Schreiber, aged almost nine.

A fortunate thing indeed that the sharp-eyed minions of the New York press did not see this family, else they would have some questions to ask of how the erstwhile son of Lord Dartington of Stowe and grandson of the Marquis de Chassagne, whose arrival in the United States had been signalised with story and photograph, had suddenly metamorphosed into the adopted son of Mr and Mrs Schreiber.

Further, among the guests were a Mr Gregson, a Miss Fitt, and a Mrs Hodge, respectively butler, parlourmaid, and cook of the household staff of the Schreibers.

And finally the party was completed by a number of the George Browns of New York who had fallen for Mrs Harris, and whom during the course of her search she had added to her ever-growing collection of international friends. There was Mr George Brown, the barker, very spruce in an alpaca suit, with a gay band on his straw boater; Captain George Brown, master of the *Siobhan O'Ryan,* his muscles bulging through his blue Sunday suit, towing his little wife behind him somewhat in the manner of a dinghy; there was the elegant Mr George Brown of Gracie Square; two Browns from the Bronx; the nostalgic chocolate-coloured one from Harlem; one from Long Island, and a family of them from Brooklyn.

The true identity of little Henry's father had been kept a secret, but Mrs Harris had apprised them all of the happy ending to the affair, and they had come to celebrate this conclusion and see her off.

If the centres of attraction, Mrs Harris and Mrs Butterfield, had worn all of the sprays of purple orchids sent them by their guests, they would have staggered under the load. As it was, Mrs Harris's sense of protocol decreed that they should wear the offering of the Marquis de Chassagne, whose orchids were white and bound with ribbons which mingled the colours of France, Great Britain, and the United States. Waiters kept the champagne flowing and the *canapés* moving.

Drink, and in particular the bubbly wine, is a necessity at these affairs, for the conversation just before departure tends to stultify, when people rather incline to repeat the same things over and over again.

Mr Schreiber repeated to the Marquis, 'The kid's going to be a great ball player. I'm telling you. He's got an eye like Babe Ruth had. I threw him my sinker the other day, figuring he'd be lucky to get a piece of it. You know what he did?'

'No,' said the Marquis.

'He takes a cut like Di Maggio used to and hoists the apple into the next lot. What do you think of that?'

'Astonishing,' said the Marquis, who had not understood a word that Mr Schreiber had said, beyond meaning that Henry had performed another prodigy of some kind, and remembering that the President of the United States himself seemed to be impressed with the young man's athletic abilities.

'Give my regards to Leicester Square,' said Mr George Brown of Harlem. 'Some day I'm going back there. It was good to us boys in the war.'

'If I ever run across the George Brown that took a powder on the kid, I'll poke him one just for luck,' promised the Coney Island Brown.

'You soi'nly desoive a lotta credit,' repeated the Brooklyn Browns.

'Some day we're gonna come over there and look you up,' prophesied a Brown from the Bronx.

'I suppose White's and Buck's are just the same,' sighed the Gracie Square Brown. 'They'll never change.'

'Dear,' said Mrs Schreiber for the fourth time, 'when you go past our flat on Eaton Square, throw in a kiss for me. I wonder who's living there now?' And then wistfully as she thought of the good days that had been when life was not so complicated, 'Maybe you'll even go there and work for them. I'll never forget you or what you did for us. Don't forget to write and tell me how everything is.'

Bayswater hovered on the outskirts rather silently and seemingly lost, for what with little Henry, who somehow no longer looked so little, his body having begun to grow to his head size, and all the sadness having been wiped for ever out of his eyes, hugging the two women, and the others all making a fuss over them, it seemed impossible to get close to give Mrs Harris what he had for her.

Yet somehow he contrived to catch her eye and hold it for a moment while he raised his own eyebrows and moved one shoulder imperceptibly in the direction of the door, but sufficient for Mrs Harris to get the message and escape momentarily from the cordon.

' 'Old the fort for a minute,' she said to Mrs Butterfield, 'while I look what's become of me trunk.'

'You won't be gettin' off the boat will yer?' said Mrs Butterfield in alarm - but Mrs Harris was already out of the door.

Down the passageway a bit, to the accompaniment of the clink of glasses, shrieks of laughter, and cries of farewell from parties in near-by cabins, Mrs Harris said, 'Whew. I didn't know how I was goin' to get away to arsk you - was it a 'airpin?'

In reply Mr Bayswater reached into the pocket of his uniform where a bulge somewhat interfered with its elegant line, and handed Mrs Harris a small package. It contained a bottle of Eau de Cologne, and represented a major effort on the part of the chauffeur, for it was the first such purchase and the first such gift he had ever made to a woman in his life. Affixed to the outside of it with a rubber band was a large and formidable-looking black wire hairpin.

Mrs Harris studied the specimen. 'Lumme,' she said, 'ain't it a whopper?'

Mr Bayswater nodded. 'There she is. Something like that gets into a Rolls and it can sound like your rear end's dropping out. I'd never have looked for it if it hadn't been for you. The scent's for you.'

Mrs Harris said, 'Thank you, John. And I'll keep the 'airpin as a souvenir. I suppose we'd better go back.'

But Mr Bayswater was not yet finished, and now he fussed and stirred uneasily with a hand in his pocket, and finally said, 'Ah - Ada, there was something else I wanted to give you, if you wouldn't mind.' He then withdrew his hand from his pocket and disclosed therein something that Mrs Harris had no difficulty in recognizing with even an odd little thrill of forewarning as to what it might be about.

'They're the keys of my flat,' said Mr Bayswater. 'I was wondering if sometime you might have a moment to look in for me, just to make sure everything's all right - sixty-four Willmott Terrace, Bayswater Road, Bayswater.'

Mrs Harris looked down at the keys in Mr Bayswater's palm and felt a curious warmth surging through her such as she had not known since she was a young girl.

Mr Bayswater too was feeling very odd, and perspiring slightly under his linen collar. Neither of them was aware of the symbolism of the handing over of the keys, but both felt as though they were in the grip of something strange, momentous, and pleasant.

Mrs Harris took them out of his hand, and they felt hot to the touch as he had been clutching them. 'Coo,' she said, 'by now I'll bet the plyce could do with a bit of a turn out. Do you mind if I dust about a bit?'

'Oh, I didn't mean *that*,' said Mr Bayswater, 'I wouldn't dream of asking you. It was just that I felt that if you might look in occasionally - well then - I'd know everything was all right.'

'You'll be a long time away, won't you?' said Mrs Harris.

'Not so long,' said Mr Bayswater, 'I'll be home in another six months. I've given my notice.'

Mrs Harris looked horrified. 'Given your notice, John! Why, whatever's got into you? What will the Marquis do?'

'He understands,' said Bayswater somewhat mysteriously. 'A friend of mine is taking over.'

'But the car,' said Mrs Harris, 'ought you to be leaving it?'

'Oh, I don't know,' said Mr Bayswater. 'Maybe one ought to take things a little easier. The affair of the hairpin came as a bit of a shock to me. Opened my eyes somewhat. It's time I was thinking of retiring, anyway. I've saved up all the money I shall ever need. I'd only signed to come out for a year. If I stay away longer I find I get a bit homesick for Bayswater.'

'Like me,' said Mrs Harris, 'and Willis Gardens. Cosy, that's what it is, at night with the curtains drawn and Mrs Butterfield in for a cuppa tea.' And then instinctively but unconsciously paraphrasing, 'There's no plyce like it.'

'Will I be seeing you when I get back?' asked Mr Bayswater, the question showing his state of mind, since he had just turned over the keys to his flat.

'If you 'appen to come by,' said Mrs Harris with equal and elaborate falseness, since she now held his keys in her own gnarled hand. 'Number five's the number, Willis Gardens, Battersea. I'm always in after seven, except Thursdays when Mrs Butterfield and I go to the flicks. But if you'd like to drop me a postcard we could make it another night.'

'No fear,' said Mr Bayswater. 'I will. Well, I suppose we'd better be getting back to the rest.'

'Yes, I guess we 'ad.'

They went. In Mrs Harris's hand was the earnest and the promise that some day in the not too far distant future she would see him again. And in the emptiness of Mr Bayswater's pocket where the keys no longer were, was the guarantee that with them in her possession he would see Ada Harris back home.

As they came back into the cabin Mr Schreiber was just finishing putting little Henry through his catechism for the benefit of the Marquis. For the first time it seemed to Mrs Harris that she saw the difference in the child, the sturdiness that had come to his figure, and the fact that all the wariness and expectation of cuffs and blows had left his expression. Little Henry had never been a coward or a sniveller - his had been the air of one expecting the worst, and usually getting it. So soon, and already he was a whole boy; not too much longer and he would be on his way to becoming a whole man. Mrs Harris was not versed in official prayers of gratitude, and her concept of the Deity was somewhat muddled and ever-changing, but he loomed up to her as benign now, as kind and loving as ever she could conceive of someone. And to her concept of that figure which looked rather like the gentle, bearded figure of the Lord depicted on religious postcards, she said an inward, 'Thank you.'

'What are you going to be when you grow up?' asked Mr Schreiber.

'A baseball player,' replied little Henry.

'What position?' asked Mr Schreiber.

Little Henry had to reflect over that one for a moment, and then said, 'Middle fielder.'

'Centre fielder,' corrected Mr Schreiber. 'That's right. All the great hitters played in the outfield - Ruth, Cobb, Di Maggio, Meusel. What team you going to play on?'

Little Henry knew that one all right. 'The New York Yankees,' he said.

'See?' said Mr Schreiber, glowing. 'A regular American already.'

The hooter hooted three times, there was a trampling of feet on the companionway without and an attendant passed by banging on a gong and shouting, 'Visitors ashore, please. All ashore that's going ashore.' Now as they moved to the door with Mrs Butterfield sobbing audibly, the farewells were redoubled: 'Goodbye Mrs Harris. God bless you,' cried Mrs Schreiber. 'Don't forget to look who's living in our apartment.'

'Goodbye, Madame,' said the Marquis, bent over her, took her hand in his and brushed it with his white moustache. 'You should be a very happy woman for the happiness you have brought to others - including, I might add, to me. All in all, it was a real lark. I have told everyone my grandson has returned to his father in England, so there will be no further difficulties.'

'Goodbye - good luck!' echoed all the Browns.

'Goodbye - good luck!' said Mr Schreiber. 'You need anything, you write and tell me. Don't forget, we got a branch office over there. They can fix you up any time.'

Little Henry went up to them with a new shyness, for in spite of everything, his experiences and his experience, he was still a small boy, and emotions, particularly those strongly felt, embarrassed him. He could not see into his future, but there was no doubt in his mind as to the present, as well as the past from which these two women had rescued him, even though the memory of his life with the Gussets was already beginning to fade.

But Mrs Butterfield had no such inhibitions. She gathered little Henry to her, drowning his face in her billowy bosom and interfering seriously with his breathing as she hugged, cuddled, wept and sobbed over him, until finally Mrs Harris had to say to her, 'Come on, dearie. Don't carry on so. 'E isn't a baby any more - 'e's a man now,' and thus earning more gratitude from the boy even than for his rescue.

He went to Mrs Harris and throwing his arms about her neck whispered, 'Goodbye Auntie Ada. I love you.'

And those were the last words spoken as they filed out, and until they all stood at the end of the pier and watched the magnificent liner back out into the busy North River, brass portholes reflecting the hot July sun, and the thousand faces dotting the gleaming white of the decks and super-structure. Somewhere forward would be the dots that represented Mrs Butterfield and Mrs Harris. The great siren of the liner bayed three times in farewell, and the Marquis Hypolite de Chassagne pronounced a kind of a valedictory.

'If I had my way,' he said, 'I would rear a statue in a public square to women like that, for they are the true heroines of life. They do their duty day in, day out, they struggle against poverty, loneliness, and want, to preserve themselves and raise their families, but still they are able to laugh, to smile, to find time to indulge in dreams.' The Marquis paused, reflected a moment, sighed and said, 'And this is why I would rear them their statue, for the courage of these dreams of beauty and romance that still persist. And see,' he concluded, 'the wondrous result of such dreaming.'

The *Queen Elizabeth* bayed again. She was now broad-side to the pier, and in midstream. Her screws threshed and she began to glide down towards the sea. The Marquis raised his hat.

Aboard the liner Mrs Harris and Mrs Butterfield, the eyes of both reddened with tears now, repaired to their cabin, whence came their steward.

'Twigg's the name,' he said. 'I'm your steward. Your stewardess is Evans. She'll be along in a minute.' He gazed at the banked-up flowers. 'Cor blimey if it don't look as if somebody died in 'ere.'

'Coo,' said Mrs Harris, 'you watch yer lip or you'll find out 'oo died in 'ere. Them flowers is from the French Ambassador, I'll 'ave you know.'

''Ello, 'ello,' said the steward as the familiar accent fell upon his ears, and not at all abashed by the reproof, 'Don't tell me now, but let me guess - Battersea, I'll wager. I'm from Clapham Common meself. You never know 'oo yer meets travellin' these days. I'll 'ave yer tickets, please.' And then as he departed, 'Cheer-oh, lydies. You can rely on Bill Twigg and Jessie Evans to look after yer. Yer couldn't be on a better ship.'

Mrs Harris sat on her bed and sighed with contentment. 'Clapham Common' had fallen gently and gratefully upon her ears too. 'Lor' love yer, Violet,' she said, 'ain't it good to be 'ome?'

A NOTE ON THE AUTHOR

PAUL GALLICO was born in New York City, of Italian and Austrian parentage, in 1897, and attended Columbia University. From 1922 to 1936 he worked on the New York Daily News as sports editor, columnist, and assistant managing editor. In 1936 he bought a house on top of a hill at Salcombe in South Devon and settled down with a Great Dane and twenty-three assorted cats. It was in 1941 that he made his name with *The Snow Goose*, a classic story of Dunkirk which became a worldwide bestseller. Having served as a gunner's mate in the US Navy in 1918, he was again active as a war correspondent with the American Expeditionary Force in 1944. Gallico, who later lived in Monaco, was a first-class fencer and a keen sea-fisherman. He wrote over forty books, four of which were the adventures of Mrs Harris: *Mrs Harris Goes to Paris* (1958), *Mrs Harris Goes to New York* (1959), *Mrs Harris, MP* (1965) and *Mrs Harris Goes to Moscow* (1974). One of the most prolific and professional of American authors, Paul Gallico died in July 1976.

Made in the USA
Middletown, DE
15 July 2022

69484950R00191